Darkness
Haunts

Susan Illene

Hope you enjoy!

Susan Illene

Darkness Haunts
Copyright © 2013 by Susan Illene
2nd edition 2014
Cover design by Claudia McKinney
Cover Photography by Teresa Yeh

ISBN-13: 978-1481861182
ISBN-10: 1481861182

www.darknesshaunts.com

To all the women who have served in the armed forces and will do so in the future. Your sacrifices may not get the recognition they most assuredly deserve, but your efforts are no less important. Maintaining the compassion and humanity common amongst the female gender, while proving oneself time and again with the big guys is no easy thing, but remarkable women do it every day. May the many women who have lost their lives in service to their country be remembered for their valor and courage.

Acknowledgments

I have so many people I want to thank for helping me get this novel ready to be published. First, to those who worked with me during the early draft stages including Angela, Mary, Tim, and Theo. Each of you had the willingness to push me to do my best and the honesty to be forthright with your critiques. All of you helped make me a better writer and I wouldn't have had it any other way. Thank you for your continual support.

To my family, who has not been as receptive to reading my work (mostly due to its paranormal contents), but has done their best to help me in any other way they could. My husband, Salam, has been an ardent supporter in getting my novel published. Though he admits it is because he doesn't want me hating him for the rest of his life, therefore punishing him even worse than hellfire and brimstone could manage, I still appreciate his (somewhat dubious) faith in me. I'll consider keeping the whip out of sight for a week or two.

My father and grandfather have also been wonderful. They've listened to me on the phone for countless hours while I talked about writing and publishing with them. My grandfather was always willing to discuss writing strategies, grammar, and spelling even if he despaired at my chosen genre. My father did take some time to read parts of my book and went so far as to surprise me with setting up my author website. He continues to help me maintain it. Thanks Dad!

A big shout out must go to Claudia McKinney at Phat Puppy Art and Ashley at Bookish Brunette for the wonderful work they did on my book cover. I couldn't have asked for a better design team. Thanks to the Author's Red Room as well for proofreading my book in a timely manner. I appreciated your ability to pick out issues with my novel without trying to change the style of my writing. It was exactly what I asked for.

Also to Angela (again) and Charity who answered all my publishing questions and have been willing to help promote the book in any way they can. You are both wonderful writing buddies and supporters. To Lynne, who hasn't read much of my book because I like to keep her in suspense, but is always happy to read the portions I give her and provide feedback. Not to mention helping me in any other way she can. I hope now she can finally enjoy the finished product! Also a huge thanks to Mark. Your last minute suggestions and corrections made all the difference.

There are so many other people who supported me in some way as I moved toward publication. I know it's been a long road since that first draft was completed one year ago. Thanks to everyone who constantly asked when the novel would be published. You all were certainly a driving force in forcing me to get it done and get it out there.

Chapter One

A true friend will always be there for you when you need them, but they'll also be the first to drag you into a pit of vipers. If snakes hung out in this place, I doubted I'd get out of here in the same shape I went in.

"The Mouse Trap" was the newest and hottest club in Monterey, California. At first glance, nothing about it appeared out of the norm. No windows broke the smooth-faced façade out front, and the loud music spilling through the open door was the same as any other establishment of its kind. But it hid a darker element.

The patrons who stood in line had no idea they shuffled impatiently to enter a place owned by supernaturals, or "sups" as I preferred to call them. Hell, they didn't even know such things really existed. They'd dressed up in their tight-fitting clothes, chains, and leather, believing they were going to have a good time. Little did they know—nothing is ever as it seems.

My nails dug into my palms as the line inched forward.

Lisette, one of my two closest friends, stood next to me. She'd picked our destination for the night, and true to form, she chose one with a mixed species element. Whenever you dealt with sups, anything could happen. I had to hope for the best and continue to play my ignorant human role with her. She didn't know that I knew.

Blinking red neon lights from the club's sign illuminated the excitement on her pale face. She hopped up and down, trying to see over the taller humans in front of her. I couldn't figure out how she kept her balance on the high heels she wore. Then again, she only came up to my chin—maybe being closer to the ground helped. Pixies tended to be on the short side.

"Ten more people in front of us."

She stopped hopping—to my relief. "Thanks. I hope they hurry and let us in soon."

I scowled, but didn't reply. My temples were throbbing. The result of being too close to a large number of sups. They'd hit my senses like a storm of fire, ice, and jagged glass as soon as we'd neared the place. I rubbed my forehead in an effort to get rid of the pain. It would pass, given enough time. My movement drew Lisette's attention.

"What's wrong, Melena?" she asked, frowning. "It's not going to be that bad. Besides, with Aniya up in Alaska, there's no one else who can come with me."

"Aniya is a stay at home and drink red wine kind of girl. You know she wouldn't come to a place like this." I paused. "Speaking of which, have you heard from her? She hasn't been answering my calls."

"No, I haven't." Lisette rolled her eyes. "But don't try changing the subject. Unless something is seriously wrong, you're going in here if I have to drag you by your hair." She reached out, as if to do just that.

I jerked the vulnerable locks over one shoulder—

the farthest one from Lisette—and edged a few inches away. I'd have to let the topic of Aniya go for now.

My teeth ground together as the line inched forward—five more people in front of us.

I had to hope this place wasn't as bad as my paranoia made it out to be. Most supernatural clubs maintained strict rules involving their treatment of humans. It was just good business, but until I went in, I wouldn't know if this one did. A risk for someone like me. It could be said my kind, *sensors*, were the paranormal equivalent of most wanted criminals. The main thing that kept us safe was that we appeared human.

In fact, we were, except a bit more enhanced. The few differences we had included the ability to sense supernaturals nearby, immunity to magic, and some empathic traits. For having those gifts, the sups had hunted us for centuries. Lisette had known me for eleven years, since our sophomore year in high school, and even she didn't know my secret. It was safer that way.

My heart skipped a beat—only three people left.

A brawny werewolf bouncer stood as the gate guard to the dark abyss beyond. His alert brown eyes checked the IDs handed to him, but he did little more than skim their details. Subtle sniffs flared his nostrils as he came into contact with each human. You could fake an ID, but you couldn't fake your natural smell, not even with perfume. A werewolf could detect your age down to a year with little more than a whiff or two.

He pulled a young brunette out of the line who wore a tiny red dress. It didn't cover up much and left plenty of curves to show. She stood off to the side with her hands on her hips.

"I'm twenty-one. You have to let me in."

He flung her ID at her. "This is fake. Get outta here."

She squealed in outrage, grabbed her ID off the ground, and stomped off. I envied her. She had an excuse to leave. Sups rarely messed with underage humans. Even they had lines they avoided crossing.

As I took my next steps toward the entrance, my feet itched to make an all-out run the other way. Even the military hadn't made me strong enough to deal with this kind of crap. One would think if I could survive being shot at and nearly blown up, a nightclub wouldn't be that bad.

It was my past experiences with them that were the problem. They'd killed Wanda, another sensor I knew, eight years ago. The memory of her murder at a sup's hands flashed in my mind often and served as a constant reminder of what could happen to me. I'd known Lisette since before the incident, making her the only supernatural I could tolerate.

We stepped up to the bouncer and handed over our IDs. I pretended not to feel the claws raking against my psyche from being so close to him. Lack of regular exposure to sups made them more difficult to be around. Slow, deep breaths brought some relief.

The werewolf did the same cursory check as he had with the others while sniffing us out. He gave my friend a subtle nod. It must have been some kind of supernatural acknowledgment. His eyes didn't even linger on me before he waved us inside.

It took a moment for my eyes to adjust to the dimness of the lengthy hallway. Black walls enclosed me tightly. Only the solitary words "Mouse Trap" written in dripping blood-red letters decorated one side. I suppressed a shiver and tried not to think of their implied meaning. No wonder I was paranoid.

Several humans crowded the corridor, already caught in the supernatural snare. They had the glazed eyes of those who had imbibed one too many drinks, or maybe more, since one fell down. I stepped over him and kept going.

Once we moved into the main room, we found ourselves sucked into a huge crush of dancers. The capacity had to be close to the max, despite it being almost the size of a basketball court. Did they want us packed in like sardines?

Lisette split off from me with a small wave. I fought my way to the bar and ordered a drink. The vampire attending it had shaggy brown hair and dark eyes. An ice-cold feeling came from him, shocking my senses with its frigidity. Deep subtle breaths pushed the feeling down. If I stopped avoiding his kind so much, this sort of thing wouldn't happen.

The vampire produced my grenadine-laced Long Island Iced Tea with a flourish moments later. His smile, though fangless, showed more than a little interest. I gave him some cash and hurried away to find a semi-quiet corner as far from any non-humans as possible. That turned out to be about fifteen feet, but it was the best I could do under the circumstances.

Lisette had already joined the throng of dancers. She fit right in while gyrating with a guy sporting tri-colored hair and multiple piercings. Her bob of freshly colored pink didn't stand out much in this place. Our styles differed as much as our personalities. I preferred to keep my dark auburn hair long and natural. She changed hers the way others did their clothes.

The level of my drink continued to go down as I leaned against the wall. A nearby vampire waitress with long blonde tresses moved about the room. She sashayed through the congested dancers with fluid grace while keeping her serving tray steady. I kept hoping she'd drop it when someone bumped into her, but to my annoyance, she didn't.

Well-placed cameras scanned the scene from above. I didn't see a single spot they didn't cover. Keeping my gaze fixed on the scene before me, my hand slid along the waistband of my black club pants. The pocket knife I'd clipped there earlier remained tucked inside. Keeping it on me for safety reasons had become natural over the years. I didn't feel secure without it.

As the minutes ticked by, nothing disturbing occurred. The pain in my head subsided to a dull ache, and my muscles started to unwind. I knew I needed to get a grip and stop being so sure the monsters would come to get me. Lisette changed partners a few times before my drink ran out. When I set it down, thinking to order another, she came over and tugged on my arm.

"You're not standing there all night," she yelled into my ear. "I'm going to make sure you have a good time if it kills you!"

"It just might," I said.

She didn't hear me, which didn't matter anyway. I let her drag me along until we found a minuscule opening on the dance floor. People pressed in close, making it impossible to move without bumping into someone. I normally liked dancing, even in a crowd like this, but having bloodsuckers and wolves at my back tended to make me edgy. Lisette didn't show any concern for the predators lurking all around. She had to have known they were there—sups had ways of recognizing each other.

We stayed together for a while until my dancing loosened up. Satisfied with my progress, Lisette moved away to rejoin tri-color hair guy. I kept her within visual range to be on the safe side. By the fifth song, the place didn't seem that bad anymore. They played my kind of music and the men who danced with me weren't the clumsy or groping types.

My enjoyment didn't last. I sensed the change in the environment before it even reached me. Swirls of magic entered the room. It curled out of the vents and surged across the crowd—impossible to see or smell, but there nonetheless. Goosebumps ran across my skin as it touched me, feeling oily and foul, but otherwise having no effect. Normal humans weren't so lucky.

As people breathed it in, the mood changed. Everyone began dancing in crude ways better suited for a strip club. Sweat poured down their bodies as they peeled their clothes off and flung them away without a care. I had to duck when a bra went flying by, cherry blossom pink not being my color.

Magic pervaded the crowd. The kind that came from a powerful witch who concocted just the right spell for humans alone. None of the sups inside the place were affected and couldn't sense it like I could. Lisette was immune as well, but she had joined in the craze by rubbing her body all over her partner. She'd always enjoyed a good scene. It didn't even occur to her that something wasn't right. That trait about her was something I both loved and hated.

I moved toward her, knowing it wouldn't be long before the club staff figured out one human stood untouched by their magical cocktail, particularly with those cameras in place. We needed to leave, now.

"I'm getting out of here, Lisette. Are you coming?" I shouted.

Lisette had eyes only for the guy holding her close. They moved against each other sensuously with no regard for those around them. She didn't even glance my way and several stubborn people wouldn't move so I could get closer.

Dancers everywhere had either stripped off all their clothes or were well on their way to it. Their empty eyes stared at nothing, but their bodies managed lewd acts with impressive skill. The heat and passion pulsing through the room grew at an alarming rate, assailing my already overwhelmed senses. It wouldn't be long before it turned into an all-out orgy.

I kept trying to elbow my way through the crowd, but the already dim room suddenly switched to strobe lights, bringing me to a blinding halt.

It took a moment to adjust to the change, but

when my vision cleared the macabre scene before me appeared something akin to a horror movie, or really wicked porn. A few of the vamps joined in to take advantage of the changed atmosphere with their own special brand of "fun". I thought I caught sight of a set of fangs flashing, but couldn't be sure.

With a final hard shove, I reached Lisette. "Hey," I yelled in her ear, "we gotta go."

Lisette frowned and opened her mouth to argue. She still didn't get it and time was running out. I grabbed her face and turned it toward the crowd. "This is not normal. We have to go now!"

She stopped dancing and took a serious look around. A flicker of realization crossed her eyes. Ignoring her partner, who'd begun to do unseemly things with his tongue to her bare legs, she shuffled closer to me. "Mel, listen. I'm going to stay, but you should definitely go. Maybe we can catch up later or something?"

"You're not coming?"

"No way." She shook her head. "This is even better than I expected, but I wouldn't have brought you if I'd known. I'm sorry."

"You're really going to stay for this?" I asked. I'd known she had a kinky side, but didn't think it went this far.

"Yes. Now go!" She shoved me in the direction of the entrance. "If I have to haul you out, it's not going to be pretty."

"Fine, but be careful," I warned.

"Always," she said with a naughty grin. There would be no changing her mind, but she could take care of herself. I had to believe that as I began working my way back toward the entrance.

Getting through the mass of people made the army obstacle courses I'd done years before look easy. Almost every inch of the floor had human bodies twisting and bending in ways that defied logic. I tripped right before reaching the entrance hall when a pair of bare legs shot out in front of me.

My chin almost smacked the floor, but I managed to stop myself a bare inch before impact. While trying to untangle myself from the loose limbs, I felt a strong presence draw close. His aura filled me with coldness and dread. I peered up through my hair, which had swept in front of my face, to see a dark-skinned vampire standing at the edge of the crowd.

"You're wanted upstairs."

I gulped. "Now?"

A flash of fangs and darkening eyes gave me the only answer I needed. My senses told me he hadn't been undead for more than ten years, but he would still be far too strong. I wouldn't win in a fight against him, but my need for escape kept me searching for a way out. I made a quick sweep of the room. There had to be another exit.

The vamp didn't wait for me to find one. He grabbed my arm in a firm grip and pulled me out of the twisted mess of limbs. Everything moved in a blur as he propelled me toward a set of stairs not far from where we'd been moments before. I almost lost a shoe in the process, but managed to retain it with the grip of my toes.

We reached the top and went straight for a door

at the end of the hall. My senses alerted me to who waited on the other side—the same witch who had concocted the magic spell. The vampire shoved me through and entered behind me before shutting the door. With him blocking my escape, I was forced to face the coldly beautiful woman standing across the room in front of an ornate mahogany desk. Only the tiny crinkles around her eyes gave away her age as being somewhere in her forties.

Waves of powerful black magic emanated from her and I could smell the putrid remnants of a recent animal sacrifice. The odor made my nose wrinkle. A quick search revealed it to be in the corner, but I didn't linger on the mess that had to have once been a bird. Brown feathers were the only thing that gave it away now. The poor creature must have been part of the ingredients needed for the spell downstairs. PETA would have a field day with this woman.

"Here she is, Madam Noreen," the vampire behind me announced. I figured him for one of her minions. All the powerful sups had an entourage of "lessers" to do their bidding.

Noreen wore a designer pantsuit, minus the jacket. The white silk shirt she had on was sleeveless and low-cut, hugging her slim curves in a flattering way, and her highlighted hair had been swept up into a fancy twist. She stood with confident authority. I set my face in a neutral expression, not wanting to give away any signs of fear. Nothing could be done about my rapidly-beating heart, though.

Her lips curled up. "Are you enjoying my club,

little one?"

"Of course, but I just remembered I left my stove on." She didn't need to know I couldn't cook a hot dog without blowing it up into chunks. "It runs on gas, so I really should get home and shut it off."

I swiveled on my heels to leave, but didn't make it more than two steps. The vampire by the door shoved me back in the direction of the witch, making me stumble before catching myself. I turned around to find Noreen had moved in closer. When she spoke next, her tone might have come off as pleasant, but a hint of malice laced its edges.

"This shouldn't take long, don't worry."

Right, I felt really reassured.

"Good to know," I said instead, glancing back at the door, "but it would really suck if my apartment caught on fire. I really do have to get going." Maybe if I said it enough times, she'd believe me.

The witch ignored my protest and hit a button on a small remote in her hand. What had been a wall in front of me slid open on silent tracks. Tinted glass appeared behind it, along with the dance floor below. The lights continued to blink in rapid succession over the contorted bodies moving with the beat. I wasn't the prudish type, but some things went beyond even my limits. It took all my self-control not to shudder in revulsion.

Two pairs of suspicious eyes bored into me, making it difficult to keep up my stoicism. I was reaching the point where I wanted them to know how I really felt. Anyone with a scrap of decency would have had a tough time pretending any of this was okay.

"Why are you not participating in the fun?"

"Fun?" I raised my brows. "They're down there licking each other's asses, among other things. Not exactly my style."

Noreen's gaze didn't leave me as she spoke to the vampire. "Give us a moment, Hector."

"Of course, Madam."

Damn, should have kept my mouth shut. Playing innocent and stupid had gotten me out of a few messes in the past, but my anger ran too high this time to keep it in check. I resisted the urge to look back when the door clicked shut. My senses told me the minion moved down the hall, but he didn't go far.

Noreen frowned. "How is it that a human could be immune to my magic?"

I cocked my head to the side. "Excuse me?"

Best to try the innocent act again.

Her eyes narrowed. "Don't play games with me, young lady."

She flicked her delicate hand out and mumbled a few incomprehensible words. Magic swept over my body before fizzling out. Noreen had cast a strong freezing spell—one that should have prevented me from moving. Any human, or weaker sup, would have been susceptible to it. I stood still. Better to let her believe the spell worked for now. One thing was for sure, she wasn't buying my act of innocence.

Noreen studied me close for signs of resistance before nodding in satisfaction at her "forced compliance". I chanted a mantra in my head, telling myself not to move yet, as she stepped up to the window.

Her back faced me while she watched the dancers below.

"Here is the problem, dear. You should be down there, participating with the others, and yet that isn't the case. This tells me you're not what you seem."

My hand slid up to reach the hidden knife. It folded open in a smooth motion, thanks to countless hours of practice, and fit in the palm of my hand. I pressed it close to my side to keep it concealed.

Whatever happened, I had to make a choice. Killing her could get me in trouble with the authorities, if the sups chose to go that route. It would be difficult to prove self defense with all her employees vouching for her, and the police couldn't be told the truth. That'd be a sure death sentence in the supernatural community and not something I wanted to contemplate. If they decided to resolve things on their own, it wouldn't be much better. They might get over me wounding her, but they'd never let me get away with killing her.

Noreen's voice carried over to me as my mind raced. "You appear to be human, yet this cannot be true. What are you?"

If she pondered the subject too long, she might come to the correct answer. Various methods of escape ran through my head. The only idea that came to mind wouldn't be foolproof, but it was the best I could come up with under the circumstances. I remained motionless, waiting for my chance, as every instinct in me screamed to act.

"Of course, you can't answer that. Can you, little one?" She smoothed her pant legs and lifted her chin. "You should know I'm the most powerful witch in central

California. The entire area around here is mine now and every supernatural creature in it will obey me. Whatever you are, you're not human. Do not doubt I will discover the truth, one way or another."

I had to suppress a flinch at the idea I wasn't human. Maybe enhanced, but still very much mortal. I refused to lump myself in with a bunch of unnatural beings. They were the enemy and pure evil. Sups preyed on humans and sensors protected them, or at least we used to.

Noreen circled my still form, studying me. The hand concealing my knife twitched, wanting to take action against her cold, slithery presence. Not all witches were bad, but this one had gone down the dark path.

She stopped moving when she came around to my front again. Her hand rose to touch my face in a light caress. I wanted to shove it away. Pressure pushed at the edges of my mind as she tried to force her way in. Noreen would discover nothing by this method, but that in itself would reveal too much. When her eyes lit up, I knew I was in trouble.

"Hmmm, there is an associate of mine who would find you *very* interesting. How would you like to take a trip up north?"

I gave up the act of being frozen, and jerked her close.

"Not very much at all," I said, looking into her widened eyes.

In a swift move made easy from practice during my army days, I thrust the knife into the region of her stomach where her left kidney should be and twisted hard. It wasn't a death blow, since it could be healed quickly by her minions, but it would be enough to weaken her until I got away. The witch screamed out in pain and rage, forcing me to cover her mouth and drive her body to the floor. I shoved a knee into her chest for good measure. Her struggles weakened, but didn't stop.

Her kind had the same physical limitations as all other humans had—unless they put temporary spells in place ahead of time. Those wouldn't work on me, even if she had used them, but my real advantage came from being stronger. I went to the gym regularly to keep my muscles toned. A part of me always knew something like this might happen.

I couldn't hold her like this for long, so I searched for something nearby to use as a weapon. A fancy bronze sculpture of entwined lovers sitting on the nearest shelf caught my eye. I grabbed it and slugged her over the head with it. She slumped onto the plush, beige carpet without making another sound. A trickle of blood ran down her head, but the rise and fall of her chest let me know she still lived.

Seeing her lying still caused a twinge of guilt, but not enough to make me feel all that bad about it. She deserved a whole hell of a lot more, considering everything she'd done. It annoyed me to know she'd live to hurt more humans, but I didn't have the power to stop her. Keeping myself alive was a full time job.

I set the statue back on the table and yanked my knife out of her abdomen, cleaning the blade off on her mint green designer pants before putting it away. She wouldn't be happy about the mess, but that wasn't my problem. I had to get out of here.

My senses told me Hector still stood at the other end of the hall. Noreen must have had the room soundproofed. It didn't surprise me since having creatures around with excellent hearing would have made privacy rather difficult.

Taking a deep breath, I pulled the door open a few inches and peeked out. He was talking on the phone with his back facing my direction. No one else stood out there, leaving me a clear path. The loud music coming from below would help cover any sounds I made, but to be safe I slipped off my heels and held them in one hand.

Staying on my toes, I raced to the stairs. He didn't turn around during my passing. His murmuring voice faded as I moved farther away from him.

My flight down went almost as fast as the one going up. I slipped my shoes back on at the bottom, wanting both hands free. The main room appeared before me. I turned left toward the entrance. A small group of newcomers walked past, but their eyes were already glazed over from the heady magic still clouding the air.

I wanted to save them and the other humans but had no way of doing it alone. A sensor I might be, but superwoman I was not. It would be impossible to go against all the sups in the place and I was nothing if not realistic. Five were in the main dance floor area and two behind the bar. Not to mention the ones I'd left upstairs and the werewolf standing at the front door.

I hesitated for a moment over leaving Lisette, but didn't think she would be in any real danger. She'd made it clear she wanted to stay. They wouldn't dare to harm a pixie anyway with so many of her kind in the area. Pixies were one of the more peaceful races among the fae until one of their own was threatened. Then things got ugly.

Reaching the entrance, I saw the werewolf who'd been standing there before. He was busy checking over humans waiting in line. I debated for a moment on how to get past him, but realized he wasn't blocking the door, only standing by it. Rushing past him in the same way I had the vampire upstairs seemed like the best idea.

It would have worked too, if he hadn't grabbed my arm right before I slipped out.

"Where do you think you're going?" he growled out. His breath stank of things I didn't want to contemplate.

A smart reply didn't come to me. I stood frozen in his vise-like grip in that way that happens when you're sure you won't get caught and then you do. He used his free hand to reach for the radio on his belt. My near escape couldn't end so close to getting away. I had to do something.

Without thinking further, my knee shot out and slammed into his groin. A grunt escaped him as he doubled over, moving both his hands to cover his crotch. I took advantage by wrapping my arm around his neck and locking him into a choke hold, using his own weight against him. Within seconds, the blood supply to his head cut off and he slumped unconscious. I dropped him, letting his body fall to the ground in front of me with a loud thump. Countless hours of training in Brazilian Jiu Jitsu had just paid off.

Those waiting nearest in line looked at me with rounded eyes and dropped jaws. Not every day a one hundred and thirty pound girl knocked out a guy twice her size.

"Get out of here," I yelled at them, waving my arms in a shooing manner. "This place isn't safe!"

Confused gazes stared back at me. Why couldn't people heed a simple warning without needing an explanation first? I didn't have time for this—escape first, worry about them later. I took off down the street and around the next corner, dashing out of sight.

Chapter Two

My townhouse resembled something a tornado stopped by to visit. This occurred to me as I trudged back and forth across the living room. My feet traced the one clear path stretching from the sitting area to the kitchen. Every other available space was covered with books, old college assignments, and recently used fast food wrappers.

Aniya, my roommate, had been away for six weeks in Alaska visiting a guy she'd met online. Because neither of us were the tidiest people, the townhouse continued to remain a mess well after her departure. When we'd decided to move in together two years before, we'd worked out a deal where she would take care of the kitchen and I would deal with the bathroom. The rest of our home was supposed to be a mutual effort, but we rarely got past our assigned areas.

It didn't bother me most of the time since we didn't invite many people over, but it irked me now. I had a lot of pent up anxiety and frustration to work out after events from the night before. Mindless chores would help me get my focus back.

The dilemma over what to do about the nightclub incident pervaded my thoughts as I worked. I imagined each piece of trash I picked up as a vampire or werewolf who needed "removal". The dirty clothes being stuffed into the washer resembled a certain witch who needed her dark magic cleansed in a more permanent way.

There had to be a solution that wouldn't require a drastic lifestyle change. I was tired of moving around. My time in the military had been a great way to avoid sups, but it didn't make me safe. Nothing did.

Life had been comfortable since coming back to California. My friends were here and classes at the nearby university would be resuming in a couple of weeks. I looked forward to school and didn't want to leave again if possible. With two semesters left before getting my bachelor's degree, it wouldn't take long to finish. There had to be a way to stay until then.

I needed to be realistic, though.

The restaurant located in the Fisherman's Wharf where I worked wasn't more than a mile from the nightclub. Keeping my job there any longer wouldn't be a good idea, or going anywhere near that area. I escaped the sups once but the odds of surviving another run-in now that they could recognize me were not high. Explaining to my friends why I had a sudden aversion to downtown Monterey wouldn't be easy, but living in the neighboring town of Marina would give me some protection by distance—so long as I kept a low profile.

When the doorbell rang a little past noon, I already knew who was waiting outside. She always lit up my mind like a bright light as soon as she got near me. I still checked the peephole, though. Caution remained uppermost in my mind—even if my senses didn't detect anyone else. The sups could always hire a human to come after me and my abilities couldn't detect them so easily. They could be standing out there now, watching my home, and I'd never know it.

No one strange appeared to be lurking about, even after I opened the door for a better view. Lisette came bounding in with her usual cheerfulness, unaware of my paranoid behavior. Her pink hair swished with her movements.

I envied that carefree attitude she pulled off with such ease. At exactly five feet, she always made me think of a tiny ball of energy. From what I'd seen, all pixies were on the short side. I frequently reminded her of my six inches of greater height—to her annoyance.

Lisette headed straight for the living room and took a seat. I plopped down beside her on the hunter green couch Aniya and I had bought together the year before, happy to take a break from cleaning and other worries. My friend wasted no time opening the conversation.

"So...did you hear what happened at the club after you left last night?"

I lifted my brow. She didn't need any further encouragement.

"The police showed up and shut the place down. Everyone ran as soon as they arrived. I managed to escape but a lot of others were rounded up. No idea who called the cops, but I'm sure the owners weren't happy. Someone told me they'll be closed again tonight. I hope it isn't permanent." She shook her head and sighed.

At least she didn't suspect me of calling them. Keeping my thoughts to myself, I replied with sarcasm.

"I'm sure they'll be open again in no time. Good thing you didn't end up in jail, though. It would have sucked to come and get you out."

"Yeah, but you would have," she said with a smirk. "I can always count on that."

"You're right...maybe." She had always relied on me and Aniya a little too much to get her out of trouble.

"Hey, did you clean up?" Lisette's eyes widened. "I can see the floor. You have beige carpet. It's a little stained, but who would have guessed?"

"The place wasn't *that* bad before," I grumbled.

She raised an eyebrow. "You and Aniya are the worst slobs I know. It might be the reason you two make such good roommates. Who else would put up with your disgusting ways?"

Of course we'd look bad to the neat freak. This was an old argument that never got old for her. We'd met in high school after I'd moved from San Francisco at fifteen years old. Lisette and Aniya gave me the friendship I'd needed after losing my parents in a suspicious car crash—an event I continued to question after discovering I'd been adopted. Who my birth parents were remained a mystery, but the man and woman who raised me felt real enough that I couldn't refer to them as being adoptive.

Wanda, a family friend, took me in after the accident. She provided for my basic needs, though she often acted distant. None of my other "relatives" wanted the responsibility, but she hadn't minded. In some ways it turned out for the best because she helped me to understand my strange abilities. She'd recognized them from being a sensor herself. Since my senses had awakened only eight months before moving in with her, I'd been lost as to what they were or how to deal with them. She taught me a lot in the time we had together.

It didn't last long, though. Three years after she took me in a sup murdered her, taking my last guardian away. I was there when it happened and couldn't do anything to stop it. After that I left for the army, hoping to get away from the danger that seemed to be stalking me. Maybe it didn't make a lot of sense, but at least the military gave me a gun and armor to protect myself. That was more than I'd had before.

It put a slight strain on my friendship with Aniya and Lisette, but we managed to stay in contact. Both women were happy when I returned to California after my six-year obligation was up.

I forced myself out of my musings to realize Lisette had changed the subject.

"So, remember how you were asking about Aniya last night? Well, I got a weird email from her."

I frowned. "What did she say?"

"Something about not coming back. She says the guy she met up with in Alaska is so wonderful that she wants to stay with him. It was short and to the point. Not like her usual chatty messages. Doesn't she have to be back for those teaching courses or something?"

"Yeah, she does," I said, trying to make out the scribbling on the calendar hanging on the wall. "They start the same time my classes do."

Aniya wanted to be an elementary school teacher. She had always loved kids and wanted to work with them. She'd delayed going to college so she could work and save money first, but now she was almost done. There was no way she would give that up. Something was seriously wrong. If I could run into a supernatural trap in a public place, who's to say Aniya couldn't have done the same in Fairbanks? Of course, my experience last night might have been making me paranoid, but it couldn't be ruled out.

"When did you get the message?" I asked.

Lisette shrugged. "It came two days ago, but I didn't check my email 'til today. Things have been a little busy and there wasn't a chance."

"Something isn't right. She might be trying to tell us she's in trouble, but can't come out and say it."

Lisette shoved her hair behind her ears. "What're we going to do? I have too much going on with the new shop and can't just close it down right now."

"I know. School starts in two weeks for me, but we have to make sure Aniya is back before then."

My cell phone rang, interrupting us. I picked it up to check the caller ID—it was Aniya's mother. Lisette leaned over to see the screen and gave me an encouraging look. Maybe we weren't the only ones worried about our friend.

"Mrs. Singh, how are you?"

"Melena, I'm so sorry to bother you, but have you heard from my daughter?" she asked, her accented voice coming through the line. "She hasn't called me in weeks and I'm worried."

"No, I haven't, but Lisette got an email from her." I went on to explain the sketchy details we'd put together.

"This isn't like her. I told Aniya not to go up there, but she wouldn't listen. She was convinced this Philip was the one, and you know there is no talking her out of anything once her mind is set. We have to do something."

"Did you contact the police up there?" I asked. An easy solution would have been nice.

"I tried talking to them but they wouldn't listen and were no help at all." Mrs. Singh sniffled. "They wouldn't even consider searching for her. I don't know what to do. Please help me."

My heart ached for the woman. She had lost her husband ten years ago when a driver high on drugs hit him one night on his way home. They'd been in the country for a little over a decade by that time, but she'd had no support system to help her. Aniya was her only child and family in America.

Since my own parents died not long before that, I understood their loneliness. We spent a lot of time being there for each other because of it. In most instances, it involved late nights with ice cream and cookies, but it had made things easier. It would be horrible if she lost her daughter as well. I was close to both women and would help in any way I could.

"Mrs. Singh, I'm worried too. Lisette is here with me. Give us a chance to talk it over and I'll call you back, okay?"

"Yes, that is fine." Her words came out muffled. "Please, do let me know. I couldn't bear it if something happened to Aniya."

"I will. Until then, try to relax. We'll figure this

out. It could be we're all worrying for nothing," I tried to reassure her.

It took a few minutes to get her off the phone, but she eventually let me go. Afterward, I filled Lisette in on the parts of the conversation she hadn't overheard. She twirled her short hair in a nervous gesture.

"If the authorities aren't going to listen, one of us has to go up there and check on her," she said.

"I agree. I could take some time off work, but I'd need to be back before classes start. A search shouldn't take more than a few days. It could be as simple as taking her back from some crazy guy. I could handle that."

"Yeah...maybe." Lisette turned her face away and pressed her lips into a thin line.

I hated it when she blocked me out. The emotions I sensed from her didn't give away much. "What is it? I know you're thinking of something."

She shook her head. "Nothing. I'm just worried and Alaska is far away. It's a big state. That guy could have moved her anywhere and it might be impossible to find her. I'm hoping you don't have to look too hard."

She wasn't telling the whole truth. My senses could pick up lies, but further pressure wouldn't get Lisette to reveal what she was thinking. A characteristic I'd learned about her long ago.

"Listen, I know you can't come with your new herb shop keeping you busy. I'll have to go on my own, but it isn't a problem. I'm a big girl. I've traveled to much worse places than Alaska. After the Middle East, this will be nothing."

She shook her head. "Don't be so sure."

"Why the negative attitude?"

"It's nothing, but maybe we should find someone else. I have an uncle who might be willing to go. You shouldn't be traveling there alone when we don't even know what happened to Aniya. It could be dangerous. That's all I'm saying."

I patted her on the leg. "I'll be fine, don't worry. I'm perfectly capable of taking care of myself."

She spent the next few minutes arguing the point, but eventually gave up and left. I called Mrs. Singh back and let her know I'd be heading up to Alaska to check on her daughter in a couple of days, after arrangements could be made. She cried at the news and thanked me. I had some savings left from my parent's life insurance, which gave me a little wiggle room since I had to quit my job now as well.

That train of thought reminded me of my own problems from last night. Maybe this could work to my advantage by going away for a while. It would allow some time for troubles in Monterey to die down. I could focus on getting Aniya home safe, and then worry about myself. If all went well, finding her wouldn't take long. Mrs. Singh had the address where her daughter was supposed to be staying. She could give me it to me before I left. At least that would give me a place to start.

***

The next day I was browsing online when a flash of golden light sparked from behind me. I almost choked on the immense power that flooded the room. The presence it indicated was not one I wanted to face right now, or at any other time for that matter. I turned to glare at him.

He reclined on my bed with his arms behind his head and legs sprawled out on my navy blue comforter. He must have lain in that particular spot to provoke me. My jaw clenched. There would be no escaping this sup.

He was my angel of death—compelling and dangerous. His looks would captivate most women. He had broad shoulders and well-defined muscles. Golden tones tinted his skin and short hair, along with a slight glow that always seemed to be emanating from him. Enough angelic blood ran through his veins to give him a stunning aura of power. In general, nephilim were not a race to be messed with, but at twenty-five hundred years old he could put up a serious fight. My senses hadn't encountered many who were stronger.

I had learned firsthand how he could use his strength. He had been the one to kill Wanda. Why he hadn't chosen to do the same to me remained a mystery. The man continued to disturb me with his presence, whenever the urge came for him to do so. Because of him, I couldn't relax, not even in my own home.

The grudge I held against him burned deep inside, with no way to lessen it. It might have been a quick death, but Wanda had known the terror of seeing him come at her with a massive sword. The blade had cleaved her body in one stroke and given me nightmares for years afterward. I'd had enough other bloody memories added since then my mind had begun locking them away in a box for my own mental protection. That one scene tended to crop up more than the others, though.

Before her death, she had warned me there were two races a sensor needed to fear more than any others—nephilim and vampires. That day this man proved her right about one of them. He became a sporadic presence in my life from that point forward. In the beginning I feared him, but that emotion turned to resignation over time. He would kill me someday, I had no doubt. It was what his kind did to mine. Lucas just wanted to draw it out and make me squirm.

"Come to finish me off, Lucas?"

"It seems you're doing well courting death without my help, sensor."

I coughed. "What's that supposed to mean?"

His eyes reflected the cold intensity I had grown used to seeing. "I know about your run-in with the witch."

It didn't surprise me. Lucas always appeared to be aware of what went on in my life. Nephilim kept their unique abilities well guarded, but he'd revealed a few things during the time we'd known each other. I had learned he could teleport wherever he wanted and track my activities without me even knowing it. How that was possible with my immunity to magic, I didn't know, but it appeared he had a way. I was half-tempted to get a full body scan done to see if he hadn't somehow managed to implant a tracking device on me.

"What do you want, Lucas?"

He ignored my question and came over to peer at my computer screen. His body moved without a sound. I reached to shut off the monitor, but he grabbed my hand before my finger could graze the switch. His grip was tight and unyielding, much like the man.

"Booking a flight to Fairbanks?" he said close to my ear. "Interesting. You do have a death wish."

I managed to jerk my hand free. Of course, it worked because he allowed it. He straightened to a full standing position, forcing me to lift my head up.

"I'm not sure I know what you mean." I scooted my chair back a few inches. "But one of my best friends is in trouble. Someone has to check on her and there is no one else who can do it. Not that it's any of your business."

Why was I even bothering to explain this to him? Lucas always had a strange effect on my sensibilities.

His eyes glinted as if he knew what I was thinking. "You do realize Fairbanks is a supernatural haven? They will not respond well to your presence."

"A haven?" I asked. "Like a hot spot?"

His face reflected disgust. "Of course. Though not all of them stay for the summer months, there are still enough to be a threat to one of your kind."

I focused on a bare spot on the wall to avoid his all-knowing gaze. "Then I'll have to make sure they don't discover what I am."

The fact he bothered to divulge such a critical piece of information made me want to doubt him, but my senses revealed he spoke the truth. One of the more useful abilities I had—neither sups nor humans could lie to me.

Not even him.

Now I had to factor in the idea Fairbanks might be a more dangerous place to travel than expected. Not as bad as staying here. At least the supernatural population up there didn't have any reason to suspect me of being anything other than a normal human, but still not as safe as I'd hoped.

"I'm not going to be the one to stop you." He shrugged. "By all means, go and get yourself killed. Saves me the trouble of doing it later."

Whenever he said things like that, it didn't settle well with my truth meter. Not to mention his past history with me didn't quite match up and that made me wonder what his real game was. It had been three years since we'd last seen each other. He'd been avoiding me until now. What had changed?

"Speaking of my impending death, want to explain why you stepped in to save my life? I've wanted to ask, but you haven't given me the chance. You could have let me die in that explosion."

His face hardened. "I had my reasons. Don't read too much into it."

"Based on the way you act, it doesn't make sense. I want to know why. Not that it will make me forgive you for killing Wanda."

"Your Wanda got what was coming to her," he growled out. "As for the rest, there are some things better left alone. Let it go, sensor."

He told the truth on that one, which bothered me. My need to understand his actions overcame my fear. I stood up so that our faces were not more than a foot apart.

"You saved my life," I said between clenched teeth. "Despite killing my guardian and threatening many times to do the same to me. I have a hard time believing there isn't something more behind these random visits of yours."

One moment I stood beside the chair, and the next he had me against the wall. One hand wrapped around my throat. I struggled to breathe while being dangled at least a foot off the floor. Maybe yelling at him hadn't been such a good idea.

"I said leave it alone. I'm not warning you again."

Unable to move, except to grip Lucas' wrist in an attempt to relieve the pressure on my neck, all I could do was stare into his golden eyes. They projected suppressed rage. Maybe it would be better not to push my luck any further—not that talking was an option at the moment. He let me go right as my vision began to blacken. I fell to the floor in a heap, gasping for breath.

"Enjoy your trip to Alaska. It may be the last place you ever see."

By the time I sucked in enough air to reply, he'd left. Why did he have to flash in and out like that? Once again he'd disappeared to avoid answering my questions. Why had he shown up that day and saved my life? I would be dead now if he hadn't shielded my body from the rocket attack.

A souvenir from the experience still remained. Thinking of it made me feel for the scar above my hip. My fingers traced the rigid path where a piece of metal had managed to find its way around his formidable protection. It was several inches long and reached across my left side. Sometimes it ached as a reminder of that day. He had taken most of the damage, so the injury wasn't as bad as it could have been.

If he'd not come when he did, though, I wouldn't be alive—a point that was hard to admit. Several of my comrades lost their lives that day. I'd seen the horrific damage done to their bodies and tried to save the ones I could, but not many had made it. The same could have happened to me, but instead I was awarded for bravery under fire. Like a cruel joke. Lucas' immortality and ability to block the worst of the blast was what really made the difference and allowed me to help them. I wished I could have done more.

Lucas had suffered plenty of injuries himself, but healed after I helped him remove all the shrapnel from his body. He didn't stay long, leaving me to deal with the rest of the mess. It still begged the question—why would he suffer even temporary pain if he wanted me dead?

I had no easy answer and it didn't matter in the scheme of things. His being a nephilim and me a human would keep us at odds. Nothing could change that. I shrugged off his strange behavior for later speculation and focused on more imminent concerns.

Discovering Fairbanks might be more dangerous than expected meant I had even more preparations to make. Its supernatural haven status wouldn't stop me from searching for my best friend, and in fact made me want to check on her more, but it would be a greater risk. I couldn't allow my fear of sups to get in the way this time.

Chapter Three

The Fairbanks airport wasn't the largest one I'd ever flown into, but it had everything a sprawling metropolis of 35,000 people needed. Okay, more like 91,000, if you counted the neighboring towns. It seemed hard to believe the city rated as the second largest in the state at that size. The temperature outside didn't feel all too different from Monterey, and according to my research, the weather in August wouldn't be too bad. It made for an ideal time to come—if you discounted my missing friend and the supernatural element of the place.

The rental car company had my four-wheel drive Nissan Pathfinder ready when I arrived to pick it up. The plane had landed close to midnight and all I could think about was getting to my hotel and falling straight to sleep. With any luck, there wouldn't be any nocturnal sups to get in the way during the short drive. At only ten days into the month, vampires were limited to about seven hours of darkness for their outdoor activities. I figured they would use every minute of it to their advantage.

Nothing eventful happened along the way. I sensed the occasional sup nearby but none worth worrying about. The sight of the motel sign flashing ahead brought a sigh of relief. It wasn't anything fancy, just a typical 1950s style complex with rooms running on three sides of the parking lot. All at ground level. The cheap price was what had sold me.

After getting the keys to my room, I hauled my bags inside. Most people would think they were filled with a ton of girl stuff, but I'd brought a few tools of the trade as well in case things didn't go as planned. Not wanting to waste time, I dumped it all into a corner and wiped my hands off on my jeans while surveying my surroundings.

The room wasn't much better than the outside of the motel. It had shabby furniture and drapes to match. I didn't care for the strong smell of cigarette smoke lingering in the air, but at least everything appeared clean. There were far worse places to lay my head. In my army days I'd had to sleep on the cold, hard ground with nothing more than a sleeping bag for protection. That made me less picky than most people.

Discovering the weak water pressure in my shower the next morning didn't start the day out well, though. With wet hair clinging midway down my back, I dug out my laptop and managed to connect to the motel's complimentary Wi-Fi signal. A glance through my email showed Aniya still hadn't responded to any of my attempts to contact her.

A check of the weather report told me it would be a warm day, for Alaska, with highs in the upper seventies. Not too hot to leave my hair down. I dressed in jeans and a light blue t-shirt that matched my eyes. My backpack came with me, filled with various essentials that might come in handy. Knives, duct tape, first-aid kit, extra cash, and a change of clothes were all inside. If things got complicated, I'd be prepared.

The cafe adjacent to the motel turned out to be a good place to grab breakfast. Some of the locals were eating in there, along with a few tourists. No one paid much attention to my arrival, which suited me fine. At least my fair skin blended in well, along with my casual attire. You could pick out a lot of the visitors based on their expensive outdoor clothing and tanned complexions.

One family sitting in a corner booth had decked themselves out in top of the line gear. You'd think they were going to climb Mount Everest, rather than gold panning, as I'd overheard them say. I'd already guessed most Alaskans wouldn't fork out the kind of cash Mountain Hardwear and North Face called for. Locals were always more practical. You picked these things up when you traveled a lot. For me, I liked the same nice stuff the tourists did but it wasn't worth standing out any more than I had to.

After finishing my meal, I headed off to check the address Aniya had given her mother. My Google maps directions took me to the edge of town and I had to check twice to verify I'd come to the right place. The "house" turned out to be not much bigger than a shack. An old, rusted car sat looking forlorn in front with grass covering its tires and grill. Other assorted junk had been left scattered around the side, including a fridge lying on the ground with the door torn off. Many of the houses I'd driven past on the way here had similar debris decorating their yards. It wasn't the classiest of neighborhoods by any stretch of the imagination.

I risked the semi-rotted steps to check the front door. My intuition told me this place hadn't been lived in for years, but I wanted to verify that before running off. The door didn't open when my hand jiggled the knob, and no noises came from inside. A glance through the broken front window revealed nothing more than trash and animal feces littering the floor. It might have been used as a teenage hangout, but nothing more than that.

My shoulders slumped as my hopes for a quick search and rescue mission came to an end. I'd been set around the idea Aniya would be here and we could resolve the whole matter with a simple explanation. I should have known better. She must have figured out early on Philip wasn't who he claimed to be. The fake address proved it. Why hadn't she told any of us this as soon as she arrived?

The possible answers worried me. She was too innocent to get caught up in something like this. The idea of sups being involved was growing on me. What had Noreen said back at the club? Something about northern climates. I really hoped she didn't mean this far up.

I trudged back to my vehicle and resigned myself to speaking with the police next. Mrs. Singh had said they weren't cooperative over the phone, but it would be worth a try to talk to them in person. Maybe my physical presence would get their attention.

I pulled into the nearest station about ten minutes later and walked inside. A dour-faced woman with frizzy brown hair pulled back in a bun sat behind the counter. She refused to acknowledge my presence while typing something into the computer. Attempts to get her attention gained me nothing more than a dismissive hand gesture. An older man, with a scruffy gray beard and filthy clothes, sat in the corner watching me with interest. I turned my gaze away from him, not liking the toothless grin he gave me.

A few minutes later, the woman raised her head, impatience written all across her face. "What do you want?"

"This is a police station, right?" I lifted my brows in question.

"Of course." She rolled her eyes. "What are you here for?"

To smack some sense into you. Of course, I couldn't say that. She definitely wouldn't help then.

"I need to report a missing woman. Her name is Aniya Singh."

The woman's thin eyebrows rose at my statement. "How long has she been missing?"

"The last contact anyone had with her was almost three weeks ago." Better to leave out the details of her last cryptic and questionable email.

The desk clerk narrowed her eyes and gave me a slow once over. "Does your friend live in the Fairbanks area?"

As if that should matter. I tried to reign in my temper and forced my hand to unclench from the tight grip it had around my keys.

"No, she came here about six weeks ago to visit a man named Philip Mercer. I'm worried he may have done something to her."

"Are you a relative?"

"No."

"Then who are you?"

"I'm Melena Sanders. Aniya is my roommate and best friend. Her mother is worried about her. She tried calling your department to let you know her daughter was missing, but you all wouldn't help her."

Glenda, according to her name tag, attempted to look down her nose at me. Her thick glasses almost slid off. I smiled. She pushed them back up and leaned forward in her chair.

"I'm sure your friend is fine and most likely on some romantic getaway with this Philip she met up with. Happens all the time. He probably lives out in the *bush* where it's difficult to get a cell phone signal. Nothing to worry about."

I frowned. "The *bush*?"

She rolled her eyes. "The surrounding area outside the city. We refer to it as the *bush* here in Alaska. Where are you from?"

I shifted my stance. Glenda was beginning to piss me off with her line of questioning.

"California. What does that have to do with anything?"

She grimaced. "You *cheechakos*, always coming in here demanding immediate attention for the littlest thing. California, humph!"

Cheechako meant an outsider to Alaska. I'd seen the term mentioned while checking out travel sites, but by the way she said the word, it sounded like an insult. I'd had enough of this woman.

"I want to speak with a detective or police officer."

She gave me another huff before raising her large frame from the chair. It let out a loud squeak.

"You have a seat and I'll get someone to talk to you. Not that it'll do you any good." She yelled the last part over her shoulder. I cringed; most of the building must have heard her. The old guy in the corner sure did since he was now cackling with glee. The heavy scent of alcohol wafted heavily from him.

Not wanting to get too close to the drunk, I took a seat on the opposite side of the small waiting area. The chair I settled into was a hideous orange color that must have been older than my twenty-six years. Something told me this could take awhile so I stretched my legs out for greater comfort. The woman came back a few minutes later and confirmed my initial assumption—no one would see me right away. A glance at my watch told me it was about noon.

An hour later I was nodding off in my seat. There wasn't even a TV to keep me distracted. About the time my patience came to an end a tall man wearing a suit, who appeared to be in his late thirties, came lumbering out. He motioned for me to come over. I hopped up and followed him past the reception area.

There was a slight limp in his gait as he led the way back to his office. Once we were inside, with the door left open, he indicated I could have a seat on another shabby chair. This one had been upholstered with faded, moss green fabric. They must have designed it so no one would want to sit on it long.

Jack Thompson, as he introduced himself, was the deputy who had the so called "unfortunate" task of dealing with me. I noted his messy desk, but that didn't come as a surprise. It's a world-wide law that no desk in a police station can be clean and free from masses of paperwork.

"Ms. Sanders, Glenda told me of the concerns you have about your friend," he spoke in a semi-placating tone. "We did receive a phone call from Aniya Singh's mother last week. It is understandable for her to worry about her daughter, but there isn't enough evidence to make a case. We can't find any record of this Philip Mercer your friend was supposed to be visiting. That doesn't mean much, since it's possible he doesn't live in the city, but without more information to go on there is nothing we can do. Your traveling up here isn't going to change that."

"Deputy Thompson...," I began.

"Call me Jack."

A little more familiar than I would like, but if it would get him to cooperate...

"Okay, Jack. You have to understand there must be something wrong with Aniya for her to not contact anyone for this long. Are you sure there isn't something more that can be done?"

He folded his hands and set them in front of him. "The problem is there is no evidence of foul play. Women fly up here all the time to meet men. Some fall in love and stay, others run screaming for civilization. Plenty of girls forget to contact their families for a while. Your friend wouldn't be the first or the last. She and this man are probably out in an area where phones and internet aren't accessible. It's nothing to get worked up about."

"For three weeks? Without telling anyone?"

He shrugged. "It could be for even longer if they went out to the bush. Maybe that's where he lives and she just hasn't had a chance to get back in touch."

Frustrated, I tried a different tactic. "Can you at least take a report of Aniya being missing?"

He sighed. "We don't feel it's worth the effort at this point."

"Okay, but have there been any unidentified women's bodies found in the last few weeks."

Jack shook his head. "None recently."

I jumped on the way he worded his answer. "There have been some that occurred before, though?"

His face closed off. "It's nothing to concern yourself about. There've been no suspicious deaths in the area in the last few weeks. That's all you need to know."

My teeth ground together. The one failing of being able to sort out lies from truth is that some people could word things in a careful enough manner that they could get by me. Non-answers and evasion tactics were always good ways to avoid being caught up. It was amazing how many people used the skill even without knowing of my ability.

I stood and laid my hands flat on his desk. "In other words, you made me wait for over an hour to speak with you, so you could say nothing wrong is going on. Is that it?"

He held his hands up. "I'm sorry Ms. Sanders, but we're short-staffed for detectives right now and I'm busy with a real case. There's no need for you to get upset."

A real case? So that's how he saw it. Why care about one young woman from out of state? I tried a few more questions, hoping to push him into cooperating, but he didn't budge. He and his colleagues hadn't even bothered to check the address Aniya's mother had given them. Jack didn't seem concerned when I pointed out its lack of inhabitants. That should have been a red flag.

After a few more attempts to gain his cooperation, I gave up and stormed out of the police department, but not before leaving him my contact information and a picture of Aniya. Just in case.

It was ridiculous that they cared so little about a woman's life. I didn't want to believe the police—in any town—could be this careless. If they couldn't be bothered with Aniya's disappearance, I doubted they'd be much protection for me if things went wrong. It looked like I'd have to watch my own back. Luckily, I'd already considered this.

A local gun dealer held the .45 Sig Sauer I'd shipped up here a couple days before. Taking it in my luggage hadn't been an option and neither had driving the long distance to transport it. That left the postal system. Mailing a handgun in the United States had been no simple task, but I'd figured it out.

After stating my identity and purpose, the man at the counter asked me to fill out some paperwork before handing the gun over. It felt good to have it back, like my personal security blanket. I purchased some hollow point ammunition for it as well. The weapon wouldn't do much good against vamps, but a well placed bullet of the right caliber could damage a werewolf, along with several other races. Maybe even kill them.

Only a few prying questions slowed me down. The nice man seemed to understand the gun being for safety concerns, which made things easier. He didn't need to know what kind of threat it was really for. Besides, I considered werewolves and vamps to be a form of wildlife.

***

A few hours and a change of clothes later I was prepared for a night out. My hopes were now pinned to finding locals who might have seen Aniya. The backpack wouldn't be appropriate for the venues I planned to visit, which meant stuffing what I could into my purse. My gun fit in the concealed holster I'd tucked into the back of my pants and a leather jacket worn over a silky tank top covered it up. A few other small weapons of possible use were also hidden underneath my clothes. If all went well, I wouldn't need them, but for the duration of my stay they would always be with me.

The first bar I found appeared to be crowded, despite it not even being dark yet. Of course, the sun wouldn't set until almost 10:30 pm. Most people wouldn't bother to wait that long before going out. The place had a rustic appearance to it with the heads of various animals hung on the walls to add to the ambiance. Hunting game was known to be a big activity up here. I had my own kind of hunting in mind, in the form of whoever took Aniya, but any resulting heads wouldn't be all that appropriate.

Almost all eyes were on me as I entered. Out of what must have been dozens of patrons, maybe a third of them were women. Maybe the male to female ratio here reflected the average American woman's living preferences. I suspected most of my gender wouldn't be caught dead living in a place where it reached a chilling negative sixty degrees in the winter.

Having dealt with even greater gender ratios in the army, I figured it could be used to my advantage. Of course, even buying a drink for myself turned into a challenge. I let the guys come; acting nice enough at first, then flashing Aniya's picture in the hopes they would recognize her. As it turned out, no one did. I had to keep running the prospective suitors off.

It wasn't my looks that drew them to me as much as my availability. No matter where in the world you go, if a woman walks into a bar alone, it draws male attention. The drunker they are, the worse it gets. After more than an hour of constant attention and no progress, I left to try my luck elsewhere.

The next two places turned out to be a bust as well. The sun had set by the time I reached the fourth at almost eleven o'clock. My senses rose to high alert with the encroaching darkness. There were a couple of werewolves in the vicinity, but none were inside the bar I entered. My range went to about half a mile. They could be at any number of places. So long as they weren't at this one, it didn't matter where they chose to hang out.

At least most witches wouldn't reduce themselves to watering holes such as this one. The vamps had yet to make an appearance anywhere nearby. It made me wonder if they lived farther outside the city limits. I hadn't sensed any of them yet.

My current locale had a mixture of military and locals inside. Despite the dim lighting, I managed to count out five women. Four appeared to be wives or girlfriends, based on the protective postures of the men next to them. The fifth woman might have been military. Her clothes were flashy and the hint of tone in her body implied regular exercise. I could see a lot of her due to the short skirt and sleeveless blouse she wore. It almost made me snicker when she tossed her long, red hair back and all the guys followed the movement, almost drooling over the sight. This young woman, who couldn't have been more than twenty-one, seemed to be enjoying the attention she received. More power to her.

I went straight for the bar, noting the impressive craftsmanship of it. The carved, mahogany wood was smooth against my touch and lined at the edges with shiny brass. A middle-aged man with a heavy beard and dark hair took my drink order while the male attention continued to be diverted to the red-head. He served it to me while I sat on a bar stool drumming my fingers and studying the place.

Two guys walked up a few minutes later. They were both close to my age and semi-sober. I sized them up in a glance and recognized their type. Before either one could speak, I started in on them.

"You two stationed at Ft. Wainwright?"

They both nodded.

The taller one with short blond hair asked,

"How'd you know? We haven't seen you around here before."

"I haven't been in town long, but you both have army written all over you with those haircuts." I smiled so they wouldn't take offense.

"Yeah, that usually gives us away. My name's Matt and this is Jason." He pointed at his darker haired friend. "Mind if we take a seat?"

I nodded at the empty bar stools next to me. "Go ahead. So what do you do in the army?"

Matt leaned back and puffed out his chest with pride. "We're airborne infantry."

It took extreme effort not to roll my eyes. Airborne infantry usually served on the front lines in battle and always had big heads. They believed their short lifespan in combat made them braver than everyone else. Little did they know I had been airborne during my career as well, though not infantry, which was reserved for men. It made it hard for me to be impressed.

Not to mention my experiences in the Middle East proved anyone could be attacked. The enemy didn't care what your official job title was, though mine would have gotten me killed faster if they'd caught me out in the open. I was an interrogator. The bad guys hated us. In the Middle East, we had high dollar price tags on our heads.

"Must be exciting." I managed to squeeze out a bit of awe into my voice.

Jason spoke up. "I didn't catch your name."

"That's because I didn't give it." They weren't going to find out either, safer for all of us.

"Listen guys, I'm not really here for social purposes." I pulled out the picture of Aniya from my purse and held it up. "Have you seen this girl?"

Jason shook his head, but Matt focused in on it before replying. "As a matter of fact, I'm pretty sure I did. Back a few weeks ago, maybe a month."

I sat up straighter. "Where did you see her?"

"Actually, it was here," Matt answered. "She was with a guy. They didn't stick around long. I only saw them on my way to the bathroom. By the time I came back, both of them had left. Jason, you were here that night too. Don't you remember her? Not a face you could forget."

Jason shook his head. "Nah, I didn't see her man. A girl like that, though, would grab my attention." He indicated the picture of Aniya. Her Indian heritage showed. She had a beautiful face and glossy, black hair. The olive tone of her skin would stand out as well.

Their answers gave me the sinking suspicion that the vamps in the area were using their mesmerization skills to wipe the memories of any humans who might have seen them. The only reason Matt remembered seeing her was because he'd been out of the room when everyone else's memories were wiped. That led me to believe a vampire might have taken her. It would make my search and rescue a lot more difficult, even if my sensor abilities could help.

Focusing my attention on my witness, I continued my questioning. "What were they doing when you saw them?"

He shrugged. "Sitting at a table having a drink.

There may have been someone else with them, but it was crowded that night and not easy to tell."

"What did he look like?"

Matt rubbed his chin. "I think he had dark hair, maybe a couple inches long. His skin was pale too, but that's the norm for this place."

Considering Matt's own skin still had a golden tan, I doubted he'd been stationed here long. The description he gave fit what I remembered from a picture of Philip that Aniya had shown me before coming up here, but I needed more details to be sure.

"How about the man's size?"

He shook his head. "I'm not sure. Maybe not that big, though, or I might have remembered. Like I said, it was crowded that night and I only saw him for a second. Wouldn't have noticed the guy at all if it weren't for the girl. So, why all the questions?"

"It's a personal matter." I waved my hand away. "Nothing to concern yourself with."

He leaned forward and spoke in a low tone. "Is she in trouble?"

My head jerked up. My senses had just sparked a warning. Two werewolves and a vampire were headed straight for the bar. Shit. I needed to get out of here. I did not want to be drawing any supernatural attention if I didn't have to.

"Look, I'm sorry to cut this off, but I gotta go," I said, getting up. "Thanks for your help."

"Wait..." Matt called out. I ignored him and hurried for the door, darting between drunken patrons as I went.

I didn't make it outside in time. The sups pulled a late-model, black BMW into an empty parking spot right in front of the bar. My SUV sat three spaces past it. I kept walking.

Please don't let them notice me.

"Hey, pretty lady," the driver said. The only vamp in the group had to be the one to notice me. He stepped right into my path.

Avoid the eyes or he'll know.

I stared at a small stain on the collar of his brown suede jacket. Dried blood?

The two werewolves snickered. "You can take that one for yourself, man. We're going inside."

Rock music spilled out as they opened the bar door. I didn't look back. The vamp in front of me held all of my attention. He appeared to be in his mid-twenties, but was actually closer to thirty. He'd been undead for about five years. I could take him...probably.

My hand itched for my gun, but I remembered Wanda's words from long ago. "Melena, don't ever bring a gun to a vampire fight. You'll get one shot off before they kill you."

Okay, fine, plan B.

I put my hands in my pockets. "You wanna get out of my way?"

"Why don't you look at me, pretty lady?" Yeah, because that would be such a good idea. He was too young to compel me with his voice. In another few years he'd have that skill, but not yet. He had to use the eyes for now.

I continued to stare at the stain on his jacket. He

had hurt an innocent human. For all I knew it could have been Aniya. I clinched my fingers around my pocket knife. This guy had to be handled very carefully.

"Get out of my way," I said through clinched teeth. "I'm not interested."

His hand shot out to wrap around my throat. I flinched, but his grip wasn't so tight I couldn't breathe. Dead prey made bad meals for vampires.

"Look. At. Me." He forced my head up, but I kept my eyes averted. In my hand, I flipped open my knife— the same one I'd used on Noreen—and pressed it hard against the bulge in his pants. The tip didn't go through, but the threat was clear. He loosened his grip on my throat enough so I could speak.

"Back the fuck off," I said, "or else this is *really* going to hurt." Some people think the bigger the knife, the better. If used properly, a three inch blade could be every bit as effective.

He backed off.

"Bitch," he spat.

I smiled and held up my weapon. "Go inside before I change my mind and use this anyway."

A muscle ticked in his jaw. I thanked God he was too young to be a real threat. He hesitated a moment longer before making a move to pass me. I stepped aside, giving him plenty of room. My knife stayed up where he could see it.

He tried to catch my eyes one more time. He kept going when it didn't work. I'd had years of practice keeping my eyes averted when vamps were around. It had kept me alive, though I preferred to avoid them altogether. One day, I'd run into a vampire who wouldn't forget he could heal from a knife wound—even if it was pointed at his groin.

Chapter Four

The next morning, cool and crisp air hit me as I stepped outside. My tank top and shorts didn't give me much protection from the cold morning temperatures of Fairbanks, but I'd warm up after a mile. Driving around town yesterday gave me a basic feel for the area, but it hadn't been enough. Fast travel usually resulted in my senses being overloaded with too much information at once. A morning run would give me a better mental picture of the demographics and what I might be dealing with. I needed the exercise, anyway.

After taking a few minutes to stretch, I took off down the road, staying parallel to the street. The muscles in my legs protested at first, but as my feet found a steady rhythm the tightness faded away. Not many cars were out yet, making the run more pleasant. I hated choking on exhaust fumes.

A mixture of businesses and homes appeared along the way, each of them in varying conditions. Some people took care of their houses by giving them regular paint jobs and having manicured lawns with beautiful gardens. Others spent a lot less time maintaining their places and had trash and junk spread all around, much like the "shack" I'd visited the day before.

My pace slowed as I neared downtown so I could

take everything in. The landscaping was colorful near the Chena River with an assortment of flower beds set in key places for aesthetics. Multistory buildings rose up to contrast with the flowing water running alongside my path.

I felt a vile presence up ahead. The sensation of the troll it represented made my stomach want to revolt. I could've taken a longer route around, but I didn't think it would be worth the effort. He'd cast a look away spell, which I sensed as I neared him, and he didn't appear to want trouble. It would disrupt fishing with the fancy pole he used. Curiosity made me take a second glance before averting my gaze. Wanda had shown me pictures before, but this was the first one I'd seen up close. They weren't that common in cities. Few of the fae races were, except pixies.

The troll was an ugly, squat creature with hairy arms and legs. He had a bulbous nose that could be used to sniff out prey. His kind didn't like anyone paying attention to them, and if they caught you looking, things would get nasty quick. A small number of young children could see them. They often disappeared if the troll caught them staring. An adult could be taken as well. I did not want to risk him noticing me. Trolls were carnivores and not picky about what kind of meat they ate.

I veered off in another direction and headed into downtown. When I reached 2nd Avenue, there were a number of gift shops, restaurants, and bars lining the street. With the light foot traffic, I was able to get a brief glimpse into places that caught my eye. One was a bakery with the sweet-smelling aroma of fruit pastries wafting from it. The scent almost made me stop my run. I'd always been a sucker for baked goods.

This was no time to linger, though. I forced myself to keep going and headed back into the residential areas. Other than the troll, there hadn't been any other sups around.

A short while later my senses picked up something I hadn't expected. A warm and tingly sensation ran over me with familiarity. It had been a long time since I'd felt anything like it. The shock hit me hard enough I almost stumbled over a street curb. A female sensor was a little south of me. We were such a rare breed that this was the first one I'd encountered since Wanda's death. I let my senses guide me to her. Anticipation thrummed through my veins at the opportunity to meet another of my kind.

Within minutes, her home came into view and the condition of it almost brought me to a halt. I slowed to a walk, not liking the scene. It was a dilapidated place that might have been decent a couple decades ago, but didn't look so great now. The decorative shutters hung loose with chips in their green paint visible even from a distance. White siding lined the outer walls; it was discolored and falling apart.

I made my way to the front where a sagging metal fence, tangled with weeds, surrounded the yard. The gate was missing with broken hinges left as the only clue it ever existed. I took cautious steps past it while trying not to trip on the numerous cracks in the sidewalk leading up to the entrance.

Part of me hadn't known what to expect, coming here without a plan. It turned out the sensor I was searching for sat on the sloped cement porch appearing forlorn and lost. She had to be about fourteen years old. Her head was bowed down while she poked at a large rock with one of her bare feet. A ponytail kept most of her brown hair off her pale face, but uneven bangs prevented me from seeing her eyes. The clothes she wore told much of the same story as the house. Whoever took care of this girl didn't do a good job of it. She wore faded jeans with numerous holes in them and a stained, yellow t-shirt.

I cleared my throat to get her attention. She lifted her head to reveal a pretty face and stark blue eyes. Surprise flickered in them briefly, making me think most people ignored her when they passed by. Not knowing what else to do, I said the first thing that came to mind.

"Hi, I'm Melena."

She continued to stare at me. I'd thought I was guarded at that age, but she had me beat by a long shot.

"Is your mother home?"

She shook her head. "Nope."

"Is she always gone this early?"

The girl shrugged. "More like she's always out this late."

"So you expect her back soon?"

She kicked the rock away from her. "She won't be back before dark."

What kind of mother left her young daughter alone all night and day? I frowned. "Do you have someone else who watches over you?"

The girl narrowed her eyes. "Who are you? Child protective services or something?"

"Um, no." I shook my head. "Nothing like that, but I do think you know we have something in common. Do you mind if I take a seat?" I waved at a spot about four feet from her on the other side of the steps.

Her brows furrowed as she looked at the empty expanse of porch. A long moment passed before she shrugged her shoulders. "Yeah, sure."

"So do you know what I'm talking about? How we are alike?"

"You feel...familiar," she said, as if surprised by the conclusion.

I nodded. "Yep, how long have you been sensing things?" It couldn't have been long, based on her age. It always started around puberty.

She stared at her hands, as if contemplating whether or not to answer.

"A few months," she whispered.

"Did you tell your mom?" She had to have inherited the ability from somewhere. Wanda had told me it could come from either parent, and could even skip generations.

"No way. She wouldn't want to hear about it and...I'm too scared to tell her."

"So your mom isn't like you?"

She returned her attention to her hands again, and started picking at her already short nails.

"No," she mumbled. "I thought maybe something was wrong with me and that she might leave me for good if I told her."

"There's nothing wrong with you," I said. "What about your father? Is he like you?"

Her thin body tensed at my question. "I never met my dad, he left after I was born."

Okay, maybe it was time for a different topic. "What's your name?"

"Emily."

"Nice to meet you, Emily." I smiled.

She returned it with a weaker version.

"Do you want to know what you are? I could help." This wasn't the time to be taking on lost little girls, but not offering might be worse. I really didn't want to think of the danger she was in while living in this town.

"I don't know." She pulled at some loose threads on her pants. "My mom will get mad if she finds out I'm talking to you. She likes for us to keep private since we moved up here." Her voice came out low and nervous.

I drew my knees up and leaned back against the post behind me. The move seemed to relax her. "Where did you come from before?"

Emily's lips curved up, as if she had recalled a fond memory, but then her face hardened. "Dallas. We lived there my whole life until we moved here a year ago. I hate this place. My mom changed since coming here and I don't like it."

"I'm sorry," I said. "What do you think made her change?"

Anger filled her eyes. "That man she came up here for, Robert. He made her into something else. I knew she changed, but since these new...."

She paused, as if unable to find the word she

wanted.

"Senses?" I supplied.

Emily nodded. "Yeah, senses. Since they started, I figured out she ain't like other people. She's like *him.*"

My fingernails dug into my palms. I suspected what she meant. Our kind tended to categorize anything inhuman as something else. Something different. We did it without thinking, as a sort of reflex.

"What do you mean by like *him*?"

She took a deep breath and blew it out, making the longer strands of her bangs fly up. She brushed them away. Her next words came out low.

"I never did like Robert or his friends. But when these senses came, I figured out my mom and those guys feel different from everyone else."

"What do they feel like?"

"Cold, some more than others, and I feel scared to be around them. Like I know they don't like me. There are other kinds too. They feel hot and...wild, maybe?"

I nodded. "Do you know what you are describing?"

"I think so," she said in a small voice. "Are they what I think they are?"

"You tell me."

She bit her lip. "Vampires and werewolves? I sense other kinds too. They feel different, but I can't figure out what they are."

I nodded. "You described how vampires and werewolves feel exactly. The others we can figure out together. For being on your own with no one to help you, you're doing pretty good."

She cocked her head to the side. "You think so?"

"Of course, though you have a lot more to learn. Do you have any plans this morning?"

She shook her head. I needed to get on with the hunt for Aniya, but giving Emily a couple hours of my time wouldn't hurt my search too much. Most of the businesses I wanted to stop by wouldn't be open for awhile yet, so it wouldn't be too big of a sacrifice.

Besides, the girl needed to learn the basics and there was no one else to teach her except me. If her mom was in deep with the sups, Emily could get herself killed if she gave her abilities away. I'd hate myself if something happened to her because I didn't help.

"Good." I leaned forward. "Let's start with any questions you have."

She gave me a shy look and scooted a couple of feet closer to me. Her voice came out low when she spoke next. "Can you tell me what it was like for you when your senses first started?"

I held back a grimace. My senses awakening was a dark time, but then again, she could say the same. I needed to tell her something about myself to earn her trust.

"Well, I was about the same age as you, so we have that in common."

She nodded. "What was it like the first day?"

I snorted. "Sex and screaming witches."

"Huh?"

My eyes drifted to the blue sky beyond the porch. "My parents were having sex in their room next to mine. I woke up to sensing waves of lust rolling off them. The faint squeaks of their bed pretty much told the rest of the story. At least it explained why they always *slept in* on Saturday mornings."

Emily shuddered. "Glad my mom hasn't done that to me."

I shrugged. "Sometimes I'd get up and go outside so I wouldn't have to sense them. At least you have to be really close to feel people's emotions, especially humans."

"Yeah." Emily's eyes lost their focus for a moment before her head snapped up. "Wait, didn't you say something about screaming witches?"

"Oh, the screaming witches." I paused to scrutinize the yard and street, as if spies might be nearby. Emily scooted a few inches closer. "A huge family of them lived next door. They got up early every morning. I could always sense their anger or excitement as they played around with each other. It felt like screaming in my head. Gave me awful migraines until I got used to it."

"Did you have any problems with them?" she asked, keeping her voice low.

"Nah," I shook my head. "Their oldest daughter, Kristen, was my age. Later we became good friends until I had to move away when my parents died."

Emily's eyes dropped down. "Oh, I'm sorry."

I reached over and squeezed her hand. "Don't worry about it. As you can see, I survived."

Her head lifted. "So what happened after that?"

"A sensor like us took me in. She taught me most everything I know about our kind. It wasn't the kind of life I'd hoped for, but sometimes you have to go where life leads you."

She sighed. "I figured that one out already."

I started to ask another question, but a werewolf heading in our direction grabbed my attention. Emily's eyes rounded at the same time. She stood up.

"You have to go," she said, eyes panicked. "He can't catch you here."

I jumped up to my feet. "Who?"

"One of the guys who hangs out at the same place as my mom."

My heart leaped in my throat. "Has he done something to hurt you?"

She shook her head and let out a short laugh. "No way. Derrick wouldn't do anything like that. Since I stopped going over to that house a few months ago, he started coming here to check on me. He worries cuz I'm here alone all the time."

"Okay," I said, still not comfortable with the idea of leaving her with a werewolf. "You sure you'll be okay?"

Emily nodded. "Yeah, he's a nice guy, not like the others. Are you gonna come back?"

He was two blocks from us. I started inching my way down the sidewalk, but gave her a reassuring smile. "Tomorrow. I'll come by and bring some cheeseburgers."

She grinned. "Okay."

After a short wave, I made my way to the street. Once there, I sped up to a light jog and managed to get two houses down before the werewolf passed in an old truck. I didn't even glance in his direction. He hadn't seen me come from the house so there was no reason for him to be suspicious. I didn't sense any emotions coming from him either. Not wanting to take chances, though, I headed straight back to the motel. At least no sups were close by there.

Chapter Five

Later that afternoon, I found myself in Pioneer Park, formerly known as Alaskaland. The travel brochures had boasted of it being a great tourist stop, but it also had a more important feature. Many locals ran shops in the park. It made the place ideal for questioning a wide range of people. It was doubtful Aniya had been here herself, but maybe someone had seen her around town or near their home. I couldn't rule out any possibilities.

Most of the buildings inside the park were old-style log cabins, painted in shades of green, brown, and other assorted colors. They came in a variety of shapes and sizes as well. Not every place was a cabin, though. Some structures were outfitted with white siding and probably built sometime around the WWII era.

I stopped by several galleries, museums, and other attractions along the way. Between those and the shops, I often found myself distracted while gazing at the various selections on display. They made me think of my missing friend and her love of shopping for unique things.

Aniya wasn't the type of woman who wanted the name brand stuff. She liked unusual jewelry, locally designed clothes, and hand-crafted knick-knacks. Malls were never her style and a place like this would have appealed to her. Too bad she probably didn't get the chance to visit.

Each time I asked the proprietors about her no one recognized the picture I showed them. The chances of her being alive and well were sinking by the minute, but I refused to give up hope yet. She had dreams and deserved a future where she could live them.

Toward the end of my rounds through the park, I came across a tarot card reading place. The older woman who ran it had a healthy amount of magic thrumming through her. Not the dark kind or I wouldn't have considered entering, but a tinge of gray was mixed in with the light. She felt warm, with an electric charge sparking out. Static raced across my mind as I recognized her as a mystic.

There weren't many more of her kind than mine. Mystics and witches didn't get along well and had been fighting each other for centuries. It had something to do with their magic clashing. I didn't know the specifics, but there'd always been more witches around, giving them the greater advantage.

The woman caught me hovering at the door and waved me inside. I took two steps in and stopped. She wasn't much of a threat, but coming near her still made me squeamish. The vampire from the night before had been a reminder of the dangers I faced with sups.

"You look lost, my dear. Are you searching for something?"

Once my eyes had adjusted to the dim interior, I saw she had kind hazel eyes, and a face framed by long silver hair. The wrinkles lining her skin accentuated, rather than detracted, from her appearance. My senses told me she was pushing seventy years old, but she had a small, nimble body that must have been more than capable.

The mystic must have been one of those types who got into the act of her profession because she wore a long, dark robe that flowed around her. Something I might have expected from a tarot card reader. Of course, she ran her business inside a major tourist attraction. She would want to cater to customers' expectations.

"Actually, I'm looking for someone." Pushing aside my trepidation, I pulled out my picture of Aniya. "Have you seen this woman?"

She leaned over the black silk-draped table she sat behind and squinted at the photo. After a moment, she shook her head.

"No, I'm sorry. She hasn't been around here."

"You haven't seen her anywhere?"

She smiled. "I don't get about town much these days. This is the one place I have a chance to see anyone aside from my family."

I supposed that made sense at her age, but this was the last place I had left to visit in the park and had hoped for better results. It was the only reason I'd been willing to take a chance on her. Vampires couldn't mesmerize her into forgetting like they could the humans around here. Not at her power level.

"Why don't I give you a reading? Perhaps that will help."

My body tensed. Sticking around a sup, any sup, for very long did not sit well with me. Never mind that I needed to work on getting past that particular problem if I was ever going to have any luck finding Aniya. I really didn't think she was with a human anymore.

The mystic cocked her head at seeing my reluctance. "If you're really worried about your friend, it could be worth a try."

Doubtful, but this was an opportunity to get a feel for the woman and see what she was made of. All the other readings in my past had been fake, done by people who had no skills at all. I went along with the show because it amused me to see how far they would go in their act. My ability to sense magic let me know they were doing nothing more than guessing. But this woman had magic—not that it would do either of us any good.

She took the twenty I handed her and stuffed it into a small opening in her robe. I contemplated asking her if she could do a spell with Aniya's picture to find her, but didn't feel ready to ask for that kind of help. One step at a time. I'd just set the photo down on the table. Maybe she'd make the offer herself.

She turned her back to get a deck of tarot cards after motioning for me to take a seat. My muscles cramped as they bent down into the chair, the kind of ache that came after too many hours on your feet. The run this morning must have taken a bigger toll than what I'd thought. I made a mental note to get myself into a better routine with my workouts. They were more important now than ever.

The mystic shuffled the cards and arranged them with care before laying them down. We both took an indrawn breath at what was revealed, or rather, not revealed. The woman's face turned ashen. I drew back in my chair. Every card she laid down came up blank—solid white, with nothing on them. It was the last thing I'd expected.

Her magic was trying to pull my information, but couldn't, so it wiped out the details of the cards. She mumbled under her breath as her hands began to shake. Guilt stirred inside me at seeing her so upset. From what I could tell, the cards had their normal illustrations on them until she laid them down, then they blanked out. She tried several times with no success. My very nature made me a void for magic, but I hadn't realized it went that far.

Our attention was so riveted on her trying a new deck that neither of us noticed the man who stepped in until he spoke.

"Those won't work on her, Yvonne." His rough voice carried over to us. I jumped.

A glance toward the open doorway revealed a man who most people would assume to be in his mid-fifties—about two hundred years short of his real age. He was large despite a slightly stooped back and he had black hair highlighted with streaks of gray. Most of it was slicked back, but a few fallen locks framed his face. I guessed his origin to be native Alaskan, based on the medium skin color he had. He was also a shaman.

I'd never met one of his kind before, but had heard of them. His magic was strong and of the earth. To my surprise, he didn't make me as nervous as many of the other sup races did. He had a sense of peace about him. His aura drifted through my mind like a cool breeze on a hot summer day, bringing relief from the overwhelming heat. I had to fight myself to not relax in his presence.

Yvonne frowned as soon as she saw him and cursed under her breath. She covered the deck with her hands, but it sounded like her failure to read the cards had been discovered already. I was more worried about how the shaman knew they wouldn't work.

"What do you want, Charlie? Can't you see I'm with a customer?"

He raised his brows. "Not much of a customer if you ask me."

I stood up. That was my cue to go. The shaman took a step back into the doorway and spread his feet apart. His face could have been set in stone.

"Let me pass," I said through gritted teeth.

He turned his gaze on Yvonne. "I said your cards won't work on her. Magic doesn't work on her."

I cursed myself for being stupid enough to allow the reading.

Yvonne frowned. "Who are you that my magic doesn't work? What are you doing to prevent it?"

Her stirrings of resentment pushed at my senses. I moved as close to the door as I dared. Charlie didn't budge an inch. He didn't show any emotion either, which made it hard for me to get a read on him. With no way out, I was stuck, but if it came down to it I'd climb over the shaman to get away.

"Don't push her, Yvonne," he said. "There aren't many of her kind left. She is rare but harmless for the most part. She should have known better than to trick you, though." He shot a disapproving look in my direction.

I shrugged while keeping my hands in my pockets where a couple of small knives rested. The gun would be too loud and draw attention. My body backed up against the wall so no one could come from behind. It allowed me to keep both the man and woman in my view—her in front of me and him to the right. I needed to be ready in case they attacked. Neither appeared as threatening as the witch in Monterey, but the shaman was far more powerful.

"How do you know what I am?" I asked in a tight voice.

"I've seen it. Trouble is brewing among the supernaturals in this area. Has been for some time, and you have the ability to make it stop."

The glare I shot at him didn't seem to have any effect. "I don't have any business with the supernaturals. I'm here to find a friend."

Charlie shook his head. "If you continue to believe that, you'll not succeed in getting her back. There is much more for you to accomplish on your quest than you realize. You have to help set things right."

I didn't want to be tied to anything of that nature. "Sounds like a problem for you supernaturals to deal with, not me."

He sighed.

"It is you, have no doubt in that." He nodded at the picture of Aniya I'd left sitting on Yvonne's table during the reading. "That girl drew you here, did she not?"

I glanced at the solitary photo laying on a black sea of silk. It looked as alone there as my friend probably felt right now.

"What do you know of her?" I asked. If he had answers, I wanted them.

"Not much, but she isn't gonna be easy to get back. I doubt they'll let her go at this point."

"They?"

"The dark ones. I did my best to make them leave when they took over a few years back, but have only succeeded in keeping most of them out of town. They need to be removed, but the only one who could do it has been put under a spell."

I scowled at him. "What does that have anything to do with me and my missing friend?"

"If you broke the spell, which binds the one we need, all will be set right and you could get your friend back."

He was speaking the truth, but that didn't make me feel better. "Who is this person that is so important?"

Charlie clasped his hands behind his back. "He is a very old vampire who ruled the supernaturals in this area for more than four decades before he was removed from power. His name is Nikolas."

I let out a nervous laugh. "And you want me to break a spell so he can come back?"

Charlie nodded.

"No."

"You'll have to do it, Melena, if you want to save your friend. Resist the things I'm telling you now, but it will make things harder for you in the future. You know this to be true. Your abilities would tell you if I lied."

I flinched. Maybe I should try a different line of questioning. "How do you know my name?"

He smiled. "I know many things."

I stepped toward the door.

"That isn't possible. Now let me pass." My voice might have come out a shade panicky, but it couldn't be helped.

"Very well. Go now, sensor, but remember my words. You'll do the right thing when the time comes."

He bowed his head and moved aside. Yvonne said nothing during this time. She had listened to our conversation, but hadn't given any feelings away. As an afterthought, I grabbed the picture of Aniya off the table before turning back to the shaman.

"Will you be warning the dark ones about me?"

"Your secret is safe with us." He nodded toward Yvonne to include her. "We are no threat to you."

He told the truth and, for now, that was enough for me. I nodded and walked out.

His parting words floated over me as I rushed away. "May the wisdom of your ancestors guide you."

What the hell was that supposed to mean?

Chapter Six

Three days of fruitless searching, along with daily lunches at Emily's, and I found myself returning to the one place Aniya had been seen. No one else had recognized her and my options were running out.

It had been frustrating, going from one establishment to another as I tried to ignore the warning Charlie had given me. No matter what my senses said about his honesty, I didn't know him or trust him. After visiting Pioneer Park, I checked other places including more bars, restaurants, and shops. To be thorough, I even stopped by a few clinics and the hospital, but not one trace of her could be found.

My ability to work around sups had become better. I'd even followed a few in the hopes they would lead me back to Aniya. They seemed to be everywhere, in one form or another, but no new leads had come up. Each day that passed pushed my sense of urgency higher until coming back here was the only choice I had left.

Everything at the bar looked the same as my last visit, except now it was Friday night and most of the twenty-plus tables were full. Luckily for me, a small table in a semi-dark corner was vacated by a young couple right after my arrival. I managed to grab it before anyone else got there.

Matt showed up about fifteen minutes later. He appeared to be alone this time, since his friend was nowhere in sight. Deciding he would make a better companion than some of the other patrons, I motioned him over. His eyes lit up in recognition when he saw me.

"Have a seat," I offered.

He smiled and took the chair I indicated. "Didn't expect to see you here after your quick getaway the other night."

I shrugged. "Something came up, sorry."

"So, what are you doing here tonight?"

"What does it look like?" I held my drink up.

"Yeah, I guess that was a dumb question," he admitted. "Any luck finding your friend?"

"No." I sighed. "Still searching."

His brows drew together. "It's weird that she disappeared like that without a trace."

"Yes, it is," I said. Of course, now I had a better idea of why. The vampires had her.

"I have to admit, if my best friend was missing, I'd be out searching too." He shook his head. "Have you tried talking to the police?"

"Yeah, but they won't help. They think she ran off with some guy she met here and will turn up eventually."

Matt took a chug of his beer. "Are you sure that isn't what happened? She looked mighty comfortable with that guy I saw her with..."

I slammed my drink down. The remnants splashed from the glass and sprayed across the table. Matt froze in his seat, face lined in shock. All the frustration I'd kept bottled inside came rising to the top. I gave him the glare to end all glares.

"Don't you think I know my best friend well enough to recognize when something is wrong? She wouldn't abandon the people she cares about. The life she was building for herself. You don't know anything about her!"

Several people nearby turned to look at us. Matt flushed at their attention and raised his hands in surrender.

"I wasn't trying to offend you," he said in a calm voice. "The first step is to eliminate the obvious. You have to know that."

I continued to glower at him, my teeth grinding to keep from saying anything I would regret. It wasn't easy, but more people were watching us now. I didn't want to make things worse. That much of my common sense still functioned.

"Look, I didn't mean to make you mad. Sorry to have upset you." Matt stood. A hurt expression covered his face. "Good luck finding your friend."

Guilt crept up as I watched him walk away. His back was ramrod straight. He wasn't the enemy, the sups were. Matt had been trying to help. It didn't make sense to jump down his throat for something he had no part in. I needed to get myself together and remember where to direct my frustrations.

Plus, I didn't want to scare him off—the arrival of several vamps in the parking lot prompted me to be reasonable. They had impeccable timing. I'd been so caught up in my anger, their presence hadn't even blipped on my radar. In a desperate bid, I called out to him.

"Wait, Matt, come back."

He turned and raised an inquiring brow.

"Please...sit. Let's start over." People were staring at us again, but I didn't care. The vamps were making their way toward the building and the tension was building in my head. They loved finding people sitting alone and I didn't want to be their next meal. In my case, blood would tell.

He wavered in his stance and I couldn't blame him. I had yelled at him in front of a large crowd of strangers. My pleading expression must have been pathetic enough because he came back.

After he sat down, I held out my hand. "I'm Melena Sanders."

A smile twitched on his face as his palm met mine, shaking with a firm grip before letting go. Matt had all-American looks, which must have attracted a lot of women. He probably wasn't used to ones like me going off on him, especially not in public.

"Matt Burrows," he replied.

We started over from there and I was glad I'd changed my attitude toward him. I had no allies in this place and having someone to talk to gave me a chance to relax. Matt kept up a light conversation with me by chatting about his time in Alaska, explaining how the climate and locale weren't all that great for him. He couldn't wait until his time ended with the army and he could go back home to Houston. I told him about my own career, allowing a few details to slip for the sake of conversation.

Matt didn't see the sups when they came in. I'd taken the best position at the corner table to observe the room. From lowered lids, I kept a close watch on the trio. At least the physical pain of being near them wasn't as difficult as it had been before. My senses were growing used to their presence.

It appeared they had come in for a drink, though not the same kind as the rest of us in the bar. I did my best to keep up my half of the conversation with Matt, not wanting him to notice my divided attention.

The vampires had made their rounds and settled across the room where a few of the younger locals congregated. I caught the darkening of the vampire's eyes as they mesmerized the group. Their guarded expressions at the vamps' arrival changed to relaxed ones after a glance from the predators.

My gut churned while watching them. The humans would walk away later with only a little less blood for their troubles. Charlie probably had something to do with their restraint. He was powerful enough to enforce some discipline on these weaker sups, but that knowledge didn't give me much comfort.

During the times I'd followed the vamps, I had learned a few things about them. My main objective had been to get a location on Aniya, but observing them had helped me learn their methods and get used to being near them. I was relieved they didn't kill any humans on my watch, but it frustrated me that none of them had led me to my friend. There had to be a central location in the area where they congregated. In most cases, it would be the master sup's home or business, but so far nothing had turned up.

Seeing these latest guys gave me hope. They were a different set of vamps than the ones I'd seen before. They appeared well dressed, in pleated slacks and dark button up shirts. Even their shoes shined. The way they all carried themselves with a degree of self-importance made me think they could be part of the master sup's inner circle. It wouldn't hurt to follow them tonight and see where they went.

"So, you've heard all about me. What about you? Aside from the military, that is," Matt inquired, bringing my awareness back to him.

"What do you want to know?" I asked. My attention was half on his question and half on strategizing a way to trail these new guys without them noticing. They looked more alert than the previous ones.

"I don't know. Simple stuff like where you live now."

"California," I replied, shifting my body toward Matt so my voice could be kept low.

"Oh, well, that's cool. Guess you like it there."

I shrugged. "It's home."

"Yeah, suppose so. How about I get us some more drinks?" he suggested. "Yours is looking a little empty."

In fact, I had gulped most of it down when the vamps came in.

"That would be great." I said with a smile. At least it would give me a reprieve from his questions. The last thing I wanted was to discuss personal stuff while vampires with excellent hearing were in the room.

Matt didn't take as long as I would have liked. A

few minutes later he returned with fresh glasses, mine with Long Island Iced Tea. His had some locally brewed beer.

"Thanks," I told him, taking a sip to find it tasted perfect. He'd asked about the mixture earlier after noticing the reddish color mine had. Not many people requested grenadine in this particular drink. I took another healthy swallow to calm my nerves.

"No problem," he said with a laugh. "Guess you needed it."

I took a slower sip the next time. It wouldn't be good to appear like a lush and I did have to drive again soon.

A serious expression spread across Matt's face, catching my attention. He took a quick glance back toward the vamps on the other side of the bar. They all seemed engrossed with their prey and paid us no attention. Matt must have seen that as well because he leaned over and whispered in my ear.

"Those guys over there in the corner, do you see them?" I nodded as if I hadn't been watching them the whole time. "One of them is the guy I saw with your friend that night."

Despite his low tone, my eyes darted over to make sure the vampires didn't hear him. Their demeanor hadn't changed and they showed no signs of listening in on us. Good, I didn't want Matt messing up my plans. This could be the night I found Aniya.

"Which one is he?" I asked. Only one fit the description, but it was better to be sure.

"The dark-haired one on the left," he told me,

keeping his tone low.

Another glance over gave me a better look at the vampires. There was only one with dark hair, while the other two had varying shades of blond. I had to be looking at Philip Mercer. Of course, that may not be the same name he went by here. Vamps were known to have multiple monikers.

"What're you gonna do?" Matt asked.

"I'm not sure yet." Better he didn't know.

"If you need help," he offered. "I'm here."

"That won't be necessary, but thank you." I squeezed his hand and smiled.

The last thing I needed was a human trying to play hero. It would get him killed and I didn't want that on my conscience. Not to mention his job as a soldier put him in enough danger without adding supernatural threats to the mix.

He frowned. "Well, the offer still stands. That guy doesn't look like the kind you want to mess with."

Before I could form a response, a new presence entered the bar—the one person who could show up in a flash without me sensing his approach. Lucas strolled in wearing jeans, a studded belt, and a black t-shirt. He wore dark leather boots as well. They didn't make a sound as he moved his large body through the crowd.

His physical appearance had been changed to include unkempt brown hair and a short beard. I could glimpse his golden form underneath the glamour, but it was disorienting to be able to see both. It was like seeing two men in the same body. The image he showed the rest of the room blended well with the locals, which was probably the point.

Why had he come here? This was not the time to get into another argument with him.

He headed straight for me—after a notable glance in the vampires' direction. I stiffened, wondering if he had figured out what I was up to. The vamps in question didn't take their eyes off their human prey. Lucas had cloaked his power so they wouldn't consider him as anything other than human. They were too young to see through it.

Matt wasn't talking anymore. I turned in his direction to find him frozen. He had a contemplative look on his face and his mouth was partway open. I glowered at Lucas as he settled down in the empty chair on the other side of me.

"Did you have to freeze him?"

"Upset I disturbed your fun with this new boy toy?" he asked. Lucas didn't bother to hide the contempt on his face.

"Matt isn't my boy toy," I said. "I don't have boy toys, as you so rudely put it."

The meaningful look he gave me said he wasn't fooled. "Tell yourself whatever you like, but I know better."

I crossed my arms. We'd had this conversation a few times before and it hadn't been any more pleasant then.

"Whatever you believe, it isn't true. I just don't like getting close to anyone. It's safer if I just keep my relationships uncomplicated." Maybe I was being a little defensive, but I couldn't help it. It seemed selfish to put a guy at risk no matter how lonely I got. Lucas knew most of my problem was his fault. He'd been poking his nose in my personal life for as long as I'd known him.

I gave him an accusing look. He laughed. Something he'd never done in front of me before. My double vision tried to make sense of what I was seeing. He'd always had such an inimical attitude toward me that it was unnerving to see him any other way, even if only for a moment, before he covered it up.

"Don't worry," he replied. "It isn't the men in your life, however briefly they may be there, that you need to be concerned about."

I ignored his barb. He said these things to throw me off. Finding out why he'd showed up tonight would be the more important thing to do.

"What are you doing here, Lucas?"

"Immortal curiosity," he replied with a shrug. "Longevity does have its disadvantages, and your short life is fascinating to observe. Speaking of which, how is the futile search for your friend going?"

I inwardly flinched. He could get right to the heart of a matter. "That is none of your business."

His eyes reflected a perceptiveness that made me uncomfortable. "You haven't found her yet, have you?"

I slumped in my chair and refused to answer. His lips curved up. Despite my annoyance, it was arresting to see. How could such an evil person's smile make me forget, even for a moment, all the bad things about him?

Every part of the nephilim drew the eye. Between his confident walk and smooth movements, not to mention his better than Hollywood looks, he couldn't be short on female companionship. I was glad to know who he really was so those things wouldn't fool me. No doubt the man had a harem of women serving him wherever he lived. If only he would go back to them and leave me alone.

It wasn't worth lying to him, though. He would know—he always did. If we could finish this conversation soon, I could still try to follow Aniya's "boyfriend". He had to be going back to her. At least, that's what I hoped.

"I found the vamp who took my friend," I admitted, nodding at my target. They wouldn't be able to hear us since Lucas had a noise dampening spell up. It made it impossible for anyone to overhear our conversation. How it was working on me, I had no idea. The magic of it clung against my skin, whereas spells of its nature usually passed right over me.

He didn't bother glancing at the group in question. "You're going to have a difficult time getting close to them. They aren't old, but neither are they newly weaned from their sire."

His voice held a warning note. It made me suspicious. "Why do you care what I do?"

"I don't," he said. "Except I consider you mine to kill...or allow to live."

He meant what he said. It wasn't the usual half-truth I got from him. What does one say to that? "Thanks, I'm sure I should feel honored."

He didn't reply, and instead picked up my half empty drink. After taking a sip, he grimaced. "Too sweet."

That made me smile. "I'm not surprised, considering your disposition. Must have tasted awful for you." I took the glass from him, keeping away from the spot where his lips touched, and slugged down the rest.

Lucas didn't take the bait. Instead he watched me in fascination. "I've never considered you a heavy drinker."

"If I'm going to die soon," I said, setting the glass down. "Might as well enjoy the time I have left."

He laughed for the second time tonight. For whatever reason, the sad truth of my life seemed to humor him.

"Can't you run along now?" I flicked my hand at the door. "Irritate someone else."

He reached across the short distance between us and pulled my out flung hand close to him. His head leaned forward so his breath grazed my ear. "Little girl, do not push your luck tonight. One day, my patience will run out—then you'll really be in trouble."

I shivered. Whether from fear or arousal, I couldn't say. I didn't want to consider it too much. Damn him for having any affect on me at all.

"Don't call me that," I said in little more than a whisper. He never used my real name, as if I was too far beneath him for that.

"Don't call you what?"

"Little girl."

"Why?" he asked, dropping his gaze to my lips.

I was not going to moisten them. I wasn't.

"It's rude."

"That's unfortunate for you, because I intend to

call you whatever I want, whenever I want." His reply came out heated.

Lucas looked at me in a way that made me want to ignore every internal warning siren going off. The golden flecks in his eyes held my attention. Did that particular shade even exist anywhere else? He moved the rest of his body close so that only a few inches separated any part of us.

The touch of his hand where he held mine tingled with a faint charge. The sensation snaked up my arm and penetrated deep within my body. It made me want to melt into him just to get more. I didn't want the feeling to stop. Ever. I couldn't move and not one part of me wanted to. It wasn't a supernatural kind of magic holding me, but something primal. How long we stared at each other I couldn't have guessed.

When he pulled away, my body moved with him before I stopped it. I had to shake my head to come out of the fog-laden daze he'd put me in. Something had changed and I'd missed it. A new song played in the background, but that wasn't the problem. Then it clicked. The vampires were no longer in the bar. In fact, they were heading down the road. I'd been so caught up with Lucas, I hadn't even noticed.

"You did that to distract me." I glared at him.

He lifted his brows. "Apparently, it worked."

Heat warmed my cheeks. I'd always been aware of his looks, but he'd never affected me this way. How could I have fallen into his trap? He'd taken my first chance at finding Aniya with nothing more than a hint of sexual teasing. I couldn't decide if I was angrier with him or myself.

He stood up. "Stay away from them."

I didn't get a chance to respond. He shoved back his chair and strode toward the entrance. People practically leaped out of his path to avoid colliding with him. He exited the building in the wake of a slamming door and disappeared from the area right after. I wished, just once, I could follow him and give him a piece of my mind.

A subtle cough drew my attention. Matt had come out of it and was reaching to take a drink of his beer as if nothing had happened. Knowing I wouldn't be pleasant company anymore, I told him it was time for me to go. It had grown late and I didn't feel up to hiding my sour mood. His face fell, but he nodded his head.

He stood up as I gathered my purse and jacket and pressed a piece of paper with his phone number on it into my hand. I stared at it, wondering when he'd written it down. Maybe in the bathroom? I shoved the paper in my jeans pocket. Matt smiled and insisted on walking with me outside. I would have refused if it hadn't been for the way I'd treated him earlier. He didn't deserve any more of my pent up anger tonight.

"When will I see you again?" he asked, once we reached my vehicle.

I shrugged. "Maybe soon. I have some things to take care of."

"Okay, well, it was great talking to you." He gave me an unexpected hug. "Give me a call sometime."

"Sure," I said, pulling away. I'd burn his number later.

He continued to watch me as I drove off.

Chapter Seven

The sound of my cell phone ringing before dawn woke me. My hand fumbled around the nightstand until my fingers grasped it and brought it close. With bleary eyes, I squinted at the caller ID to see who could be calling this early. The name on the screen brought me wide awake. I answered it at the same time I jumped out of bed. A familiar voice, sounding more frightened than I'd ever heard it, came through the line.

"Mel, you have to leave Fairbanks now," Aniya rushed out.

"Niya? Where are you?"

"It doesn't matter, but you need to leave town as soon as possible."

"What have you gotten yourself into? Your mom is worried sick. I promised her I would bring you home."

A choked sob came before her next reply. "Tell my mom I love her, and that I'm fine, but you have to leave..."

"No, not without you."

"Just go," she pleaded. "They know you're looking for me and they'll get to you too if you don't leave right away."

A cold chill ran through me. I should have known they would figure it out sooner or later. My aggressive search methods had increased those odds.

"What is going on, Niya?"

A faint but angry voice rose up from her end of the line—it was growing louder by the second. Her breathing picked up so I almost didn't catch her next words.

"I have to go, they're coming. Please, get out of town before it's too late."

The connection broke before I could respond.

My attempts to call her back failed. The phone had already been turned off. I sighed in frustration, wishing she could have told me more. I felt better knowing she was still alive, but for how long? Despite the danger, I couldn't leave her with the sups to die.

It was time for an alternate plan. Staying in a motel room was no longer an option. I needed to find a more permanent place to stay. Fast.

***

Later that day I walked into my new "home". A small cabin located a short distance from the city limits. The position of it was far enough away from other people so no one else would get caught in the crossfire—if it came down to that.

The average person wouldn't consider it fancy, but it would work well enough against most types of supernatural assaults. After I made a few small changes, anyway. My one month contract guaranteed it would be considered a private residence in my mind, meaning vamps couldn't get in. The trick was you had to think of it as a home, and a motel room would never have done that for me.

This place had cost me more than I had wanted to spend, which is why it hadn't been my first choice. The functioning bathroom in it made the cabin even more expensive. Many of them had outhouses and no running water. That wouldn't be practical under the circumstances. The last thing I needed was to be caught outside with my pants down.

Though the cabin wouldn't be considered large, it did have a decent size bedroom, large walk-in closet, and a small kitchen with a pantry. The living room spanned about ten by fourteen feet, which would be more than enough for my needs. The owner had furnished the place with stuff that might have been around since the eighties.

The couch had brown, flowery print on it and the wood end tables on either side were scratched and worn. The rest of the furniture came in varying shades of dark wood, not really matching, but close enough. Lamps provided lighting everywhere except the kitchen and closets. The yellow-tinted shades covering them had seen better days, but would serve their purpose. I did purchase my own blankets and sheets, considering them a necessity. The ones that had been left here were now sitting at the bottom of the bedroom closet.

After settling in and making sure everything worked as it should, I began my preparations on the cabin for withstanding a supernatural assault. I'd hoped to never need to use the knowledge of how to go about it. There wouldn't be much time to get things ready before sundown, but every moment counted. My first move was to spread my stash of wolfsbane around the place. The cabin's small size worked to my advantage or else my supply might not have been enough. I couldn't perform magic myself, but the herb acted on its own—a natural repellant werewolves couldn't go near.

It had been one of the few things I'd known could give me an edge when coming to Alaska. Wolfsbane had to be reserved for emergencies, though, because otherwise you would be letting the sups know you were on to them. No one carried it around just for the sake of it. Any were or sup with enhanced smelling abilities would smell it if you came near them. Never a good idea if you wanted to keep a low profile.

My personal stock still had the flowers on the herbs, but that would add to their effect, so I didn't remove them. Their purple petals might have stood out except I was tossing it all into the crawlspace under the cabin. The weather forecast predicted a thunderstorm tonight. I hoped none of it would get blown away.

After sprinkling the last of the herb, I began the next task of preparing for witches. With no way of knowing who might come for me, it seemed like a good idea to take every precaution. I grabbed an IV catheter from my first aid kit, along with a band to tie off my arm and set to work collecting a portion of my blood.

For magical spells, you had to cut yourself as part of the sacrifice, but I didn't need to do that. Cutting myself when I didn't have to wouldn't serve any purpose and it would be more difficult to collect all the blood needed, not to mention the mess a deep wound created. Needles proved far more efficient and clean if they could be used instead. A pint of it would cover the perimeter of the cabin and do the job I needed it to.

Long ago sensors discovered their blood, on its own, could negate spells. Since then, my kind had used the secret to protect their homes. By spilling fresh blood once every few months around the perimeter of a dwelling, the place could be kept safe against all types of magical attacks. Sups, aside from vampires, could still enter but they couldn't use their powers against the residence or its occupants. That gave a definite advantage in most cases.

Wanda used to protect our home this way, which is how I learned of it. It couldn't stop a physical attack, but at least it negated magic from being used as a weapon. I'd once tried using my blood to keep Lucas from flashing in, but that didn't go so well. He kicked down the door and threatened to destroy my home if I ever did it again. I had to hope he wouldn't hold to that promise under the circumstances.

In a methodical manner, I smeared my blood in thin lines around the bottom edges of the cabin, between the crevices of the logs. The stains didn't stand out this way, and would have some protection from the elements. Even diluted, sensor blood could protect well so long as it was laid fresh, but I preferred to err on the side of caution.

About the time I finished covering the cabin, a crunch of tires caught my attention. It came from a vehicle heading down the drive in this direction. The standard red and blue lights on top sent me into a panic.

With no time to spare, I dashed in to wash the

blood off my hands, scrubbing hard at my fingernails where some red spots didn't come off so easily. I also pulled a long-sleeve fleece top over my t-shirt, not wanting the cop to see the needle mark on my arm and make me out for a drug addict. With my luck, it would inspire him to search the property.

"Ms. Sanders," a male voice called out. He sounded familiar.

I looked through the living room curtains to find the deputy who'd spoken to me a few days before outside. He stood by his car, leaning on his good leg, wearing pressed khaki pants and a white button-up shirt. Voices from his police radio blared from the open window of his vehicle.

My palms were sweaty as I made my way out to greet him. The blood stains on the cabin walls didn't look too visible, a quick glance assured me of that, but I still didn't want him getting close.

"Hello Deputy, what brings you here?" I stuffed my hands into the back pockets of my jeans, and pasted a sweet smile on my face.

"I heard you moved out here and wanted to check on you," he said, studying the area around us.

Aside from the cabin and my SUV, trees and vegetation dominated the scene. Not much to look at. There were a few neighbors some distance away, but none of them were visible from where we stood.

"Where'd you hear that?" I asked.

"Fairbanks isn't that large, Ms. Sanders. People talk."

Right. He didn't need to spell it out any clearer.

He was keeping tabs on me and I needed to watch myself. Something about him felt off, but I didn't know what.

"Moved in today. Thought I would stick around for a while."

He gave me a skeptical look. "You're not still searching for that friend of yours, are you?"

I opened my mouth to deny the accusation, but stopped myself. He wouldn't buy any excuse I gave. Considering my recent activity, he must have heard about my ongoing search efforts. I shrugged instead. "She's here. It's just a matter of finding her."

He shook his head. "It's a wasted effort. She'll turn up when she's ready, they always do."

Somehow, I doubted that, but didn't have time to debate the matter. Daylight hours were burning. "Is there something you need deputy?"

My question brought his eyes back around from where he had been studying the cabin. I crossed my arms at his penetrating stare, not liking the suspicion reflecting in his gaze. The movement drew his attention to my hip.

"Is that a gun I see on you?"

His observation made me twist my neck around to look at the object in question. I had forgotten it was still tucked in my pants. Carrying the weapon at all times in recent days had made it feel like a part of my attire. In my haste, I must not have pulled the fleece top over it all the way. Damn the deputy for noticing.

"It's for protection," I explained, falling back on the excuse I'd given the gun dealer. "I heard about all the wild animals roaming the woods and figured it might be a good idea to have one with me."

His face relaxed. Maybe I wasn't the first woman to take that kind of precaution around here.

"A young girl like you, that's understandable, but do be careful. A gun isn't a guaranteed way to stop big animals."

"Of course, but better than nothing, right?" I asked with a raised brow. A good firearm could kill anything if aimed well, so long as your target didn't have immortality as part of its make-up. Then things got tricky.

"That's true," he frowned. "Do you know the Alaska laws for carrying concealed firearms?"

Had this become an interrogation? I was familiar with those and didn't find it amusing, especially since I was on private property. The guy seemed determined to draw out our conversation. At least I had an answer for him. If you were going to skirt the law, you needed to know it first. I stated the basics off the top of my head.

"No permit required, but don't bring it into schools, courthouses, or bars?" Not that I followed that last part, but he didn't need to know that.

"Yes, but next time, remember that you should always inform a police officer when you're carrying it. Otherwise, you can be charged for failure to do so."

"Sorry about that," I apologized. "You surprised me with your visit and I wasn't thinking."

He nodded, accepting my excuse like all men who underestimated women. Most of the time that annoyed me, but in this case it worked to my advantage. I had forgotten to tell him about the gun, so my answer had been the truth.

"It's alright," the deputy said, "but do be more careful in the future. A young girl such as yourself shouldn't be living alone out in the bush."

"It isn't that far out from the city, deputy, but thank you for your concern," I replied, taking a step back toward the cabin.

He tipped his hat. "I'll let you finish settling in."

After his car disappeared beyond the trees I went inside to finish cleaning up the mess from my earlier bloodletting. Better to hide the evidence in case any more nosy people came around to "check" on me. I couldn't be sure if he came for the reasons he'd stated or if he had an ulterior motive. Human minds could be manipulated by vamps, leaving me unsure. My truth meter worked best against sups, whose minds usually couldn't be tampered with. The deputy could be a pawn for all I knew.

Chapter Eight

An hour before sunset, the cabin stood ready for whatever might come. I typed a short email to Lisette and Mrs. Singh updating them with my progress, or lack thereof, but left out Aniya's recent phone call. No point in worrying them further. Both had been checking with me almost daily since I arrived. I gave Lisette my new address, wanting someone trustworthy to know my location in case the worst should happen. At least she could pick up my things since my body would have little chance of being found. A morbid thought, but my optimism wasn't very high at the moment.

To keep up my strength, I ate some spaghetti I'd cooked earlier for lunch. The meal settled into my stomach like lead. Staying calm hadn't been easy since discovering my life was in imminent danger. At least in the military it had been a general threat as opposed to this time, where the enemy had singled me out. They would be coming sooner or later. All the different types of painful torture methods they might use if they captured me swirled through my head.

The hours rolled by with no sign of them. By midnight, I lay on the couch near the front door. The Sig rested on my lap, with a round loaded in the chamber, its cold metal a small comfort. It had no safety. One pull of the trigger would do the job. I kept my fingers away from that part of the gun. No point in saving the sups the trouble by taking myself out.

Would they really come for me? I had this morning's phone call to go by, but nothing more. Part of me wanted them to show up so we could get this confrontation over with. Sitting here waiting in anticipation was going to drive me crazy.

My senses lit up about the time I began to doze off. Vague sensations of dread rolled over me as they came, moving at a steady speed in my direction. The group consisted of three vampires. They couldn't get inside, but my hand still gripped the gun. Having a sword right now might have been helpful. Beheading was one of the few ways to kill a vamp. I doubted I could strike fast enough for it to work. Stakes to the heart could hold them immobile so you could finish them off, but getting one in the chest would be almost as difficult as simply cutting their head off. They were too strong and fast for me to do it without the element of surprise.

The vampires closed in on the cabin, slowing to a walking pace as if they had all the time in the world. Their ages ranged from twenty to one hundred. Just strong and experienced enough to be a problem. My combat training gave me the proficiency needed to fight newly turned vamps, but these were beyond my skill level. The protection of my new home had better work.

Within moments, they arrived and sent the youngest one ahead to the door. The knob sizzled when the vampire jiggled it. He let out a shocked yelp and a string of curses. The idiot should have known that would happen, even if I had only moved in twelve hours ago.

Chuckling came from across the yard. Did they think this was some kind of game? I was tempted to go to take a peek out the window, but didn't want to be near it with one of them so close. The idiot standing in front of the window always died first in the movies.

"Melena," the oldest vamp drew out my name in a compelling voice, "why don't you come out here and talk to us."

Of course, the compulsion in his voice didn't work—not even with using my name. Names could have power over a person, but not mine. I ignored their repeated calls and remained silent. They might have been able to hear my heart beating faster, but there was no point in talking to them yet. All three began calling to me at once, so that "Melena" echoed across the yard with an eeriness that made me shiver. It went on for a few tense-filled minutes before dying down.

Uncertainty rose to fill in the sudden silence. There were rare humans born resistant who weren't sensors, but they numbered at a fraction of one percent. Maybe they would think me part fae or something. Some people appeared to be human but had a trace of the supernatural from their ancestors crossbreeding with humans. It gave enough of a boost so they couldn't be compelled, except by the very old immortals—who held enough power to do it anyway. Except on sensors.

"You can't stay in there forever," the first one called out.

I'd had enough of playing the quiet girl.

"And you can't stay out there forever," I yelled

back.

"We can stay out here long enough," he replied. "We know you're looking for your friend. She belongs to us now, but don't worry, you'll be joining her soon."

Not if I could help it. They must have made her a blood slave, which sickened me, but drinking my blood wouldn't have quite the same affect on vamps that a human's did.

"You're not getting in, so go away." Not my best come back, but I couldn't think of anything else.

"Come out now and we'll go easy on you." His voice came out cajoling. "I give my word of honor." Right. He said this while his buddies stalked around the cabin. It didn't take my senses to see the truth.

"Not a chance," I shouted back.

"Very well, the choice was yours."

They were far enough away from the front window that I could take a peek. The vampire I had spoken to, the oldest of the group, stood about fifty feet away near the trees. The moonlight illuminated him enough for me to see some of his features. He had the same dark hair as Philip, Aniya's kidnapper, but his shape was leaner and he had a more arrogant posture.

"Some choice," I muttered.

He smiled, looking straight at me through the window. "Better than none at all, little human."

There was no point in replying.

The vampire and his friends backed away from the cabin at least a hundred feet, probably so I couldn't hear them. The oldest one held his phone to his ear, no doubt calling for reinforcements.

I stepped away and let the drapes fall back in place. While the bedroom had blackout curtains to block sunlight during the height of summer, when the nights were short, the living room window had sheer fabric. It made it easy to peer out so long as I stood close. I grabbed a bottle of water from the refrigerator to relieve my dry mouth and paced the living room.

Thirty minutes later, I sensed half a dozen werewolves enter the area. Their signatures raked over my mind like sharp claws digging at my skull. It took me a minute to adjust. They moved at a semi-rapid pace, but were close enough together to make me think they rode in a vehicle. I didn't worry too much. The wolfsbane would hold them back. At least in theory—I'd never actually tried it myself. Wanda had kept the herb around, so she must have believed it worked.

I sunk into a chair near the window that matched the couch. In a habit formed during my childhood, my fingers crossed hoping they wouldn't get close. The herb had to have a range of effectiveness, but I didn't know how far it might be. They didn't seem bothered by it yet.

For now, the werewolves stood speaking with the vampires, their postures rigid. A casual observer would think they were about to head off to war. Ten minutes passed before they moved toward the cabin. When they came within thirty feet of the walls, they started sneezing. A little closer and their breath wheezed in and out as if their airways were closing off. Those in wolf form went into convulsions. Maybe the animal form came with a heightened sense of smell.

I snickered, unable to help myself. They'd come

in with so much confidence that they never guessed a well placed herb could keep them away. One of the vamps, who had come forward to help the werewolves, glared in my direction.

"Think you're smart don't you?"

"Not at all, just prepared," I said, not bothering to raise my voice. Vamps had no better sense of smell than humans did, but he'd proved his hearing worked more than well enough.

"We'll see," he yelled back over his shoulder.

Once they had the werewolves out of the "danger zone", the vamps stalked their way back towards me with determination written all over their faces. They spread out, getting as close to the cabin as possible. Sizzles sounded all around when their hands tried to reach underneath the structure. Their muttered curses confirmed my suspicions.

They were trying to remove the wolfsbane, but soon discovered it was out of their reach. I had expected they might try that when I decided to put it outside. It would be impossible for them to get to so long as it lay within the confines of the home's support structure. I wanted to thank whoever laid the curse on the vampire race a few millennia ago, preventing them from getting into any human's residence without an invitation. As soon as they got close to the borders of a home, it was nothing but sizzles for them if they weren't welcome.

The vampires moved back to where the wolves stood. They shouted threats on the way involving something along the lines of being drawn and quartered. As if any of them had been alive when that was still a practice. Did all younger immortals try to sound older than they were?

One of them began speaking on their phone again. They were running out of options and would have to give up soon. The predicted thunderstorm loomed in the distance and the wind had begun to pick up. It would be an hour or so before it reached us, but I hoped it would scare the sups off sooner.

A lightening strike, if direct, could kill them. Not only that, but they were a natural magnet for them whenever they were outside. Much like an antenna on top of a tall building. If they valued their lives, they wouldn't stick around to get hit.

Twenty minutes later, two witches showed up. They drove a large SUV with headlights blazing, not bothering to hide their entry onto the gravel drive. When the werewolves had come, they had shut their lights off as soon as they turned from the main road. I could sense annoyance from the sups who were forced to cover their eyes. It almost blinded me with my normal vision.

One of the witches had a good amount of power, not as much as Noreen back in California, but enough zing coursed through her to be considered formidable. The second witch had about half that strength. They both appeared cocky as they got out of their vehicle. Their high heeled boots looked out of place and impractical, but they wore them with a certain grace and fluidity I couldn't have managed out in the woods.

The two women arrived at the congregating point and settled into wide stances with hands on their hips and disapproval stamped on their faces. Most modern witches tended to avoid the outdoors, being forced to come here must have irritated them. They liked their creature comforts. One spoke in a boasting voice that she had never seen a human so easily best werewolves and vampires. I grinned to myself, thinking she would be eating her words soon enough.

With a cocky sway of her hips, the stronger witch moved toward the house, her long blond hair fluttering in the breeze. Even through the dark, I could see that the golden locks were the one decent feature she had. Her skin appeared far more aged and wrinkled than it should for a woman in her mid-thirties and her lips had a permanent down-turn. She also had the famous hooked nose Hollywood portrayed bad witches as having. It stood out from her face, but this time it wasn't a cliché. She used a simple illusion spell to prevent anyone, aside from me, from seeing her true appearance. Her forays into the dark arts must have caused the loss of beauty. It had to have been a nasty spell to cause this much damage—most required a different sacrifice than personal looks.

I could tell she wanted to show her apprentice how superior witches were to the other races. She moved to the door and I sensed her attempt at an unlocking spell. Of course, it didn't work with my blood in place. She tried opening the doorknob without magic, but that failed as well since the door remained locked. Her feet stomped on the porch. After a moment, she tried to shove the door open with the weight of her body, but it didn't budge.

"Unless you want this cabin destroyed," she

growled out. "I suggest you come out now. Otherwise, I will not hesitate to use force."

"Give it your best shot," I replied. The cabin could hold against any magic she tried against it. If her first spell hadn't worked, none of the rest would either.

Her rising anger pricked against my senses, but I was too amused by it to care. She tramped over to the side of the house and attempted a spell to knock a hole in the wall. It bounced back and knocked her on her ass ten feet away. She had packed quite a punch into that one and hadn't figured it would spring back on her. I caught her fall from the kitchen window and waved at her. She shot me a rude gesture in return.

To her credit, the embarrassing display didn't stop her from trying again. A series of spells came hurtling through the air in rapid succession. I could feel the power of each one, but none of them did more than make me flinch a little. The blood protection held. Her magic didn't. She'd tried everything, including water and air, only to have them fail too. It had to have taken a great deal of strength to perform so much at once. She didn't have a lot left. I imagined it would take her days to recover after tonight—all magic had its limits.

This group of sups didn't understand what a sensor could do to protect themselves. Of course, they couldn't have known what they fought against before getting here, which made things easier on me. The knowledge of my race had eroded over the centuries as we stayed in hiding and none of the ones here had been around when sensors were still prominent. It gave me the advantage I needed.

A frustrated scream came out of the witch when she finally stopped trying to put a hole in the cabin. By this point they were all laughing at her. She had brought it all on herself. I had to laugh too when she started kicking up dirt as she made her way back to the group. She shot me a venomous look that would have terrified most people, especially if they saw what she hid under the spell, but it didn't bother me. I'd seen more scorn from human enemies while serving overseas.

They started another discussion in hushed tones. By this time, the storm had reached us and loomed overhead, darkening the whole scene so I could barely make out their figures. It would start any minute. Lightning flashed nearby, but as yet, no rain fell. The sups glanced a few times toward the threatening weather, but didn't stop talking. One of the vampires picked up a tree branch that was about the thickness of a baseball bat and broke it into a three-foot long piece. What did they plan to do now?

He carried the branch in a determined grip as he and the two witches moved toward the cabin. The women had daggers in their hands and an idea of what they might be about to do formed in my head. My feet took several steps back until I stood at the border between the living room and open kitchen area.

Faster than I could see, the vampire swung the branch at the window, shattering it. With swift movements, he swept the glass away using the same tool. He might not be able to put his hands inside the cabin, but the branch didn't have that problem. I stood frozen, watching him closely. It didn't take a genius to figure out why the witches had come with him. They didn't need an invitation to go through the opening he'd made.

I raised the gun, which had been in my hand the entire time, as soon as the vamp stepped away. In his place came the older of the two witches. As she began to climb through the window, I knew I couldn't hesitate. It was a matter of her life or mine. Sometimes, you don't get the luxury of a choice if survival is at stake. When her foot crunched on the loose pieces of glass, all my focus went straight to her through the sights of my weapon.

The witch's gaze froze on me. I let out a calming breath as my finger squeezed the trigger. The gun kicked back at the same time as a loud report hit my ears, making them ring. Horror flashed on her face right before the bullet hit its mark, erasing her expression. She had seen her death coming.

All of these details registered in my mind, as if it happened in slow motion. I never took my eyes off the open window and immediately reacquired my sights in case I needed to shoot again. The witch's body had fallen back onto the porch, but the vampire continued to stand there, a shocked expression on his face.

The younger witch began to scream. I leveled the gun at her, but she turned her back on me and bent down to check on her friend. It put her out of my sight and she appeared too distraught to be a threat. She wailed loud enough to hurt my ears. The two must have been close for such a visceral reaction.

The woman I shot had to be dead, she wasn't immortal. Nothing came to my senses to indicate she might still live, her life force had left within moments of the bullet hitting. I assumed the vampire would be trying to heal her with his blood if there was a chance of saving her, but he made no move to do so.

Instead, he gave me a look filled with so much hatred it left little doubt he'd kill me in a slow, methodical manner if given the chance. I stood my ground with the gun now pointed in his direction, and gave him my own cold stare.

No emotion touched me, only the will to survive.

If the gun could have done any real damage, my finger might have been pulling the trigger again, but it'd be a waste of a bullet. Even giving him a temporary wound wasn't worth the trouble. Besides, he couldn't get in to harm me anyway.

I kept the weapon raised until he picked up the body and moved off the porch. The other witch followed right behind him, continuing to sniffle. She paid no attention to me, her sole focus on the woman whose body lay lifeless in the vamp's arms. In my military career, I had shot at enemies before, but never watched them die. I wasn't sure if any of them had since we never stuck around to find out. My limited experience came from ambushes that occurred while driving the streets of war zones—our goal had been to fight our way out and get to safety, not hang around checking for bodies. Staying in one place for too long in situations like that tended to invite more danger.

This experience had very little in common with those from my past. Part of it may have been the location—I should have been safe in my own country. Instead I'd been forced to kill. Even if the witch hadn't had the best of intentions toward me, it still didn't feel right.

One moment she had stood before my eyes and in the next she didn't. A mere blink in time altering all that would go forward. Her existence came to a sudden halt the instant I pulled the trigger. The memory flashed before my eyes and the look on her face imprinted on my soul.

While the sups dealt with the ramifications of their latest plan, I let the scene play several more times in my head before shoving it into my special box. The danger hadn't gone away yet. Lingering on what had happened wouldn't change anything and I didn't need to be putting myself at further risk. I couldn't let them capture me because then there would be no one to rescue Aniya. Mrs. Singh needed her daughter and I wanted my friend back. *They* were not going to stop me.

As the group talked amongst each other, their collective anger rose. It seemed perfect timing, as a crack of lightening came down not far from our location. Rain followed the loud boom and flash of light. It didn't start as a drizzle, like some storms do. This one came as an immediate downpour. Wind swirled around and blew through the open window into the cabin. My hair whipped about my face, blurring my vision for a moment before I used my free hand to hold it back.

I could still make out the group, standing among the trees. One of them pointed up at the sky. Dawn would be approaching soon, perhaps less than an hour, and the storm would be too dangerous to stay out in. They'd lost this round, but it was an empty victory for me. Taking the witch's life had been an unexpected turn of events. The protections I'd placed around the cabin were my way of preventing bloodshed, but they hadn't been enough.

The entire group, including the vamps who'd come on foot, got into their vehicles and drove away. Tires spun on the wet gravel as they went. My senses quieted once they reached beyond the half-mile mark. I let my shoulders sag with relief that they had finally left.

A mess of glass and debris surrounded me. The owner would wonder about the cause, but the storm's convenient arrival could explain the damage. For now, I went out back and grabbed a loose piece of plywood that had been left behind the cabin. It would fit over the window well enough to keep it covered for the night. I took down a few cheap pictures of wildlife from the wall and managed to use the nails they hung from to fasten the board. One of my talents lay in improvising, which came in handy now.

A while later I had the place cleaned up. A whistle of wind still made its way through my make-shift window barrier, but it held the worst of the storm back. My instincts told me the sups wouldn't return too soon. The vamps were limited to the dark hours and the werewolves were weaker during the day, unable to shift to wolf form. The witches could come, but they wouldn't dare after what had happened tonight. There was one thing I was certain of—this was only the beginning, they weren't gone for good.

Chapter Nine

I stood in the shower, trying to wash away the memory of the night before, when the walls and floor began to shake. A thunderous roar came over the cabin and I nearly slipped on the wet tiles. The ominous sound had me grabbing a towel to wrap around my body as I leaped out. My heart thumped heavily against my chest as I reached for the gun on the sink counter, ready to shoot anything that came near. Had the sups come back already? My senses didn't pick up anything dangerous nearby but something had to have made that noise. It couldn't have been my imagination.

I moved in a methodical manner through the cabin using standard military search techniques. Nothing turned up by the time I'd finished. My confusion came to an end when realization hit me. I almost threw my gun against the wall, annoyed at myself for not figuring it out sooner.

In my weary state, I'd forgotten about the Air Force base nearby and their regular flights over the area. The roar of the planes going by annoyed everyone, particularly the locals who had to deal with it the most. This wouldn't be the first time military aircraft had disturbed me, but I still wanted to run outside and raise my fist at them. Of course, they were long gone by now while I was left standing in the kitchen dripping water onto the floor.

I forced myself to set the weapon down on the table. It freed my hands, which were still shaking, to make coffee. The hot, soothing brew would help calm my nerves and wake me up—something I needed right now after last night's events left me with little more than fitful sleep.

The memory flashed in my mind again.

It wasn't something any decent person could forget. The dead witch's face floated before my eyes, her gaze now haunting. It transformed to become one covered in blood. How many others had I killed overseas and tried to forget? Now I had an image to go with all the other deaths because I knew I'd hit some of my targets when we were ambushed. Feelings of remorse rose up before I shoved them back down. Not now, definitely not now. I tossed the key on my mental lock box for extra security.

There were bigger issues to worry about. The group had been angry when they left and would no doubt be back for more. My protections had held, but the sups would find a way around them, given enough time.

Make a run for it.

The thought flashed through my mind, no doubt fueled by self-preservation. It wouldn't work. In all likelihood, they were more determined than ever to capture me and running away wouldn't change that. Not to mention I couldn't leave Aniya behind on the remote chance escaping the area might save me. She deserved better. She'd always been there for me. If I could at least get her out of there, maybe we could both hide.

One new advantage would help. Last night I'd taken extra care to memorize each of the sup's unique signatures with my senses. It would allow me to know if any of them were nearby. All I had to do was find one of them and tail that guy back to their home base. They would have to be staying at the same place as Aniya. At least, I hoped they were. It was the one way I could think of to find her.

First, I needed some more wolfsbane. Most of it had been blown or washed away by the storm last night. The wind had been worse than I expected. What remained wouldn't be enough to keep the werewolves out if they came back. I didn't want them near the cabin, whether I was here or not.

I grabbed a phone book the cabin owner had been thoughtful enough to leave for my use. There appeared to be several herb shops nearby, but I didn't want to be out in public any longer than necessary. Calling first seemed like a good idea.

I considered tossing the phone book after discovering the first two stores didn't have wolfsbane. It didn't seem right. The herb wasn't uncommon and most places would carry it. They did in California—Lisette's shop sold it. Not that I'd bought it from her place. She would have asked too many uncomfortable questions.

I tried the third and last one, hoping for better results. A woman answered the phone with a polite greeting. Her voice had a melodic tone to it.

"Yes, do you have any Aconite?" I gave the more proper name so as to not alert her to my true purpose.

A distinct pause followed my question before she answered. "I'm sorry, no, we don't sell that here."

A small tremor had been notable in her voice. She was hiding something, but I couldn't come out and accuse her of it. "Do you know anyone who does?"

"It isn't...commonly used in Fairbanks. You won't find anyone who sells it in the area. Is there an alternative herb I could help you with?"

"Um, no, thanks." I hung up.

The conversation told me a few things. First, the other shops hadn't hesitated to inform me they didn't have it in stock. I knew they were telling the truth. Next, this woman seemed to be a little too aware no one carried it.

She had to know why.

Maybe the sups forced local stores to get rid of the herb and to not sell it anymore. Humans could have been compelled and supernatural owners threatened. The practice might not be all that unusual for a place with a high supernatural population. It wouldn't surprise me.

The woman had felt "other" but my detecting abilities had their limits over a phone line. Intuition was all I had. She had to be carrying it in secret because the feel of her words made me believe she told a half-truth. If that was the case, it would be worth the risk to find out.

After ditching the towel and getting dressed, I headed over to the store. It looked nice on the outside, despite its small size. Most herb shops weren't that large so it didn't surprise me. My senses picked up on her nature long before I reached the door, a fairy—one with a good thrum of power emanating from her. My senses told me she had been alive for about sixty years, but she appeared to be no more than twenty-five. Amongst the fae, fairies and elves tended to live the longest, measuring their lifespans in centuries instead of decades. I'd never seen an elf and this was only my second fairy.

The woman turned out to be as beautiful as her voice. She had flowing red hair reaching past her curvy hips and porcelain skin that brought out striking green eyes. If not for my ability to detect glamour, I might have believed magic made her look that good, but she didn't need it.

A fairy's natural appearance was a direct reflection on how they lived their lives. Those who did bad things were ugly and covered it up with glamour. The ones who acted good and kind became beautiful. Everything they did turned their looks one way or the other, so they had to consider every action. Maybe I could use that to my benefit. She wouldn't want to tarnish her image.

I gave her a bright smile, which she returned with one of her own. It almost blinded me. Wow, she had to be really good to have that kind of wattage.

"Can I help you?" She asked in an even more lyrical voice than what had come across the phone.

"Yes, I called earlier about the Aconite."

The skin on her face tightened a fraction. "I'm sorry, but as I said, I don't sell it here."

She avoided lying again by using the same half-truth. Fairies were good at that. She wouldn't get off that easy with me, though.

"I know you said you didn't sell it, but do you have it?"

Her eyes turned down as she started to fidget with a colorful floral arrangement on the counter.

"There is none available that I can give you." She glanced up at me before averting her face again. "Is there something else I could help you with?"

I moved forward and put my hands on the counter in front of her. My next words would be a risk, but one I had to take. A glance at her business cards by the register gave me a start.

"Felisha, please don't lie to me. I know you have it."

The worry creasing her features melted to surprise, then denial. She backed away.

"I told you already no one sells that herb here. Please leave if that is all you are looking for because I can't help you."

She had a thread of fear coming from her that made me feel a tinge of guilt for my tactics, but there wasn't time to be soft with her.

"I know you're a fairy and don't bother looking surprised." I could see that she was. "Why are you taking orders from the vampires and werewolves around here?"

She gasped.

"You're the woman they're searching for, aren't you?" Her voice came out little more than a whisper.

I shrugged. The word on me must have gotten out. "Unless there's more than one woman who they're searching for, I'm probably the one you're thinking of."

Felisha shook her head. "If I were you, I'd run as far away as possible."

She paused for a moment. "Don't use the airport, they'll be watching for that."

Wasn't she helpful.

"Running from them won't save me, we both know that. I came here for a reason. You have to have some wolfsbane back there." Might as well use the real term for the herb now that my secret was out.

Pity reflected from her eyes. I supposed she figured me for a dead woman.

"Your being a sensor doesn't mean you can beat them. Unless you have an angel or two around to protect you, they will get you."

The one thing close to an angel I had would be more likely to kill me than save me. Of course, she didn't know that, but something else she said worried me more.

"What makes you think I'm a sensor?"

Her lips thinned. "I have the sight. It might not work on you, but others have figured out what you are. I can 'see' them discussing it. Whatever you did last night sealed your fate. They want you more than you can imagine."

A fairy that could "see" things. There weren't many of them with that ability from what I understood. A few other races tended to have the monopoly on that skill.

"Please, sell me the wolfsbane. I need it to protect myself. Would you really deny me such a small thing considering all I'm up against?"

Her conflicting emotions—both fear and

sympathy—bombarded my senses. These sups must have had her scared.

"Why don't you leave, rather than live here in fear?" I asked. Seemed to me she had more of a choice than I did. There couldn't be that much holding her to this town.

She opened her mouth, and then closed it with an audible snap, appearing to be in deep thought. After a moment of contemplation, she waved me over.

"Come with me, I'll get you the wolfsbane, but you must leave after that. I have to hope they didn't see you come in."

"They didn't," I said. "You're the only supernatural around here right now."

"Oh, right." She turned back and gave me a weak smile. "You would know."

I smiled back, trying to reassure her. Not an easy thing under the circumstances. Her nervousness was making me nervous. I imagined both of us wanted to get this over with.

There were clear storage bins of varying sizes for the herbs in the back room where she led me. She pulled one open and took a sealed bag of wolfsbane out, handing it over while keeping an eye on the door. It was like a backroom drug deal, except of the supernatural kind.

"This is all I can spare. They've prevented us from getting any additional supplies into the area. I wish I could give you more, but you're holding half my stock in your hands as it is."

The bag weighed a couple of pounds with the

herb packed tight inside. If I took extra precautions this time, it would be enough to do the job.

"Thanks," I said, putting the herb in my backpack. "How much do I owe you?"

She waved her hand. "Nothing, don't worry about it. Please, just don't tell them I gave it to you."

"Don't worry, they'll never know."

She nodded and led me back to the front. Before I could go, though, she stopped me at the counter.

"There is one other thing I may be able to help you with. As a sensor you can handle using it, but save this as a last resort."

She brought out a small white pouch that had been tied off with a golden string. I took it from her when she handed it to me. The pouch felt smooth, like velvet, and didn't weight much.

"What is it?" I asked.

"Fairy dust. Are you familiar with its use?"

Wanda had covered some fairy mythology in her lessons, not a lot, but she'd explained enough for me to know their dust could be used as a protective measure. It stunned the victim for a brief period and made them forget the seconds before it hit them. Most of the time, only fairies could handle it since no others could touch the dust without being affected. Sensors were the exception. So long as our blood didn't touch it, the substance would remain active for use on anyone else.

"Good, then please be careful. They want you now that they know what you are. I'm afraid of what purpose they think you could serve. Avoid them at all cost."

I was touched by her concern. Not to mention she'd taken a serious risk giving me such a precious gift. If the sups found out, it could cause her a lot of trouble.

"Don't worry. I'll take care and they'll never know you helped me," I promised.

She managed a weak smile and surprised me with a warm hug. We were about the same height. I got a good whiff of her floral scented hair as it rubbed against my nose. It had a calming effect that had nothing to do with its magical properties. It should have been awkward to embrace a supernatural creature, but it wasn't with her. Maybe there were a few sups out there that didn't have to be classified as all bad.

I broke away from her with a smile and headed out the door. The one way I could return the favor was by leaving.

***

Two hours later, I had the fresh wolfsbane laid out under the cabin. This time it was divided off into cloth sacks and tied to the supports underneath so it couldn't be blown away. I tried to learn from my mistakes. Maybe it would keep me alive.

The landlord had come by during my trip to Felisha's shop and patched up the window. I'd called him before leaving the cabin earlier, wanting to get it taken care of as soon as possible. He came faster than expected and left a message saying the glass was on order and would take about a week to arrive. I had to give him credit. He did a better job boarding up the empty space than I did. He even stapled some plastic on the outside to seal it better.

Satisfied my home was as safe as it could be, I left again to begin my search for the sups who could lead me to Aniya. The best defense would be a good offense. They wouldn't expect me to search for them. Most sensible people would be running away right now. There was nothing sensible about my actions lately.

The sun rode low in the sky as I drove around. It didn't take too long to cover all the major areas of the city, considering its size. Over two dozen sups blipped on my radar, but none of them were the ones who had been at the cabin last night or the bar the evening before. I decided to drive farther out in the hopes of finding them elsewhere.

My next stop was a town called North Pole. Not the actual North Pole, which was much farther north, but a town that went by that name. Even in August, it had a festive atmosphere and catered to the Christmas season. I had read somewhere the townspeople here received all the letters sent to Santa via the post office and replied back to the kids who wrote them. I wondered if the letters I'd sent as a child ever made it to this place. Assuming my parents really did mail them.

My attention was diverted while driving on Santa Claus Lane by the very thing I was hunting. There had been a few sups in the vicinity, but none I recognized until now. One of the werewolves who attacked the cabin the night before was inside the Safeway grocery store. I decided to pull over at a nearby gas station and grab something to drink while waiting for him to come out.

About the same time I got back into my vehicle, he got in his.

I didn't move until he got a few blocks away. My SUV glided into the light traffic as I picked up speed to follow him. He drove out of town and headed north for awhile, making a few turns onto other highways before I sensed his vehicle pull off and come to a stop. I couldn't come up behind him, so I picked out a dirt road that didn't appear like it was used much. It was far enough out of the way no one would notice my vehicle while I continued on foot.

I grabbed my backpack before heading into the woods. The hiking boots on my feet turned out to be a good choice for the terrain, along with my jeans, long-sleeve shirt, and jacket. The air had already begun to cool outside. The temperature would be dropping further as the sun set. All I needed to do was verify Aniya stayed at the same place the werewolf had gone and get a good look at the set-up. With luck, I'd be back at the cabin before dark to plan my next step.

The sups couldn't sense me like I could them, making it less risky to sneak up on their house. There didn't appear to be any other homes nearby, which reduced the risk of nosy neighbors. Despite not sensing anyone too close, I moved cautiously all the way until the house came into view through the trees.

There were a lot of sups in there. All of their contrasting signatures pushed at my senses, making me sway for a moment before getting myself under control. All the recent exposure to them had reduced the effects, but there were enough of them here to make my temples throb.

I counted at least seventeen in the place—eight werewolves, seven vampires, one witch and...a witch-vamp? That came as a surprise. From what I understood, it was an almost unheard-of occurrence. No vamp would want to turn them, and most witches wouldn't ask for it. The transition could kill them, and even if they did survive to become a hybrid, their magic was reduced considerably from what it had been before.

Despite that, this one had been turned long ago and had to be around four hundred years old. She wasn't super strong, but she still ranked higher than anyone else in the area. Some of the older vamps would have killed her on sight if they'd found her, believing a hybrid to be too great a threat, but she seemed to be doing well for herself up here. Of course, Alaska wouldn't be a bad place to live if you wanted to avoid notice.

I maneuvered myself to about two hundred yards from the house and settled into a position with plenty of bushes where it would make it easy to hide while observing. No outdoor activity could be seen, and the werewolf had already gone inside. It was a large home that looked to be in good shape with light blue siding, and a deck along the back. It branched out over a down-hill slope and no doubt provided a nice view while standing on it. I imagined it cost a fortune to build the entire place. There were two above-ground floors and I could sense a couple of sups down in a basement below, both of them younger vampires who were probably resting until nightfall.

The tricky part came in attempting to sense any

humans at this distance. Most of the time, I could only detect them at a very close range. Even then they had to be feeling strong emotions, but sometimes my ability could be stretched further with deep concentration. Minutes passed as I forced my mind to focus. All at once, a burst of fear came from the house. It had to be from a human, but I couldn't get enough of a lock on the signature to know if the person was Aniya. The emotion strengthened to a high pitch and sent a shot of pain through my head. It had to be her.

A few moments later six werewolves came dashing outside in human form and raced straight for me. I sucked in a breath. How could they have known I was here? Not wanting to stick around and ask, I took off running through the woods toward my vehicle, fumbling with my backpack as I went.

The crack of broken twigs behind me let me know the group had sped up and weren't bothering to be subtle about it. My feet practically flew across the uneven terrain as my pursuers gained on me at a terrifying rate. I could see the Pathfinder up ahead and pushed hard to reach it. My heart pounded hard in my chest. The SUV was close enough that I thought I could make it if I didn't slow down.

The weres weren't going to make it that easy, though. To my dismay, one of them pulled ahead of the others and closed the gap between us within a few seconds. As I came within a dozen strides of reaching the vehicle, he leaped forward and knocked me down. The air left my lungs as his weight collapsed over me.

It couldn't end like this.

I had the fairy dust in my hand, having already grabbed the pouch from my backpack. It had to work. The werewolf pulled his weight off mine enough that I was no longer being crushed by him. I took advantage of it and flipped myself over. My hand flung a pinch of the dust into his surprised face.

It froze him on contact. I pushed his body off to the side and jumped up, ready to make the last stretch to my vehicle, but by this time the others had caught up. They circled around me, their postures wary.

My lungs dragged in air as I tried to catch my breath. Most of the fairy dust remained in my hand, but there would only be one chance to use it. When one of the weres turned his head to give an order, I took advantage.

With several flicks of my hand, I cast the powdery substance over their faces while pivoting on my feet. Some moved to stop me, but not quickly enough. The whole group stood frozen within seconds. I propelled myself to the SUV again and almost made it, but the first werewolf had come out of his trance. He had been the strongest one in the group.

It gave me a jolt when his hand took hold of my fallen hair. It had been in a bun before to keep it out of the way, but it must have unraveled during the chase. He rolled half of it around his hand and dragged me back to him. I struggled, not ready to give up yet.

He grunted when the sole of my boot slammed into his shin.

"You had to do this the hard way," he said in a gruff voice.

A hard knock to my head made everything go black before I could reply.

Chapter Ten

Consciousness came back to me in slow increments. Sharp pain lanced through the crown of my head, and someone must have glued my eyes shut. I couldn't move my arms either. The chains suspending them might have had something to do with that. A light rattle when I shifted gave them away. The manacles around my wrists were set high enough that my feet barely touched the cold cement floor, as if they were designed for someone taller.

A physical check told me I had no other wounds. They had removed most of my clothes, leaving me in a bra and underwear. Chills ran across my bare skin. The temperature outside had been in the fifties when I left the cabin, but in this underground room it was much cooler. How long had I been out? Night might have fallen already.

With some concentration, I forced my eyes open to take a look around at the small room. It took a moment to focus before I could make out a few small details. It didn't appear to be a large room, maybe eight by twelve feet, with cinder block walls. A small glow came from underneath the door behind me, lighting up the lower portions of the room. Everything else was hidden by darkness. It was as if I was stuck in a tomb.

What were they planning to do to me?

I fought the chains, twisting and turning in an effort to get loose. They were well-built and probably meant to hold prisoners much stronger than me. It took a few minutes of struggling before I wore myself out. They weren't going to break. I was stuck. The sound of my ragged breaths echoed against the walls as I tried to get control of myself.

A magic eight ball would no doubt say "Outlook not so good." The sups had won this round and now they had me trapped with no way out. Flashes of those scary movies where the heroine finds herself in a dark place where she can't hear anything except her own heavy breathing bombarded me. I had become that girl and did not like the implications. Those scenes never ended well.

I needed to calm down and think.

Years ago, I underwent training in the military to learn how to deal with this type of situation. In SERE (Survival, Evasion, Resistance, Escape) school, they captured and held us in primitive prisons, all to simulate the environment we could face if caught by the enemy in the real world. There were limits on how far instructors could go, but no one would call the experience pleasant. The more they put you through in a controlled setting, the better prepared you would be for a real one. I had hoped to never need the training, but it looked like I would now.

One thing was for certain—panicking would get me nowhere and could make things worse. They had me locked up tight with no way to get out, but that didn't mean opportunities wouldn't come. I needed to bide my time and figure out my options. If they were going to kill me, they would have done it already. Not to mention Felisha had said they wanted me for something. They would have to keep me alive for that.

There was one problem with that line of thinking.

No one had come to check on me, though a guard stood nearby. With his werewolf hearing, he must have heard the racket I made trying to get free. Were they planning to let me rot down here in a slow death? With no food, water, or way to get warm, it wouldn't take more than a couple of days. If hypothermia set in, it could be even less.

Hopelessness hit me with the realization I had failed Mrs. Singh and my best friend. I never even got close enough to see Aniya. My senses told me there were several humans in the house, but I didn't have the energy to figure out if any were her. It wouldn't matter anyway, if getting out of my own situation couldn't be done. What would they do to her if I didn't save her?

Did my actions make things worse?

Following that train of thought wouldn't do any good right now. I needed to focus on my immediate problems. Like the fact no heat reached this room and it had to be freezing. I began to shiver and couldn't seem to stop myself. My teeth were chattering so hard it was a miracle they didn't knock themselves out. After what might have been hours, I grew tired and weak from exhaustion.

Dark thoughts ran through my mind as I hung there with nowhere to go and nothing to do. My body stopped shaking after awhile, whether from shock or adapting to the environment, I didn't know. The manacles continued to dig into my wrists and my toes grew numb. Staying awake became difficult. My eyelids drifted closed. I'd sleep—just for a little while.

***

Time stood still. I'd fall asleep only to be woken soon after by sharp pains shooting through my arms. Breathing in this position wasn't easy either. A day must have gone by since my arrival. I had sensed both vampires and werewolves outside the door, and guessed they were rotating according to daylight hours.

A werewolf waited outside now, pacing back and forth along what must have been a corridor of some sort. His emotions were volatile. He had been there the other night at the cabin. I suspected he held a grudge. Funny how the bad guys always got angry at people who defended themselves.

The lack of food and water, along with the constant pain and discomfort, was wearing me down. I couldn't think clearly. In a strange and twisted way, the room became both my prison and my sanctuary. So far, nothing had hurt me here, excluding the chains holding me in place. If I had to die, it wouldn't be such a bad thing and maybe even for the best. Anything would be better than staying stuck in this room for much longer.

The werewolf stopped his pacing and unlocked the door. It opened inch by inch, creaking along as it went. Before my eyes could adjust to the brightness, he closed it behind him, taking the light away. He stood there in silence. I barely breathed.

He took a few steps closer, moving in behind me. I wanted do disappear. His werewolf vision gave him an advantage. I could sense lust rising from him. It felt like his eyes were roaming over every inch of me. I desperately wanted to cover myself and tried shifting in my chains. It wasn't the cool temperature in the room making me cold now.

I jerked when his rough fingers traced over my skin, starting at my shoulders and moving downward. My body recoiled, but I couldn't get far from him. He laughed and reached around to my breasts, squeezing them hard. I cried out. It hurt. I wanted...no, I *needed* to make it stop. I was a fighter. I couldn't let one disgusting werewolf do this to me.

"Get your dirty paws off me, you stinking mutt," I gritted out.

He smacked me hard on my ass. The sound echoed against the walls.

"I don't think you're in a position to talk, little whore," he said before continuing his explorations. The sick bastard.

Both his body and breath stunk. I grew nauseous from the combined assault on my body and senses.

"Don't touch me."

His darkened shape moved into my view. "You'll learn to enjoy it."

"I will never enjoy it, you sick fuck."

I kicked my leg out, trying to nail him anywhere I could. He side-stepped out of the way. The lanky man could move fast. Lacking any other options, I spit in his face.

"Stupid bitch." He swiped the dribble off his cheek. "Try that again and I'll shackle your legs…apart!"

He smacked me again. My head swung to the side as pain exploded in my cheek. Okay, that really hurt. At least one of my back teeth had been knocked loose. I had to press my lips together to keep from making any kind of sound. No point in giving him that pleasure.

He froze when the lights came on. The door flung open, banging against the wall. Another werewolf entered. Though I couldn't see him, he had the feel of an alpha about him. It was the same one who had captured me in the woods.

"That's enough, Kevin," he growled out.

"Ah, come on Derrick," he said. "She has it coming after the trouble she caused us. You weren't there when she killed Janice or you'd understand."

Derrick? That was the same guy who visited Emily. Was his showing up a good thing or a bad thing?

"Doesn't matter. I allow you a lot of freedom but molesting women, regardless of who they are, isn't one of them. We don't treat females—any females—that way. Now get out of here and don't let me catch you in this room again."

I could feel the command in his voice. The weaker werewolf responded to it. He huffed, but he left without further argument. Smart thing since the alpha wolf had to be about five times his strength. In fact, Derrick registered on my senses as being almost two centuries old. I hadn't paid attention to his age that day he passed me by on the street, being in too big of a hurry to get away, but it bothered me now. Werewolves, on average, didn't live past a century, if that. How had he managed his longevity?

The alpha followed the other guy out and shut the door behind him. The light remained on, though, and a few minutes later he came back holding a bottle of water. Saying nothing, he held the opening to my mouth. Not knowing when another chance might come, I accepted it, enjoying the taste after having nothing to drink for too long. The werewolf remained quiet while I chugged it down.

At least there were no lusty vibes coming from him.

With lowered lids, I studied the man. He looked like a typical alpha werewolf with a stocky build made large by heavy muscle. Unlike the other guy, this one was well-groomed with a fresh-shaven face, and his long brown hair had been pulled back in a ponytail at the neck. I guessed it to be about shoulder length or a little longer. When his brown eyes turned to mine, my gaze jerked away, focusing on the nearby wall instead. That might be considered a submissive move to his kind, but I was the one stuck without any clothes on, chained tight. It made it kind of hard to act all that tough.

His mouth opened as if to say something, but he grunted instead and left without a word. The light stayed on, a small favor to me. I wasn't afraid of the dark, but I'd discovered I didn't like it much in this place. Derrick stationed himself not far from the door.

I let out a silent breath of relief.

At least one person here had some decency. He

might have knocked me out during our scuffle in the woods, but his stopping a man from molesting me still upped my opinion of him. It would have been nothing for him to ignore it. Not to mention his care of Emily. She hadn't talked about him much, but what little she did say had been good.

My opinion of sups had gone on a roller coaster ride since arriving in Fairbanks, meeting the good, the bad, and the questionable among their ranks. I couldn't settle on whether the good ones counted or if it was better to consider them all bad—no matter how moral they first appeared.

No one else came again for a long time. Doubt and worry set in as the hours trickled by and nothing else happened. When new visitors did arrive, I wanted to go back to my solitary existence. The human witch and two of the werewolves from the attack on my cabin entered the room. Derrick had left his station outside the door not long before that. There wouldn't be anyone to intercede for me this time. Whatever this group wanted, it couldn't be good. The three came in with revenge on their minds. I could feel it in their moods as they circulated around me.

The witch stood off to the side, the furthest away, and wore a sickening grin. She had a long, narrow face with icy blue eyes and long, stringy black hair. Her frail body didn't have a hint of curves, which was made worse by her being on the tall side. No one would ever call her beautiful.

The one thing that saved her was a pert nose and full lips. If she'd ever bothered to look friendly, the two features would have softened the harshness making up the rest of her. I didn't think that would ever happen, though. She might be young at twenty years old, but she had already been dabbling in the black arts. It would make her appearance and disposition grow worse if she continued down that path.

The witch placed her hands on her hips, attempting to appear tough. It didn't work with her slight body and under different circumstances I might have laughed.

"You killed my sister. I'll make sure you pay for that, you little bitch." Her voice came out in a screech.

"You tried to invade my cabin. What did you expect? A welcome party?" I asked.

Her eyes lit up with rage. "How dare you!"

I could feel the waves of maliciousness coming off of her. She nodded to the two weres, who stepped closer to me. The witch no doubt wanted to watch me get hurt without having to get her own delicate hands dirty.

I shook my head and let her see the pity in my eyes. "This won't bring her back, you know."

She tightened her jaw and waved at her companions.

The first strike to my chest took the breath right out of me. One of my ribs must have cracked, if the piercing pain was anything to go by. There was no chance to focus on it further. Successive blows rained down on me after that. Each man took a turn holding me in place while the other took his shots at me. They rammed fists into my back, chest, and legs—along with the occasional strike to my face.

They weren't using their full strength, but it still hurt like hell. Death might have been preferable under the circumstances. The torture of waiting for them to come didn't compare to the physical punishment I was getting now.

My body jerked like a puppet on strings as they worked me over. It was methodical and brutal. Blood poured from my nose and down my face. I could taste it on my lips. My manacled wrists were being gouged from holding up most of my weight. They'd crushed one of my knees and the other one was having trouble keeping up.

The witch laughed and smiled the whole time, encouraging them to hit me more. I passed out twice, but they threw buckets of ice water on me to solve that problem. One of the vampires from the other night brought the ice in and stayed for a few minutes to watch. My senses gave me a vague impression of him, but my eyes had swollen to the point I couldn't see well anymore.

Every sup in the area had to have heard my torture-filled cries until my voice grew too hoarse to make much noise beyond a whimper. Through ragged gasps, I begged them to stop—my dignity having long since fled out the windowless room, but my tormentors laughed at my pleas. They found my pathetic mewling to be a source of amusement.

A person in deep pain has no pride; only the desperate will to make it stop. I was no longer Melena Sanders—I was a stranger. A woman who felt nothing, saw nothing. Nothing but the intense pain coursing through her body. A broken creature with no hope of survival. If there was a light at the end of the tunnel, the flickering bulb above my head wasn't it. The faces of my tormentors were no angels—they were hell's minions and I'd stepped into their purgatory.

Hours might have passed before it ended, maybe it had been less. There was no way to be sure. I was having difficulty breathing, but enough breath reached my lungs to somehow keep me alive. They freed me of the chains and one of the weres caught my body before it fell to the floor. Even his lighter touch hurt to the point it brought visions of blackness.

He set me up against the wall in the corner. I slumped, but managed to stay semi-sitting up so I could breathe easier. He stepped back to examine the damage he and his cohort had done. I could just make out his shape through my cracked eyelids. After seeming satisfied with my condition, he turned to the witch.

"You think that was enough?" he asked.

The coldness in her voice reached me. "It will never be enough, but it will have to do. Variola wants her later tonight."

The witch swept out of the room without a backward glance. The two werewolves followed, shutting the door behind them. My blurry vision barely allowed me to notice when the lights turned off. My awareness was fading fast. Within moments I passed out, unable to keep myself conscious any longer.

***

A hand rubbing my arm disturbed me from an

uncomfortable sleep. I came awake and moaned when the pain from my injuries came rushing back to hit me with full force. It must have been too much for them to let me sleep for long. My eyelids were swollen and gritty from the dried blood and tears encircling them. I managed to open one of them enough to see who kneeled before me.

A couple of slow and agonizing blinks later I recognized her. She was the last person I expected to see. Why would the sups have let her come down here?

With a shaking hand, I reached out to touch her tear-filled face. Sharp pain shot through my shoulder. I gritted my teeth through it and managed to graze her cheek. Wet drops ran down my fingers, leaving streaks through the grime. She didn't seem to care about the filth covering me. A mixture of guilt, sadness, and fear reflected in her eyes. After days of searching, I had found Aniya, and now my body was too broken to help her. The irony of it was not lost on me.

She looked good, which made me feel somewhat better. No bruises or scars marked her skin. Her long, dark hair had been left loose and framed her tear-streaked face as she looked down at me from a crouch. She grabbed my hand as it began to drop.

"I'm so sorry," she murmured over and over again.

"It's okay, Niya," I whispered. Not much of my voice remained after all the screaming I'd done earlier.

"No, it isn't, Mel. You've been hurt because of me. I never meant for this to happen and wouldn't have come here if I'd known about Philip. He can control me in ways

I can't..." she stopped.

I followed her gaze to the alpha werewolf standing at the open door. Disappointment emanated from him, but I couldn't figure out the reason for it. Did he disagree with my friend being here? His arms were crossed as he observed the two of us with a shuttered gaze.

I directed my one good eye back to Aniya. "What did Philip do to you?"

She lifted her shoulder in a small shrug, still not looking at me. "He...he influenced me somehow. For awhile, I didn't notice that he never went out during the day and didn't eat food. It didn't bother me in the beginning, though it should have. Eventually, his influence wore off. They said compelling a human too often can cause that. The others can still make me do things, but not him."

I hadn't known about that, but it made sense. As a younger vamp, he probably didn't know his limits yet or what to do with a human girl like Aniya if he wanted to keep her around long-term.

"So he tricked you and then wouldn't let you leave?"

A blush crept up her cheeks. "Yes, but at first we were staying somewhere else—a smaller house a few miles from this one. After his influence wore off, I tried to get away, but he caught me and brought me here. I've been stuck in this place ever since." She pinched her lips together as she glanced up at the rest of the house. What had they been doing to her for all this time?

There were so many questions I wanted to ask,

but it was getting harder to concentrate. The werewolf's growing impatience was clawing at my senses as well. Aniya and I didn't have much time left. Whatever we wanted to discuss, it had to be now.

"Has he hurt you?" I had to know that much.

She shook her head and blushed. "No, not really. I think...I think he loves me."

Of course he loved her. Why else keep her in good health for so long? I tried to take a deep breath before speaking again, but my ribs protested, making me groan. Aniya rubbed my arm in light strokes. I wanted to tell her to stop, but didn't. When the pain subsided to a more manageable level, I continued.

"What do you think of him?"

"Mel, I don't know. Before I found out what he was, I thought I was in love with him. Now...it all seems so wrong."

She bent her head down, allowing her hair to cover the new tears that were no doubt falling. I wanted to be mad, but Aniya could be so innocent sometimes. She didn't have the luxury of knowing how to protect herself against the darker elements of the world, and it seemed stupid to be angry with her over something she couldn't have known about.

Part of me wished I'd told her what was out there, but everything Wanda had taught me said to never reveal my knowledge of the supernaturals to anyone. I still hated knowing my friend was trapped here and my chance to help her had been taken away.

"Niya, take care of yourself, all right?"

Her eyes rounded at my words. I had spoken in a

rush after seeing the werewolf move toward us. She jerked when he grabbed her arm, but he forced her up anyway.

"Time to go. Variola gave you ten minutes," he said in a gruff voice.

Aniya refused to move at first and nodded her head toward me. "What about her? What are you going to do to her?"

A little of my friend's inner strength came out in that moment. Most people would think of her as a soft woman, but she had a backbone when it came to those she cared about.

"She'll be taken care of," he replied.

"Mel's my friend. She needs medical treatment. You can't leave her down here like this!"

Aniya kept arguing until Derrick whispered something in her ear. She stopped yelling at him but continued to sob. He guided her out the door and handed her off to some unseen vampire in the hall. The sniffling went away after that. The vamp must have silenced her, but I couldn't tell because the door closed after the werewolf came back inside.

The light above cast a shadow on him. His hair had been left down this time and covered the sides of his face. The straight, silky locks gave his features an even harder edge than when they were pulled back.

I braced myself as he came closer with a small vial in his hand. Was he going to drug me now? It wasn't like I could go anywhere in my condition.

Derrick held the vial to my lips, urging me to drink. The blood had a spicy flavor that didn't sit too well on my tongue. It had come fresh from a vampire. I jerked away, wanting no part of it, but I didn't have far to go with the wall behind me.

"You have to drink it before its effect is lost," he said. "You can't go to the hospital and your injuries are too severe to survive long without medical help."

"No," I croaked out. "I'm not drinking their blood."

He shook his head and growled at me. "You're being stupid. Do you want to live or not?"

"I don't want it." The idea of it made me nauseous.

"This is for your own good."

Derrick forced my head back and tipped the vial so it came rushing between my lips. Thanks to my broken nose, my mouth was the only opening I had to breathe. He took advantage of it and clamped my jaw shut. I almost choked on the blood, but managed to swallow. The aftertaste didn't leave a very pleasant flavor on my tongue.

It didn't take long to work. The injuries across my body began to heal right away, even down to my toes. The pain intensified in the beginning, as bones reset themselves, forcing me to grit my teeth through it. Derrick took my hand and encouraged me to squeeze his until it was over. I hated needing his reassurance, but it didn't stop me from taking it.

The process took several minutes. Moans escaped my lips a few times when it got to be too much. In the end, my body had been restored, but the vampire blood wasn't able to cure my malnourishment. The healing process had left me weak. At least I could finally think with a semi-clear head.

"So what now?" I asked him.

Derrick's nostrils flared while his brown eyes focused on me. His heightened sense of smell must have picked up on the blood and dried waste that clung to my body. Even my human nose, newly healed, could smell it. Under normal circumstances, the filth covering me would have been horrifying. This situation wasn't anything close to normal. It still bothered me enough to curl into myself.

He sighed—his annoyance flaring across my senses. It made me wonder what kind of man was behind the impenetrable mask. For being such a tough looking guy, he didn't seem as bad as expected.

"Now?" he responded in a gruff voice. "We get you cleaned up and ready before Variola comes down."

"Who's Variola?" I asked as he pulled me into a standing position. I hadn't wanted his help, but he didn't give me much of a choice in the matter.

"She's the leader for this region. Not a woman you want to anger, which you already have."

Chapter Eleven

Two hours later my body had been restored to a more presentable state. Derrick returned my clothes, after allowing a warm shower in the basement bathroom. My underwear and bra were tossed into the garbage since they were too soiled to ever be used again, but the rest of my garments were clean and warm. It felt better than I could have imagined.

With some encouragement, Derrick convinced me to eat a warm bowl of beef stew. It had more broth than anything. He swore it'd help me get some of my strength back. I knew he was right. It would take time and a lot of food to get back to normal, assuming they let me live after this and weren't just toying with me.

I wouldn't put it past them.

The alpha werewolf had stayed with me after my meeting with Aniya. He'd given me some space to recuperate, but not so much as to allow me to think I could make a break for it. He had an air of displeasure surrounding him that made me wonder if it was directed at me or someone else. His eyes revealed little and his words even less.

He eventually left me sitting in the far corner of my prison, alone and as far from the door as possible. Someone had hosed the room down, removing the filth, but I still made sure to find the cleanest spot before settling in. Derrick had warned me any attempt to escape would put me back in the chains. With the number of sups in this place, I already knew it would be impossible to fight my way out. I was desperate, but not stupid.

When the door opened, two vamps I hadn't seen before entered. I stood slowly, keeping my eyes on both of them. They had dark skin and short cropped hair, along with matching black pants. Nothing covered their well-toned chests. They could have been twins. Their ages came in at about a hundred years old, so they might have at least been brothers. The woman who sauntered through the door after them grabbed my attention right away.

She had to be the dreaded Variola. Her presence was like poison stinging my senses. She didn't go with the sophisticated vampire look I expected of a leader and instead leaned more toward the "Queen of the Damned" style. Maybe she'd seen the movie. She was also the vamp-witch I had sensed in the house before.

She stood there in a blatant pose of confidence and sensuality. Black leather pants hugged her hips and legs, and she wore a matching bustier with silver studs. The woman looked more like a dominatrix than a powerful vampire leader and even had a short whip attached to her belt. My eyes shot a quick glance at the chains, which had held me before. I got a good mental picture of what they might be used for under different circumstances.

She flowed forward in steps so smooth I couldn't be sure if she was touching the ground. Her hand waved the two minions back when they moved to follow her. She studied me with an intent expression. Her black eyes were set in a stern but beautiful face framed by dark hair falling in dozens of tiny braids well past her thin, muscular shoulders, almost to her waist. I got the impression she was a mulatto due to the tint of her skin, which was neither black nor white. It had paled over the four centuries she'd been a vampire but it continued to give away something of her origin.

Variola didn't bother to breathe until right before she spoke.

"You, little sensor, have caused quite a lot of trouble," she hissed the words out, reminding me of a snake. "If we'd known what you were sooner, we would have handled your capture quite differently."

My body shuddered at the pure evilness emanating from her. I stayed silent, not believing she wanted a response anyway.

"Why did you come for your friend, so far from home?" A trace of an accent in her voice led me to believe she may have been from the Caribbean in her youth. I'd had a friend from that part of the world in middle school, who spoke in a similar way, minus the hissing effect. He had picked up an American accent after a couple years, but you could still hear the slight difference in his pronunciation of certain words. At least that guy had been nice, unlike this woman.

"Because that's what a person should do when their best friend goes missing," I said.

She laughed. "You would be amazed how many I've taken over the years and no one came for them."

Something told me I didn't want to know how many, exactly, that had been.

"Not everyone is the same," I said.

"Perhaps." She ran her fingers along one of her braids. "That leaves us with what to do with you. You've been punished for killing my witch, but it could be made into a reoccurring event."

Variola's thin lips shaped into a sadistic smile. "Did you enjoy your visit with your friend? She is quite the delectable little morsel. It's the one reason why I allowed Philip to keep her."

The bitch.

"I saw her."

Variola put a hand on her cocked hip. Something about her didn't seem natural. Most vampires made a point of breathing in public. She didn't, except to take in air to speak. For someone like me, who had always avoided being around them, it was unsettling. Breathing meant life, something this woman no longer had. At least, not in the normal sense of the word.

"Good. Then you will want to keep your friend alive, yes?"

"I would," I replied, wondering where she was going with this.

"Smart girl." She nodded and began speaking in a clipped tone, the hissing no longer present. "There is a job for you. One that suits your abilities and will give me a reason to keep both you and your friend alive. Do you wish to hear it or is dying preferable?"

She asked this question as if the answer didn't mean the difference between life and death. I leaned against the wall for support, but otherwise tried not to show any weakness.

"Go ahead, tell me."

She nodded, her braids swaying with the movement.

"Very well. After speaking with an associate of mine in Monterey—you may remember her as Noreen..." Variola paused to give me a knowing look. I didn't take the bait, not wanting to feed her need for a reaction.

"...we have decided you can be of use to us, despite your troublesome nature."

It didn't surprise me that they knew each other. The witch community wasn't that large—if you cut out all of the imitators. My problem was with the two of them discussing me. The Monterey witch couldn't be a big fan of mine after getting my knife stuck in her gut. All these years I'd worked hard to stay off the radar. The last couple of weeks had seen that ruined.

"What is it you want me to do?" No point in beating around the bush.

"We want you to find a vampire, one who escaped from us five years ago. We put him under a sleep spell, but haven't been able to locate him since. He's somewhere in this area. We know he couldn't have traveled far before the spell went into effect." Waves of irritation rolled off of her as she said the last part.

My arms crossed. "You put a sleep spell on a vampire but can't find him. How'd you manage that?"

If venom could have shot from her eyes, I'm pretty sure it would have.

"Don't worry about how. The spell worked,

despite his trying to run from it." She slapped the wall hard. Dust flew out around her as she turned back to me. I tried to pretend I hadn't jumped at the show of violence. "He couldn't have gone more than twenty or thirty miles from here, considering how fast one such as he could move, but someone used magic to cover up his location. Our attempts to find him have failed. You do not suffer our limitations and could give us what we want." Her eyes gleamed in anticipation.

"What's to say the same person using magic to hide him didn't break your spell?"

She shook her head. "This is not possible. It took myself and four witches and warlocks, all very powerful, to put this vampire down. There is no way it could have been broken."

I couldn't help but ask. "Would you know if it had been?"

She moved so fast I didn't even see the blur. One moment she stood five feet away and the next she appeared right in front of me, inches from my face.

"Do not get snide with me, sensor. I will make you regret it. The spell could not have been broken and that is all you need to know."

She ran a slow finger down the side of my face and throat. It was ice cold. Instinct made me want to turn my head away, but that would expose my neck. I kept my eyes locked on her.

Variola moved her head in closer, forcing my chin to the side. I couldn't help but swallow. She sucked in a breath at the movement. Her lips pressed against my skin. She ran her tongue in a trail up my neck, leaving faint traces of saliva behind. I clenched my fists, wanting to fight her, but knowing it wouldn't do any good.

Her voice whispered close to my left ear. "I've heard sensor blood can be so sweet in the beginning, before it turns nasty and takes more than it gives. I am too smart to fall for that lure, but remember, a small taste would do little harm, and it could be made rather unpleasant for you."

I remained quiet, focusing on my breathing. It took all my willpower not to slide away from the witch-vamp. To my relief, she backed off and moved a few feet away, closer to her stoic minions who still hadn't moved a muscle. They hadn't bothered to breathe either and could have been mistaken for lifelike statues. She must have cowed them into submission at some point.

Variola's attention returned to me after a full minute of silence. She'd regained control of her blood lust. I suspected the only reason she didn't bite me was because she couldn't be sure she could stop at one swallow. I understood—apple fritters had the same effect on me.

"Will you take the job or not, sensor?"

I rubbed at my neck, wanting to get the icky feeling off. "If I'm going to find this vampire, then you're going to have to at least give me a few details about him. I need to know what to look for with so many of you in the area."

Her mouth stretched into a triumphant smile, thinking she had me already. I knew how to play the captor vs. captive game. Hell, that had pretty much been my job as an interrogator—except with the roles reversed. I needed her to believe she was getting what she wanted. It could buy my freedom out of this place.

"Smart of you not to argue further," she said. "His name is Nikolas and he is almost twelve hundred years old. Comes from England originally. Is that enough?"

I drew short at the name. It sounded like she wanted me to hunt down the same vampire Charlie had mentioned. What was it about this one man that was so important?

"It's enough." I nodded. His age and gender was all I really needed. "What do you want me to do once I find him?"

"I'm assigning my second, Derrick, to you. He will accompany you at all times during the search and contact me when the vampire is found. You are to do nothing more than locate him. Is that understood?"

It sounded simple enough, assuming I could achieve my own goals.

"My friend, Aniya, and I will go free after I find him for you. Right?"

Variola stiffened. She'd lived during the time of the inquisition and had to know she couldn't lie to me. "Find the vampire and your friend will go free, but don't assume the same for yourself. Not yet anyway. There are many other potential uses for you in the future."

Damn, there had to be a way around this. I might be able to get Aniya free, but Variola had no intention of letting me go. Would she force me to do other things that could be even worse? I opened my mouth to argue, but she held her hand up.

"No, there will be no negotiating on this. Either

you agree to the terms or we can kill your friend right now in front of you—in the slowest and most painful manner possible. Then we will proceed to spend however long it takes to convince you to work for us. The last beating you received is nothing compared to what we could do."

The expression on her face said she would take personal pleasure in bringing me around to her way of thinking. I looked up at the ceiling, trying to think of a way out, but nothing came to me. It was either sacrifice Aniya, and receive endless torture until I begged to work for them, or skip that and at least gain some freedom.

I couldn't handle another beating or allow someone else to be hurt because of me. As a former interrogator, I knew what they were doing. We'd studied all the methods, even the forbidden ones since you had to know what you could and couldn't do legally. It was a common tactic by some countries and groups to use a person the prisoner cared about as a weapon against them. It usually worked, but if all else failed, they could always resort to violence. I felt fairly certain no one here followed the Geneva Conventions guidelines for treatment of prisoners.

Very few people on earth could resist torture for long. Any former prisoner of war could testify to that. Intense pain, disfigurement, sensory deprivation...all those things could break a person. The real trick to surviving was to give your captors just enough of what they wanted to satisfy them. Even if it meant lying—so long as you didn't get caught. For now, I'd play along until I found some other way to get myself and Aniya out.

"Fine, I'll find this vampire for you, but Aniya goes free after this is over," I said through gritted teeth.

Variola gave me a brief nod, turned, and walked out the door. Her two minions followed her. The lock screeched into place behind them. I slumped to the floor, my body too weak to stand any longer.

Chapter Twelve

Derrick drove me back to the cabin in the Pathfinder the next night after further arrangements were made. At some point during my stay they had picked up my vehicle and moved it to their house. I tilted my head to watch the fast moving landscape going by the window. A seemingly endless number of trees rushed past us through the darkness.

Derrick hadn't spoken much since handing me my weapons and backpack after we'd made it out of the house. Returning my stuff might have been some kind of peace offering, but I didn't bother to thank him. Nothing much mattered at this point except getting Aniya free. Both my mind and body were numb to everything else.

Variola, in her infinite generosity, said I could have one day to recover but after that I had to begin the search for Nikolas. I planned to do a lot of sleeping and eating during my short break. A warm, comfortable bed had never sounded so good after my long stay in the basement. When the cabin came into view, it appeared like a beacon. I had left the light on in the bedroom, as well as the one on the porch.

As soon as the vehicle stopped, I hopped out and went to unlock the door. Derrick grabbed his stuff from the back. He'd brought a bag of clothes and some blankets with him. I'd warned him there weren't any extras in the cabin. My attempts to convince him to sleep outside in wolf form hadn't worked. I figured he better find the couch comfortable because that was all he was going to get. I wasn't giving up my bed, not after what I'd been through.

He started toward the cabin, but began sneezing violently the moment he got close. I glanced back at him from the door, wondering why he had a sudden case of the sniffles, but then realized the problem. The wolfsbane.

"Sorry." I suppressed a smile. "I'll get rid of it."

Through a face red and swollen with irritation, he managed a grunt. I wanted to feel bad, I really did, but forcing my weak body under the cabin took what little sympathy I might have had away. My muscles protested the awkward crawling in a way that let me know I was nowhere near recovered yet. At least the herb bags were easier to remove than my first method of distribution. After gathering them up, I walked out toward the woods and dumped them in some bushes.

Derrick stood in the doorway when I got back, surveying the living room. At least it didn't look too bad. After being gone for three days, the only thing different was a mustiness in the air. While he arranged his things, I moved to the kitchen for something to eat, washing the dirt off my hands first.

A bowl of cereal seemed like the simplest choice. Feeling generous, I offered some to Derrick. It must have been a brand he liked because he accepted the offer right away. Of course, werewolves did have a high metabolism and needed to eat often. He might have wanted it no matter what it was.

We sat at the table, eating in silence, with only the sound of our food crunching between our teeth to break the quiet. Irony struck me. It came from that place inside that could still find humor in a bad situation. If anyone had told me a few weeks ago I'd be eating in a peaceful manner with a werewolf, I might have considered them insane.

His presence didn't irritate my senses nearly as much as I thought it would. The constant influx of sensations that bombarded me at Variola's had worn me down, but being around him didn't feel that bad. He was like a circle of heat wrapped around my mind. I wondered who this man might be besides Variola's second. It couldn't hurt to get to know him before we began working together. I didn't want him here, but for now I had no choice.

"So, how long have you lived around here?"

"About five years," he replied between mouthfuls of cereal.

"Do you like it?"

He shrugged and poured himself another bowl. Mine was still more than half-way full.

"Know the area well?"

"As well as I need to."

Okay, I'd landed myself a real conversationalist. He had a trace of an accent, maybe southern. During my captivity, I hadn't noticed it, but now it seemed more obvious to me.

Derrick had brown hair and skin with a bare hint

of a tan, but that didn't tell me much about him. Nothing stood out to give me a clue. His looks were average, neither ugly nor handsome. Maybe a bit brutish. His clothes were nothing special either. He wore a long-sleeve flannel shirt, dark blue jeans, and a pair of worn boots that had seen better days. Rugged would be the best way to describe him.

One thing could be said, he smelled good. A few people I'd run into in this area didn't bother to bathe all that often. It could have been due to all the dry cabins around that didn't have running water. Then again, it could have just been my poor luck. I seemed to find the worst kinds of people wherever I went.

At least Variola hadn't saddled me with a stinky guy, if I had to look at the bright side. The werewolf who'd tried to molest me would have been a far worse alternative. I might have decided to shoot him after getting back to the cabin, consequences be damned.

After finishing my bowl of cereal, I put it away in the sink and let him know he was welcome to whatever else he could find. Despite my reservations with having him here, the last thing I wanted was a hungry werewolf in the cabin—that would be a recipe for disaster.

He nodded his head and continued eating, now on his third bowl. I forced myself to put his presence out of my mind so I could get cleaned up and ready for bed. After being in a house full of sups for the last few days, dealing with one shouldn't be as bad. At least, that was what I hoped.

***

The next morning arrived with the smell of bacon and eggs. My hunger rose at the tantalizing scents. I mentally checked over my body before getting up. There was still some weakness, but it was better than last night. Knowing a good meal would help, I crawled out of bed. Maybe Derrick would take pity on me and share. The old pair of boxer shorts and shirt I wore covered me enough I didn't feel the need to put anything else on. I just ran a brush through my hair and put it in a ponytail before leaving the room.

Derrick looked up from where he stood in front of the stove. There were no shoes on his feet, but he did have jeans and a red t-shirt on that stretched across his chest. He'd left his hair loose. A few strands fell over his face and almost hid the dark circles rimming his eyes. I supposed a big, muscular guy like him wouldn't have had the easiest time sleeping on an old springy couch.

He nodded at one of the kitchen chairs. "Take a seat. Food's 'bout ready."

I froze in my steps. "You're cooking breakfast...for me?"

"And myself," he said.

"You didn't have to do that."

"Sounds like I do after what your friend said."

"Aniya warned you about my cooking? Why would she do that?"

These were the bad guys. It didn't make sense to warn him. I'd be willing to admit my cooking skills left something to be desired. They were limited to simple pasta meals and sandwiches—everything else was beyond my abilities. I could even ruin eggs, which is why it surprised me he had been cooking them. There hadn't been any here before, or bacon for that matter. He must have made a run to the store while I slept.

"She said she didn't want me dying of food poisoning," Derrick said while stirring the eggs around.

My brows furrowed. "Werewolves can't get food poisoning."

Unfortunately.

He cleared his throat. "No, but we can get an upset stomach. She also said the taste of your cooking was something best not tried."

"That little snitch," I grumbled under my breath.

He shot a sharp look in my direction, but I ignored him. It annoyed me that my own best friend had ratted me out to a sup. She must have liked Derrick to even bother telling him, which made me wonder what he'd done to get in her good graces. If I ever got the chance, I'd ask her—and berate her for spreading vicious rumors about me to the bad guys.

Deciding it wasn't worth arguing over food I didn't have to cook, I slumped into my seat without saying anything else. The man had even made toast, though that must have been a trick since the kitchen didn't boast an actual toaster. Maybe he used the oven.

Derrick put a plate in front of me before sitting down with his own. He'd loaded mine with food that made my mouth water. Wanda had told me at one point to never eat food a sup prepared, but she didn't have a love for home cooked meals the way I did. They say the fastest way to a man's heart was through his stomach. I may not be a man, but a well-cooked meal could win me over a lot faster than anything else. Anyone who'd had to eat military rations for weeks on end, or my cooking for that matter, would feel the same way. Though I didn't think my culinary skills were as bad as Aniya made them out to be.

We ate in silence. Both of us concentrating on our meals and not each other. Everything tasted even better than it smelled, which came as somewhat of a surprise. Could evil people make food this good? Maybe I could put up with him for a little while if he kept feeding me like this. At least Variola hadn't given me a vampire.

"How far out do your senses go?" His question startled me. Guess the man could open a conversation.

I shrugged. "About a half-mile."

He finished chewing his food before speaking again. "Guessin' you haven't sensed Nikolas before. You'll need to show me the places you've been on a map so we can narrow things down."

"No problem, I've been through most of Fairbanks. Same thing with North Pole. That town's small enough I would have picked up on him during my brief drive through there. Other than that, though, I haven't covered much."

He nodded. "I got some maps we can mark up. We'll start with the most likely places and work it out from there."

"Sounds fine," I replied. At least he had a plan.

After finishing my meal, I went ahead and started on the dishes. My parents raised me to believe a cook shouldn't have to do the clean-up job if there was anyone else to do it. I'm not one to bother washing dishes until they pile up to a height comparable to the Leaning Tower of Pisa, but something told me Derrick would do them if I didn't. Enemy or not, I didn't like others doing my dirty work.

The rest of the day was spent in recovery for me and planning for Derrick. He appeared to be on top of things and I still didn't have the energy to insert my own opinions into whatever plans he was making. The man appeared to be organized, if nothing else.

He had me up and out of the cabin the next morning by nine o'clock, after another filling breakfast of pancakes, eggs, and sausage. It was a good thing I needed to gain weight after my stay at Variola's because he cooked several times a day. The lasagna he made the night before was the best I'd ever had. Even my mom hadn't been that good and I remembered her meals being amazing.

I insisted on driving. He started to argue, but I gave him the glare all women are capable of giving if they are determined to have their way. He must have been familiar with it because he let the argument go. Smart man.

He guided me to a place north of the house where Variola lived, calculating Nikolas might have headed that way. We drove down all the paved roads in the area, but out in the bush it didn't take long. There weren't that many of them. I decided to go for some off-road driving after that, ignoring Derrick's protests.

"I know what I'm doing," I told him.

He turned his head forward and proceeded to

grip the "oh shit" handle. I set my iPod to play Creed songs so we'd have something to listen to. He shot me a surprised look, maybe not expecting my choice of music, but settled back in for the bumpy ride without saying anything.

After a while, we came up to a deep puddle that had to be at least twenty feet long and as wide as the road. With trees and brush on both sides, there would be no going around it. I stopped the vehicle and jumped out. Finding a lengthy stick nearby, I tested the depth. The puddle was about two and a half feet deep, plus or minus a few inches.

Derrick shook his head. "We'll have to turn around. Not worth trying to get through that."

I shrugged and went back to the SUV. He was studying the map when I shifted the vehicle into four-low, applied the gas, and eased it toward the water. The forward momentum caught his attention right away.

"Don't you wanna go backwards to get outta here?" He said as he tried to take control of the gear shifter.

"No," I said, slapping his hand away.

The front tires entered the water. I pressed harder on the pedal. The vehicle surged forward and went fully into it. Water splashed on both sides as I maneuvered through, never letting up on the gas.

At one point the tires began to spin in place, but I refused to let the pedal go and kept turning the wheel back and forth. The vehicle managed to gain traction again moments later. Seconds after that we were on the other side and on dry land again.

"You could have gotten us stuck."

I smiled. "But I didn't."

He grunted. "No, you didn't. Wanna tell me where you learned to drive like that?"

"Guess Aniya didn't tell you I was in the army, huh?"

He lifted his brows. "No. For how long?"

"Six years. They sent me to an off-road driving course. I've driven through lots of stuff like this since then. Give me a decent four-wheel drive and I can get through almost anything."

"Huh, well in that case," he told me with a wave of his hand, "carry on."

We drove for some time with me splashing through more puddles and going down some hills Derrick claimed made his life flash before his eyes. That seemed a bit of a stretch, considering how difficult it would be to kill a werewolf. The inclines had been a little steep, but it had surprised me how freaked out he got over them.

As time passed, I began to get the idea our search might be hopeless. Then my senses picked up on something unusual. Not the vampire we were looking for, but something else. When it comes to detecting sups, I could track them for up to a half-mile away, but the same couldn't be said for magic. For that, I had to be closer. This one felt to be a few hundred feet off the overgrown trail we were driving through.

Derrick lifted an inquiring brow when I stopped the vehicle and opened my door. I ignored him and climbed out. He followed me as I began trudging through the brush.

"You sensing somethin'?" he asked.

"Yep," I answered without explaining further. He might have stopped me if he learned the place I was going to investigate didn't have anything to do with our elusive vampire.

A little farther in we hit the first circle of spells. Derrick stopped, emitting a low growl. I gave him a wary glance and hoped it didn't mean he was about to turn violent.

His eyes had darkened and his fists were clenched tight. The sun wouldn't be setting for several more hours so at least he couldn't shift. That would be dangerous for me since weres had less control over themselves in their wolf form. I hadn't considered a "keep away" spell would cause this kind of fear in him. It didn't affect me at all, but then again, it wouldn't.

"I ain't liking this," he stated in a gruff voice, his eyes alert and searching for unseen enemies.

How do you calm a werewolf down? I missed the class on that one.

"Derrick, it's just a spell," I spoke in a calm voice. "If you can hold yourself together, it will pass after we walk about fifteen more feet. Can you do that?"

As an added precaution, I kept my eyes directed down and away from his. My lessons served me well enough to know looking a werewolf in the eye when he was upset or angry could result in disastrous consequences.

"I'll manage," he replied after a minute of breathing through the fear.

Hoping to set the example and get him to follow, I resumed walking forward. His light footsteps let me know he wasn't far behind. Fifteen agonizing feet later we made it past the thick band of magic. I sensed his immediate relief when the spell no longer affected him. A glance back showed his eyes and posture had returned to normal.

"Sorry about that," I told him. "There was no way around it."

"Are there more?"

I shook my head. "Not like that, but there is another one that will affect you."

"How?"

I pointed to an area up ahead. "Past that bank of trees, there is something there, but it's covered with an illusion spell so no one can see it. You'll think there is a deep, dark hole in the ground that you could fall into—but really, there is no hole. The idea must be to keep people from seeing, or walking into, whatever is there. Don't believe what you see. Just stay close to me and you'll be fine."

He nodded his head. A look of resolve settled on his face. He didn't come off as the type who liked to appear weak.

My senses could locate a spell and identify its purpose, but I couldn't know what the magic intended to hide until I saw it with my eyes. Derrick followed me as I headed toward the area in question. When we broke past the trees, the open field beyond came into my view. I gasped. Derrick would see a giant hole, which must have spanned a hundred feet, but I got to see what really lay there.

Chapter Thirteen

As my nose took in the putrid smell, my stomach lurched in protest. The visuals didn't help either. Bile rose up in my throat and I promptly bent over the ground to throw-up. Not even in my military days had I seen something this bad.

Derrick came over and rubbed my back in a soothing motion, helping to ease the cramps that had started in my stomach. I wanted to pull away, not trusting him so close while I kneeled on the ground in a vulnerable position, but the horror of what I'd seen had me stuck in place.

"What is it, Melena?" He couldn't understand what I was seeing, but his concern must have overcome his fear of the gaping hole he had to think he was standing on.

I attempted to breathe through my mouth to avoid the worst of the stench. It was the most awful thing I'd ever smelled. As a werewolf, he should have scented it too, but the illusion spell must have prevented it.

It was far too horrific to describe. He'd have to see it for himself, so I took my knife out of my pocket. He glanced between me and the blade, but didn't say anything. I pricked my finger to draw out blood and let it hit the ground until several drops mixed with the magic.

It was enough to break the spell. The illusion came crashing down around us. Derrick took a few steps back and covered his nose.

His eyes turned wild and he trembled. I couldn't blame him. The sight of dozens of bodies piled up in a massive mound had been an unpleasant surprise for me too. Once his initial shock wore off, I felt his anger replace it. Disgust and revulsion reflected in his face, making me think he might not have been a part of this.

"You know whose spell was covering this up, don't you?" I asked him in a tight voice.

"No," he answered.

Truth. I stood up and moved over to stand in front of him, wanting to know how innocent he was in all this. "Variola and two of her witches set this up. Any idea where all these bodies came from?"

He shook his head. "I had no idea they were here."

Derrick moved forward to study them closer.

I believed him, but figured there had to be an explanation. Most of the corpses weren't fresh, and in fact, quite a few skeletons poked out from underneath the others who were in varying stages of decay. One of the fresher bodies looked to be a vamp kill based on the fang marks dotting the neck. Another must have been from a werewolf attack because of the way the torso had been ripped apart. Maybe animals got to it, but I couldn't be sure since the spells surrounding the place could affect them as well. They were powerful and few natural species had immunity to this kind of magic—except insects, which were swarming all over the mound.

I turned to question him. "How could you not know about this?"

I had to work with Derrick and needed to figure out where he stood. It wouldn't change that I was stuck with him, but it would let me know how much of a distance to keep.

Derrick's voice came out low. "I had no idea they'd done this. Variola must of kept it from me, knowin' I wouldn't agree with it."

Truth again. "You have no idea who all these people are?"

He stood silent for a moment. I figured he must have been studying the bodies and where they might fit in with what he knew.

After a few minutes, he answered me. "I'm guessin' the oldest ones are from when Variola took over. There were some humans stayin' at the house who belonged to the last leader when we moved in. They would've remained loyal to him. She said she sent them away after compelling them to never speak of what they knew. She must've meant a different kind of sending away than I assumed."

I continued to hold my nose as I spoke. "How can you be sure?"

He nodded at a small silver bracelet with a distinct Celtic pattern lying around one of the skeleton's arms. It poked out from the pile. "I remember one of the humans wearing that. There's only one way it could of got here now."

"So that first group was left here and they continued to use this place as a dumping ground after that for all the kills they didn't want to have to explain away."

Derrick dipped his head. "It looks like it."

"With my luck, it'll be my body here next."

Irritation rose up from him. It made me take a step back, plus one more. His eyes followed my movements. I needed to stop. With him being a predator, backing away only made him want to attack more. My feet froze and long minutes passed as he fought to regain control of himself. Facing away from the carnage, he took deep breaths in and out. I really hated being around sups, even if they could cook well.

"Melena," he paused. "I wouldn't do something like this. Variola knows that. It's why she probably kept it from me. I can promise you, I'll be havin' a word with her about it."

He meant what he said. It made me feel a little better. I didn't want to be around a man all day, every day, who considered this kind of thing acceptable.

"How can you be sure you can stop her and the others? I'm thinking the evidence says she doesn't care all that much for human life."

He let out a short growl. "I'll do my best to convince her."

"And if that isn't enough?" The man needed his blinders taken off.

Derrick rubbed his face. "We're all forced into situations we don't care for. Just like you are now. This ain't somethin' I would allow in my presence, but I don't have the power to make Variola do what I want."

"So you would keep working for a woman as evil

as this?"

Anger flashed across his face. "Don't make presumptions about me, little girl. There are things you can't know about, or understand. I'm not here to explain them to you."

Despite his predatory stance, my hackles rose at the term "little girl". I threw up my arms in the air.

"Fine, it's your life. You have to live with your choices. It's not my business."

I stomped off in the direction of the vehicle, unwilling to discuss it with him anymore. Let him get through the "keep away" spell on his own. I wasn't shedding more blood to break it.

He followed right away at a short distance, but managed to get himself through without my help. Derrick didn't say anything when I drove us straight back to my place. Seeing the body dumping ground had been enough for one day. Neither of us spoke until I pulled the vehicle up to the cabin.

"Give me the keys," he said.

"Why?" I asked.

"Sensor Girl, a man can only take so much. Today you had your turn, but from here on out I'll be doin' the driving. Live with it."

He jerked the keys from my hand before I could get them out of his range. I gave him a growl that would have done most werewolves proud before shoving my door open. Some men's superiority complexes never ceased to amaze me. Why couldn't they understand a woman could do most things as well as they could?

Speaking of difficult men.

Charlie came walking out of the woods as we climbed the few steps leading up to the porch. The shaman's timing appeared a little too convenient; making me think he must have been waiting. I couldn't read his expression to determine what he wanted.

Derrick appeared to recognize him.

"Charlie," he said by way of greeting.

The older man inclined his head. "Derrick."

"You have a reason for being here?"

The shaman nodded toward me. "I came to speak with her."

"Why?" The werewolf crowded close to me.

"You know I don't have to answer that. Go on inside, I won't take much of her time." Charlie had a hint of steel behind his words you had to respect. He wasn't going to take no for an answer. Derrick must have known that because he sent me a cautionary look before using the keys he'd taken to unlock the cabin. The door didn't close gently behind him.

I hesitated on the steps as Charlie beckoned me to follow him. My senses didn't have any negative reactions to him, but they weren't reliable for that anyway. Today's events had amped up my wariness of all sups, particularly mysterious shamans.

"It's alright, Melena. I'm not here to hurt you," Charlie said in an encouraging voice. His words came out as truth.

I stood there for a moment longer in indecision before choosing to follow him and see what he wanted. If he appeared trustworthy enough, I'd consider telling him about the bodies. Someone needed to know, outside of

Variola's circle, and he would be the best choice. If he tried anything funny, though, I'd shoot him. My gun was tucked into my pants and begging to be used after the day I'd had.

The shaman relaxed his stance when I took the first steps off the porch. I followed his lead as we walked for some distance away from the cabin before he broke the silence.

"Melena, I know you were missing for several days. Now you've come back with Derrick keeping a close eye on you. Want to tell me what happened?"

Though his voice sounded concerned, I wasn't sure how to react to him. Did he need to know what happened? And even if I told him, what good would that do? It's not like he could change what had been done to me and I hadn't known him long enough to cry on his shoulder about it. I gave him a glare instead.

"Want to tell me how you knew where I lived?"

His lips spread into a grin. "You rented this cabin from my grandson. It wasn't difficult to find out."

I stopped walking. "Your grandson?"

He shrugged. "Well, a few generations removed perhaps, but he is my descendent."

I didn't know what to think about that, so I reverted back to the original topic.

"Why do you want to know?"

He gave me a patient look. "If you tell me what happened, I may have a way for you to get out of your current predicament."

I covered a cough. "Somehow, I doubt that."

"Try me," he said. "What do you have to lose?"

He had me there. Telling the shaman wouldn't make things worse in any way I could see. No one had ordered me to silence. What if he did have a way to get me out of this and I didn't take it because of my prejudices? Did I want to risk spending the rest of my life working for an evil vampire-witch who would use me until every part of my soul eroded away?

My earlier conversation with Derrick made me wonder if he wasn't trapped by Variola in some way as well. He hadn't lied, but he had been hiding his reasons for staying with her. Maybe she had something on him too.

Charlie listened as I filled him in on most of the gory details covering the past few days since my capture. He frowned during the worst parts, but didn't say anything until I finished.

"This could be turned to our advantage, if you're willing to hear me out."

I had a feeling I already knew what he meant, but nodded for him to continue.

"The vampire you're looking for is the same one I told you about before. Nikolas led the supernaturals in this area before these dark ones took over. During his time, he kept his people in line. Humans were safe. Variola used deceitful methods to remove him from power. Now you have a chance to bring him back."

I leaned against a tree behind me. "By waking him up?"

"Yes," he agreed. "Find Nikolas, and use your abilities to break the spell keeping him asleep."

I huffed out a breath. "You're serious. You want

me to wake a twelve hundred year old vampire who has been sleeping for five years?"

Charlie nodded. "Exactly."

I downgraded my opinion of the man to lunatic status.

"How do you propose I do this?"

"The same way you protected your cabin and broke the spell in the field today, with your blood. It will end the curse if you feed it to him."

"Wait, how do you know about the attack on the cabin?" I'd told him about my kidnapping and finding the bodies, but not the preceding assault.

He lifted his shoulder in a shrug. "I watched your place that night and saw how you protected it from those who came. It was the most entertainment I'd gotten in decades."

He chuckled, as if the memory brought him great enjoyment. That irritated me.

"So you stood out there," I gestured toward the woods, "and witnessed all of that happen without stepping in to help me?"

"You had it under control."

"I had to kill a woman," I gritted out. Maybe she wasn't a good person, but it still bothered me.

Charlie put his hand on my shoulder. It made me flinch, but I didn't push it off.

"Melena, you're meant to be a fighter. There will be many more lives you'll have to take with the path laid before you."

I studied the ground. Would it come down to that? Hadn't my battles in the Middle East been enough?

"In other words, I need to wake the vampire and let him fight Variola, assuming he doesn't kill me in the process. What about my friend, Aniya? She could die in all this. That much was made clear when I was forced to take the deal."

Charlie let his hand drop from my shoulder. "Don't let Variola find out. If you can wake Nikolas without Derrick alerting the others, the werewolf can be "influenced" to stay quiet and he can help protect you. After that we can work to save your friend. You'll see these things have a way of working out."

"Easier said than done, but I'll consider it."

He lifted his arm and indicated we should move back to the cabin. I walked beside him, kicking up twigs and leaves as I went.

"That is all I can hope for, but remember this," he paused for a moment with his much older eyes boring into mine.

"The significance of your decisions may seem minor in the scheme of life, but the ramifications can reverberate through time, impacting the future in ways you cannot imagine. Some people get the luxury of never having to make difficult choices, but you are not among them. Follow your instincts."

I looked away. Nothing about this situation appeared easy and taking the path of least resistance didn't mean I would get the results I wanted.

"Good night, Melena," he spoke softly, as if his voice floated on the wind. "May the wisdom of your ancestors guide you."

Not that ambiguous line again. A glance in the direction

he had been a moment before made me turn around in place. The shaman was no longer there. Wanda had never mentioned his kind being able to teleport or cloak themselves. Apparently there were plenty more surprises in store for me.

Chapter Fourteen

For the next two days Derrick and I searched for the missing vampire without so much as a hint of where he might have gone. I suspected someone might have moved him, but that idea was shot down, along with my previous one implying he may already be awake. Variola stayed confident that his supporter, whoever the person was, would not have been able to get him out of the area. It seemed like wishful thinking on her part, but I kept trudging along, sending my senses out as far as they could go in the hopes of finding him.

We had covered most of the passable roads in the area, which wasn't hard since there weren't many of them. Hiking would be the next step if we didn't find the vampire soon. I'd had plenty of that in my military days and didn't feel all that inclined to do it again. In the meantime, I came up with an alternative for the day that would get us through some territory with less work.

Derrick and I would be taking the morning tour on the Riverboat Discovery Cruise. It began in Fairbanks, but would pass along one area we hadn't reached yet. I looked forward to doing something different and it gave me the excuse to get a little sightseeing in. Derrick admitted he had ridden the boat before, but gave grudging agreement to do it again. He claimed he was allowing it because I needed a break from the stress. Maybe I did.

To my dismay, our plans were delayed as soon as we opened the door. In front of us, blocking the porch steps, stood a huge moose grazing on the grass growing there. Spiky antlers with sharp ends branched off from his head. He gave us a disdainful look when we froze at the entryway. Derrick grabbed my arm, pulled me back inside, and shut the door behind us.

"What was that all about?" I asked, shrugging off his rough handling.

We could go around the moose. It would mean getting close, but still doable.

He glared at me. "Do you have any idea how dangerous those animals can be?"

I shrugged. "He doesn't seem all that scary."

Derrick shook his head. "I'm sure the last guy who was trampled to death by one would say the same thing if he was still alive to tell the tale."

Somehow, I doubted that many people died from moose attacks. It seemed even more ludicrous when I considered my company. Derrick was an alpha werewolf. A moose couldn't be that much of a challenge for him. I told him as much.

He snorted. "You think the answer is to kill the moose? This is his home too and he has as much of a right to be here as we do. The only reason to attack him is if it is for food or defense. Otherwise, it's best to leave the wild animals alone."

Should have known a werewolf would be sympathetic to animal rights. I'd never been much of an animal lover myself. My allergy to cats made them impossible to be around and dogs were too much trouble. My parents gave me a parakeet for my birthday when I turned nine and it hadn't survived long. Apparently birds needed to be fed on a regular basis. Fish died even faster when left in my care. I was a little too generous in adding the chemicals to their water.

Animals and I did not go well together. Something as ugly and big as a moose rated even lower in the scheme of things. Especially when we needed to leave in the next ten minutes to get to the tour on time. I wished I could shoot the damn thing.

I glanced at my watch. Make that five minutes. Too bad the cabin didn't have a back door. "Fine, we can't hurt the moose. I get it, but can't you at least scare it off?"

Derrick leaned back against the door and gave me an incredulous look.

"What would you have me do? I assume you know I can't shift during the day. Attempting to scare a twelve hundred pound bull would most likely result in serious injury, *for me*." He pointed a finger at his chest.

I sighed, realizing he wasn't going to budge on the matter. In the last few days we had learned to set aside our differences and get along. Neither of us wanted to be stuck in these circumstances, so a truce had been called. I didn't really want to see him get hurt. The man had been a lot nicer to me than expected. Besides, if he was injured, it might be a while before he could cook again.

"Sorry, you're right," I said. "We'll wait it out." *However long that took.*

Derrick relaxed. Seeing no further argument from me, he settled into a comfortable position on the couch and pulled out a book to read. Something having to do with the Civil War. Yeah, he knew he'd won this round. I skulked off to the bedroom to reschedule the tour for the afternoon.

After getting new tickets, I sifted through my email account while keeping an eye on the door. Derrick had a tendency to watch all my communications, making me think that must have been part of Variola's orders. Over the last week I'd gotten a ton of frantic messages from Lisette. She hadn't heard from me since the day I'd been captured. There hadn't been a chance to call or write her back. She had to be going crazy.

Derrick stepped into the room. I closed the window and opened another one that would be less incriminating. He peered at my screen.

"California State University of Monterey Bay, why are you looking at that site?" he asked.

I gave him a disgruntled look. "Because I couldn't get back in time for classes to start so now I have to cancel the ones I was enrolled in."

He lifted his brows. "You were going to college?"

"Yeah," I sighed. "Planned to graduate in the spring too. Guess that's not going to happen now."

With a few clicks of the mouse, my schedule was cleared, along with my dream. It didn't seem fair. I supposed the fact I was still alive should count for something—it could always be worse. Aniya was going to have the same problem if I didn't save her. Derrick gently patted me on the back. I read sympathy in his eyes, making it hard to put much of the blame on him.

"Don't give up yet, Sensor Girl. There's always hope."

I gave him a wan smile before shutting down the laptop. There would be no chance of getting a message out as long as he didn't stop watching. It wasn't worth trying to come up with more delay tactics in the hopes he'd walk off. I chose to go sit by the bedroom window where I could play a staring game with the offensive animal who ruined my morning plans.

Derrick left me alone. We didn't speak again until the time came to go. The moose had wandered off by then so we had no further complications getting out. I figured the dirty looks I'd shot at it had sped things up.

The sight of the boat, a sternwheeler, lifted my spirits. This would be far more enjoyable than riding in an SUV all day. It had four decks for passengers to choose from, though the lower two were enclosed in glass. I wanted to be as high as possible. We climbed to the top, along with a couple dozen other passengers. At the back of the boat I could see the large wheel that would be churning the water as we moved along the Chena River. The tour would last three hours, but not all of it would be on the boat.

Derrick stood beside me, hands stretched out to grip the rails. At least he didn't act annoyed to be there. I leaned forward as the ship began to thrust forward, enjoying the light breeze blowing across my face and hair. The tour guide gave us a running commentary while the land passed us by.

I had to keep my attention divided between the

sights along the way and scanning for Nikolas, but still managed to enjoy the moment. As part of the tour, a bush pilot took off from a small runway next to the river and came back to land. Having been around larger military planes before this, it impressed me how short a distance it took for the pilot to get into the air. They called it STOL, short take-off and landing, in aviation terms. Some of the planes appearing along the way had floaters attached so they could land on the water. Their usefulness gave me an idea I would have to discuss with Derrick later.

A child calling loudly for her father brought my attention back to the deck. The six year old girl was hopping up and down pointing at a moose—of all things—that grazed near the river bank. A few feet beyond the girl stood Matt. He was staring straight at me from across the deck. He had an unreadable expression until our gazes met. A smile lifted his lips as he began walking straight toward me.

Crap.

Derrick's body went rigid and a low growl came from his throat. No need to wonder if he'd noticed the younger guy walking our way. I needed to get rid of Matt fast. It had never occurred to me I'd run into him here.

"Melena, haven't seen you in a while," he said after reaching us. He stood with his legs wide apart and his arms crossed. I got a sense of disgruntlement from him as he shot Derrick a distasteful look.

"Been busy." I shrugged. "How about you? What are you doing here?"

A slight blush colored his cheeks. "I'm trying to get in some of the tourist stuff. Figured I might as well do that much while living up here."

"Makes sense," I agreed.

"So, who's this?" Matt nodded at Derrick. Despite the wording, I got the impression he really wanted to know why I was with the man. There was a definite undercurrent of hostility passing between them.

The werewolf stirred beside me. He didn't give me a chance to answer, or at least make something up, and instead put out his hand toward the younger man.

"Derrick Wilson," he introduced himself.

Okay, so they were going to at least act like they hadn't met before.

"Matt Burrows." He winced when the werewolf gripped his hand.

"You know Melena?" Derrick asked in a gruff voice, letting the younger man go.

I wanted to interject at this point, but Derrick put his hand behind my neck and squeezed lightly. With my long hair in a ponytail, it made it an easy place to reach. I understood the warning, but didn't care for the methods.

Matt gave an affirmative nod. "Yeah, we've seen each other around a couple times."

"Oh really?" Derrick turned his head to give me an inscrutable look. His voice sounded curious—too curious for my liking.

I opened my mouth to speak, but he squeezed me again. If he did it one more time, I was going to stomp on his foot. All this posturing was ridiculous.

"She's a nice girl." Matt replied in a tone loaded with a meaning I didn't understand. He turned his gaze to me. "Did you find your friend?"

"Um, not yet." I put my hands in my jeans pockets to keep from fidgeting. "But Derrick is helping me now so we should find her soon."

I hoped my voice sounded more confident than I felt. Derrick had converted to caressing my neck, making it difficult to think. His hands were warm and rough against my skin but somehow managed to be gentle and soothing as well.

"Oh, that's nice of him." Matt's expression conflicted with his words, "Last night I saw the guy who was with your friend before. Looks like he is making a habit of going to that same bar. It might be a good idea to try and catch him so you can ask a few questions. He has to know where she is."

Derrick's gaze swung toward me and the caressing stopped. Time to end this before it got ugly.

"I'll check that out, thanks." I implored Matt with my eyes to leave.

He frowned and gave me a worried look. "Are you alright, Melena?"

The caressing began again and I did my best to give a reassuring smile. "Of course."

"Well, if you need help, you have my phone number."

"Yep, sure do." It'd been burned over a week ago.

"She's with me now," Derrick interrupted with a growl. "I'll help her get her friend back. You just need to stay out of it."

I started to retort, but he squeezed my neck again. That was it. I stomped his foot hard and squished my heel around for good measure. The damn man didn't even blink.

Matt put his hands up in a gesture of surrender. "If you say so. I just wanted to let her know the offer stands."

He dropped his gaze from the werewolf and I recognized it as a submissive gesture. Derrick had won that round.

Matt's next words came out low. "You take care, Melena. I'm still here if you need me."

He walked off before Derrick could say anything further, which was probably a good thing since the tide of anger rolling off him made me think the werewolf was close to his limits. The whole confrontation left me angry with both men. If I'd had my way, neither one of them would have been involved.

Why couldn't this trip have been a simple rescue of my friend? Instead, I ended up with people all around trying to manipulate me toward what they wanted. Meanwhile, Aniya continued to be trapped by dangerous sups who could be hurting her even now and there was nothing I could do about it.

I shot Derrick a dirty look and jerked on his grip. He removed his hand, but didn't seem all that apologetic about it.

"If Variola finds out that kid knows anything, she'll kill him. The best thing to do is run him off before he learns too much. Melena, you're smart enough to know that."

The muscles in my throat tightened. He had a point and the logical side of me knew that. I should have been grateful for what he did, but it could have been handled better. Besides, there was something more to that exchange than what they had let on.

"Do you know Matt?" I asked.

He shrugged. "I've seen him in passing."

His answer came out as a half-truth.

"Just in passing?"

A muscle in Derrick's jaw ticked. "Let it be, Mel. The guy is human and ain't got no business in all this."

There was no trace of a lie that time. I turned back toward the river, hating the situation I'd been put in.

Derrick rubbed my back. "Concentrate on the tour and finding Nikolas. The sooner we do that, the sooner this is over."

I followed his advice and pushed the meeting with Matt to the back of my mind. We visited the sled dog kennels for a famous Iditarod champion next, followed by a mock native Alaskan village. I tuned out the guides much of the time, preferring to concentrate on the scenery. The tour turned out to be a fairly good distraction from my worries.

It didn't go as far as I'd expected, only about four miles. I had hoped to cover a lot more ground. Derrick later told me he'd known the distance wouldn't be worth the trouble but decided to humor me since I appeared so excited about the idea. I chalked it up to a lesson learned and figured we'd have to get back to more serious searching tomorrow.

Both of us were hungry after finishing the tour and decided to travel to the far north side of town to a restaurant Derrick wanted to visit. Along the way, we passed by the University of Alaska Fairbanks and their recreation area. The forested area was a good place for students to ski and dog sled during the winter, and hike during the summer. That wasn't what grabbed my attention, though.

I grabbed Derrick's arm and forced him to pull off the road and into a parking lot set up for visitors. He gave me an inquiring look, but there was no way to explain what I sensed. Emily was out there. As soon as the vehicle came to a stop, I dashed outside and ran for the woods. It couldn't be safe for a girl her age to wander alone on these trails. Any number of things could happen.

As I neared her, my inner warning system shrieked. Emily's emotions had turned to high levels of terror. I took off as fast as I could with Derrick staying right beside me. While my breathing began to grow heavy from leaping over logs and passing through brush, his was smooth and even. We broke through a section of woods to find Emily being attacked. A large, black bear roared over her frozen form lying on the ground. My heart nearly stopped at the sight of it. Blood covered her upper body and her arms were pulled up to protect her face.

Derrick didn't hesitate to race forward and jump in the fight. If he had been in wolf form, it might have worked, but in his human form he was at a disadvantage. He did manage to draw its attention away from Emily. Derrick slammed the bear in the muzzle with his fist, striking over and over, as he took careful steps back. He was drawing it away. I supposed with his unnatural

strength it would be a lot more painful for the animal
than if I had tried that. It wouldn't be enough to scare it
off, though.

I pulled my gun, which was tucked into the back
of my pants, and aimed for the bear. Its head was too
close to Derrick and I couldn't get a good shot. I gave up
on a clean kill and aimed for its side instead. Just before
the bullet tore into the animal, it gave a powerful swipe,
hitting Derrick's head hard. The werewolf slammed into
a tree behind him and passed out. Blood covered the side
of his face.

The bear turned toward me with a roar of rage—
my bullet had hit him, but not enough to do severe
damage. I pulled the trigger again, this time aiming for its
head, but the bear dropped to all fours at the last second
and I missed. By the time I reacquired my sites again it
was too late. The animal had almost reached me. It
rammed my body into the ground and jerked my arms
over my head. I lost my gun in the fall. Sharp claws raked
across my torso, sending screaming pain up my side. I
thrashed, hitting anywhere I could in an attempt to save
myself. I was losing the fight.

Lucas appeared larger than life with a flash of
golden light. He grabbed the bear in one hand and tossed
it like a rag doll into a thick tree thirty feet away. An
audible crack sounded as the animal's head collided with
a heavy thud. His large form slumped to the ground,
unmoving. I doubted it would wake up again. The tree
suffered some minor disfigurement and seemed to be
leaning more than it should, but it remained standing.

My gaze moved over to Lucas, who appeared as if

he'd come straight from a business meeting. He wore black pants with a matching jacket, a designer blue shirt, and shiny black dress shoes. After his move with the bear, you would think he might have gotten a little messy, but not one hair was out of place. He hovered over me with his intimidating form.

I pulled myself up to a sitting position, hoping to maneuver away and put some space between us. Sharp pain shot up the side of my torso and a groan escaped my lips. I had to lie back down to catch my breath. Damn. The claws had dug deep.

Lucas bent down to examine me, his brows furrowed in what might have been concern on a normal person. I lay still, feeling as if I'd exchanged one predator for another. The touch of his warm hand sent tingles along my body while he checked the extent of the damage. My blood clung to his fingertips where he had grazed the deep gouges. After he finished, he stood up and cleaned his hand off with a handkerchief he pulled from his pocket.

"You'll live."

The blood loss must have made me light headed because his pronouncement made me smile.

"Making a habit out of saving me, Lucas? It's shining my tarnished image of you."

He lifted his brows. "Your day will come— but it isn't today. Do make an effort to try and stay alive, sensor. Saving you is getting tedious. I may decide to put you out of your misery myself if this keeps up."

More half-truths, but he didn't give me a chance to call him on it. One moment he stood there and in the next he flashed away, the bear's body was gone with him. At least with the evidence taken away, I could claim the animal had run off after I shot at it.

I forced myself up again, managing to suppress a groan this time. Derrick lay with his eyes closed not too far from me, but it was Emily I was worried about. A sigh of relief came over me when she turned her head and looked my way with clear blue eyes. Pain reflected in them, but at least she appeared lucid.

I crawled over and kneeled next to her. While she might be awake, her injuries were much worse than mine. The bear had bitten her deep in the arm and clawed her left shoulder and face. Blood seeped from her wounds and covered her clothes. Though nothing appeared immediately life threatening, I knew I needed to call for help.

We were on the side of a trail wide enough for a car to pass through. I figured an ambulance should be able to make it to us without too much trouble. My cell phone was in my pocket so I made the call. The dispatcher assured me they had already received reports of shots fired and emergency crews were on their way.

After hanging up, I sat down next to Emily and used my jacket to put pressure on her worst wound where her shoulder had been gouged deep. I cursed myself for not bringing my bag with the first aid kit inside. All those preparations and they meant nothing now.

Emily couldn't talk with all the damage done to her face. At first she tried pushing out a few syllables, but stopped after it caused her too much pain. I soothed her with nonsensical words and held her hand. A wave of despair came over me at seeing her torn up so badly. What had she been doing out here in the first place?

Derrick came over to us a few minutes later. The visible damage he'd taken appeared to be healing already. I could see the cuts on his face weren't as bad as before. Werewolves could heal much faster than humans, though it still took some time to fully recover. He kneeled on the other side of Emily, checking her over. I updated him on my call for an ambulance and he nodded his head.

He had a haunted look in his eyes while gazing down at Emily. A tear might have fallen from him, but I couldn't be sure. The anguish he was showing made me wonder what was going on in his head. He began murmuring his own assurances to the girl, and it was clear he knew her well from his regular visits to her home. At least she seemed to respond to him. I supposed they must have built up some kind of bond, but it didn't occur to me how much until now.

Emergency crews found us a short while later. Derrick and I insisted on them checking over Emily first. Only after she was tended did I let them near me. Derrick refused altogether, saying he would take the SUV and meet us at the hospital. They would notice his rapidly healing injuries if they were around him for long. A quick clean up job would erase the evidence of his wounds altogether once they healed.

I chose to ride with Emily, telling the EMTs I was her aunt. They didn't question it. The entire time we rode in the ambulance, she kept giving me strange looks. Derrick and I showing up together had probably thrown her off, but explanations for that would have to come later. She had her own explaining to do.

Chapter Fifteen

I received twenty-two stitches while Emily received over sixty. They separated us while we were getting treated, but I went to her room as soon as they let me go. It had been a close call and the doctor wanted to keep her overnight for observation. At least she looked better now that the blood had been cleaned off.

Derrick sat with her the whole time after convincing the hospital staff he was a relative as well. Once we were alone, he'd asked me how I had met Emily. I'd had to simplify the story about us running into each other while I'd been out searching for Aniya. It was kind of true if you took out the sensor elements. He hadn't questioned it—to my relief.

Stitches covered the left side of her face and the doctor ordered her not to talk. I still wanted to know what she had been doing in the woods, but that would have to wait. With dusk growing near, her mother would be coming soon. Derrick had called her, arguing she had a right to know. It made me wonder what kind of mother, even a vampire, could take so little care of her daughter. If she had done the right thing, the girl wouldn't be in the hospital now.

Derrick smoothed Emily's hair while whispering reassuring words to her. She had been sedated and slept peacefully for the moment. He, on the other hand, had a forlorn look on his face.

"Derrick, are you okay?"

He turned his gaze toward the wall and cleared his throat. I almost didn't think he would answer.

"I had a daughter once about Emily's age. Her name was Judith."

His voice came out low, but the words were filled with a soul-searing pain. A tear slipped from his eye, and he brushed it away with a swipe of his hand.

"What happened to her?" I asked.

"She was murdered, along with my wife and two sons."

I sucked in my breath. That had not been the answer I'd been expecting.

Derrick's face filled with rage as he spoke his next words. "I'll get my revenge one day. They've dodged me so far, but if it takes another century to find them..."

Determination like that, I could understand. "I hope you do."

He nodded and turned back to Emily. "Seeing her injured today, it reminded me of that time. We survived the Civil War, only to be slaughtered in our home a few years later. My daughter looked much like Emily did today—covered in blood. Except Judith was dead by the time I found her body laying outside where they'd left her."

I leaned forward. "How did you survive?"

"Variola found me while I was breathing my last breaths, and saved me with her blood. Unlike the rest of my family, I'd had my werewolf side battling to heal me.

My body would have lost the battle, though, if she hadn't come. The injuries were too much to recover from. The attackers had expected me to die soon after, so they hadn't even bothered to finish the job."

He shook his head, as if that could clear his thoughts. At least it explained why he stayed loyal to her.

"Do you know who did it?"

Derrick's jaw ticked. "There were three vampires. I hadn't seen their kind before, but figured it out real quick when their fangs sunk into my neck. They must have known what I was but it didn't matter none to them. A woman was there too. I never figured out who she was, but she smelled like somethin' different. Ain't none of them shown their faces again, but I'll keep lookin' for them."

He cracked his knuckles as if he was ready to fight them right then. I'd heard the resolve in his voice and realized revenge must have been the only thing left to keep him going after all these years.

"If you ever need my help, you only have to ask," I said. "Not sure what I could do, but I understand what it's like to lose people you care about."

Derrick's eyes met mine. His had a trace of surprise. Perhaps he hadn't expected my offer, but something made me to give it. The man had been trying to avenge his family for well over a century. If there was something I could do to help, I would.

"Thank you," he said, giving me a solemn nod.

I was about to say something more when my senses picked up Emily's mother. It had to be her based on the age and gender. I let Derrick know of her impending arrival. His face transformed into an expressionless mask. What was he expecting?

When she arrived at the nurse's station, her shrill voice reached our room from forty feet away. I heard her give her name as Stephanie Druthers. The same surname Emily used. She informed the staff that she would be checking her daughter out right away and told them to give her the paperwork. They argued, but she compelled them to do what she wanted. The doctor went through the same process when he was called over. She used her vamp powers to convince them all Emily was fine and to annotate the records to reflect it.

It took a little while, but they got everything in order faster than the normal time it should have taken. Stephanie headed our way after finishing—even vamps had to make sure records appeared legit or else they'd have a bigger mess to clean up later. If it had been me, though, my priority would have been to see my daughter before anything else.

First impressions can have a big impact on how we see people, good or bad. I didn't like Stephanie as soon as she stepped through the door. Perhaps there were some preconceived notions already in my mind, but she made them worse in person. She strode into the room, hands on her hips, and lashed out at the first person she saw. Luckily, it wasn't me.

"Derrick, why was my daughter in the woods alone?"

Irritation flashed across his features. "Don't know. She's been too injured to tell us. If you had bothered to look at her, you might've noticed that."

Stephanie let out an exasperated sigh and threw her hands up. "That's easy enough to fix."

She strutted over, used one of her long nails to slash her own wrist, and forced her daughter's mouth open to pour blood into it. Emily started to choke, which drew protests from both me and Derrick.

"She's my daughter and I'll do whatever I think is necessary for her. If you paid attention you'd see she is fine now." Stephanie gave us a pointed look.

Emily had stopped making the gagging sounds, but it had been a close thing there for a moment. She was still barking out short coughs, trying to clear her lungs. I wanted to wring her mother's neck for being so callous. Nothing about her said "warm and loving" mom in any way.

Stephanie had been turned in her late-thirties and would be stuck with that age forever. She used a ton of make-up and brushed out her shoulder length brown hair to a shine, but her age still showed.

Most women still looked great in their thirties, but if they lived a hard life of drugs and drinking, it usually showed by that point. Stephanie hadn't escaped the damage she'd done to her body before gaining immortality. Her eyes sagged underneath, taking away from what would have been beautiful blue ones like her daughter's. She had some extra weight around the middle, and her skin was worn. When you combined that with her personality, it made me wonder what vampire in their right mind would have wanted to turn her. They tended to be picky about who they doled immortality out to.

It took a few minutes more for Emily's injuries to finish healing. Derrick sat next to her and pulled the stitches off the fading wounds as the threads came loose from her skin. Fear froze her face when she opened her eyes to see her mother.

"What were you thinking?" Stephanie started in right away. "I told you not to do anything stupid and now I've been dragged into this mess! How hard is it to keep out of trouble, Emily Jean?"

No concern whatsoever for her daughter, who could have died. My fingernails dug into my palms. Things might have been a lot worse if Derrick and I hadn't showed up when we did.

Emily shrunk into herself, something I remembered her doing when we first met.

"I'm sorry, mom," she said in a tiny voice.

"Sorry doesn't cut it this time." Stephanie paced back and forth by the bed as she spoke. "I'll have to think of some kind of punishment for this. You'll learn to listen when I tell you not to do something."

Emily turned her face away, but her shaking body and defensive posture told me all I needed to know. Derrick and I exchanged looks. Neither of us liked the direction this was headed.

Stephanie shook with anger and outrage as she continued to strut about, waving her arms. When she stopped, she turned back to her daughter and pointed a finger at her.

"I'm getting rid of the house, Emily. You'll stay with me and Robert at Variola's. That way I can be sure you'll stay out of trouble. There is a cook there. As part of your punishment you can help her in the kitchen for the next month."

Disturbed blue eyes met mine. She did not want to go to a house full of sups and I couldn't blame her. Emily sat up with a pleading expression on her face.

"Please don't make me go there, mom. You know I hate being around a bunch of creepy people. School is starting and I want to be closer to my friends."

Stephanie slammed the side table. Her fist cracked the surface, making us all jump. Her fury had risen with vampiric swiftness. I sensed not an ounce of sympathy or love from this woman and doubted she had much even before her change. Vampirism only enhanced the personality that was already there.

"You'll do what I tell you and not argue with me. I'm not in the mood to hear it."

"But mom..."

In a move too fast to see or anticipate, she slapped her daughter's face. The sound of it echoed through the room. Emily cradled her cheek and fresh tears spilled from her eyes. Derrick and I both stood up in unison. This had gone too far and we had to put a stop to it.

He spoke before I did. His anger rose as he enunciated each of his words in a tone that would have made most people quiver in fear. "Stephanie, that is enough. The girl just survived a bear attack and you're makin' things worse. There was no need to hit her."

Stephanie didn't bother to look at him. "Derrick, she is my daughter and no concern of yours. Someone has to discipline the ungrateful little wretch and I'm the only one around to do it!"

Red colored my vision.

"You bitch," I spat out.

Stephanie turned at my words. She had nothing but disdain in her expression. "I know who you are, sensor. Don't think you can step into my business. I'll clean the floor with you."

I stared at her coldly. "Give it your best shot."

Stephanie spread a nasty grin before flying forward and knocking me into the wall. We collided with a thud. I figured she might do something like that.

My hand clutched a six inch blade I'd pulled out before drawing her attention. It had been hidden behind me. While it might be illegal in most states, including Alaska if concealed, I had opted to take my chances in carrying it and was glad I did now.

Stephanie clenched her hand around my throat, trying to choke me. I ignored the pressure and shoved the blade through her torso and up into her heart. The sharpness of it made the move easier than it might have been. The pressure released from my neck as she froze in shock. Her heart had stopped beating in order to preserve her life. My free arm grabbed her when she started to collapse. Derrick stepped in to help by propping her up from behind.

My hand twitched with the urge to draw another weapon and remove the stupid woman's head. As a vampire, she'd turn to dust and there wouldn't be a body for anyone to find. A broom and dustpan could remove any evidence that remained. But she was Emily's mother. The young girl might be permanently traumatized if she watched her mom die in front of her. Especially after what she'd already been through. Kids tended to love their parents, flaws and all.

The frightened blue eyes staring at me from the hospital bed kept me from it. Stephanie might not be able to move, but she was aware of her surroundings. Derrick stayed close as I mulled over what to do. His lips twitched. I sensed amusement coming from him. It reassured me he wouldn't interfere.

I stared deep into the eyes of the woman before me and gave her my coldest look. Never again would she touch Emily if I could help it.

"That door you came through," my head nodded toward it, "you're going to walk right back out of it as soon as this knife comes out."

She blinked.

"When you leave, don't look back. I'll care for Emily from now on so you can go on being the stupid bitch you are without affecting a young girl's life. You've done enough to her already."

I drew the knife out enough so that it was no longer all the way in her heart.

"Say 'yes' if you understand."

"Yes," Stephanie gritted out between clenched teeth.

No doubt the blade continued to cause some discomfort. Good. She needed a wake-up call and a little pain would give that extra special jolt to push her along.

"Don't try anything stupid either. I promise...you will regret it."

My hand twisted the blade for emphasis. She

cried out as the hole in her chest widened and blood trickled down her shirt. I smiled. "Please, give me a reason to really hurt you. It wouldn't be all that hard to take you down."

At my nod, Derrick stepped back to give me space. I shoved her toward the door, letting the knife come free of her chest. Stephanie stumbled, but didn't fall before reaching the exit.

She paused to give me a venomous look. "One day, I'll make you pay for this."

My brows lifted. "Is that supposed to scare me?"

"It should," she replied.

A wave of my knife had her fleeing out into the hallway. Good thing she wasn't one of those vamps who enjoyed pain—that would have made things more difficult. I'd noted a stagger in her step—it would take her a while to heal.

"Nicely played," Derrick told me with a grin. "I'll make sure she doesn't cause any more trouble."

"Thanks," I said.

He took the knife from me and cleaned it before returning it. My hands still shook with anger. There were few times in my life when I'd ever been that furious, but seeing Stephanie hit Emily pushed me beyond my limits. I took a few calming breaths and turned to the girl in question.

Her lip quivered as our gazes met. "Did you mean what you said, Mel? That I could stay with you?"

I went over to her and eased myself onto the side of the bed. My chest was beginning to hurt again. The pain killers must have started wearing off.

"Of course I did, Em. Why would you think otherwise?"

Tears filled her eyes once more. "You didn't come. I waited for days and it was like you disappeared and left me. Even Derrick wasn't coming around. That's why I was out in the woods. It seemed like no one cared about me anymore, so nothing mattered."

I rubbed my face in frustration and wanted to kick myself. Things had gotten so crazy after Variola and her crew captured me that I hadn't had a chance to deal with anything else. Not to mention with Derrick so close all the time it didn't seem like a good idea.

Not knowing what else to do, I hugged her. She gripped me tight, as if hanging on for dear life.

"I'm so sorry, Em. Something happened and I couldn't come visit you, but I'm here now. Please don't cry." She was sobbing into my chest as my hands rubbed her back in comfort.

Taking on a teenager at this point in my life was not the best idea, but letting her stay with her mother would have been worse. Besides, based on Derrick's concerned gaze, he would watch out for her too. We'd figure the rest out after everything was over and see what to do from there. No way would her mother ever get near her again if I could help it.

After Emily calmed down, I pulled away. She had red, swollen eyes and one very puffy cheek, but otherwise didn't look to be in too bad of shape. The fear was gone and she even managed a small smile for me.

"Let's get you changed and leave this place, okay?"

She nodded in agreement. Ten minutes later we were headed to her house to grab all her belongings before going to the cabin. Tomorrow, I'd take her shopping for anything else she needed. At least she appeared happy to be coming with us. I wondered how I kept digging myself deeper into the drama surrounding Fairbanks.

Chapter Sixteen

Two days later I found myself sitting in a Cessna 180 bush-plane. The engine roared in my ears and took me back to my days of jumping from planes. Only this time, I didn't have a parachute. Derrick had assured me the pilot knew what he was doing after I'd eyed the old plane with wariness.

We'd dropped Emily off at school that morning so at least she wasn't sitting alone at the cabin. A bus could bring her back, which worked out in case we couldn't return in time. She had wanted to come along with us, excited by the prospect of flying, but I didn't want her missing her first day of class. Summer break was over and she needed some normalcy in her life.

I'd gotten the idea of using a plane after our tour on the riverboat cruise. Derrick had agreed it would be a faster and more effective way to search. We were both tired of driving through endless forests and wanted to get the hunt for Nikolas over with.

Derrick called in a favor from a hunting friend of his and we were able to find a pilot to fly us around. To our benefit, the guy had nothing more important to do and the money he got out of the deal made it worth his time. He didn't mind our non-specific purpose for his services. All he knew was he had to fly certain patterns, which Derrick gave him as we went along.

The one drawback to flying was the large amount of sups popping up on my radar gave me constant mental whiplash. Some of the fae inhabited areas outside of Fairbanks, along with quite a number of werewolves, vampires, and other creatures who might have given me nightmares if I ever came across them in person. I supposed if you wanted to live in Alaska, it wasn't for the civilization, but for the remoteness and privacy.

My senses were going into overload because of it, though. The plane moved much faster than a car and it stayed close enough to the ground so that everything popping up hit me harder than usual. I rubbed my temples trying to ease the ache. It had been an hour, and though there were some older sups around, none hit the millennia mark.

I gazed out at the scenery and a wave of awe came over me. Nothing could have prepared me for the beauty of Alaska until I viewed it from a bush-plane. There were dense forests all over; along with swamps and open grass areas to break the sea of trees up and give some variety. The immediate land around the city was mostly flat with some rolling hills interspersed around it, and in the distance, mountains rose to make for an amazing backdrop. When you added the rivers, lakes, and streams that could be seen all over, the place took on a mystic quality.

Derrick ordered the pilot to turn east toward the town of Fox. We'd been flying over the land west of Fairbanks and had turned up nothing. It had been a long shot for the vampire to have come this far, but it had been an area we'd needed to rule out.

Our next destination came much higher on the list of potential areas. It had a large amount of private property that couldn't be crossed on the ground without risking trouble. Flying alleviated this problem. If we found something, we could plan a way to avoid notice when checking it out.

My senses fired up not long after we passed over the town to continue north. I pulled my gaze to the area below and found an old mineshaft dug deep into the ground. No activity appeared to be there now, so they must have stopped using it. This region was well known for gold mining operations, including the Ft. Knox gold mine, where they continued to produce a hefty amount of U.S. gold. That wasn't what drew my interest, though. It was the twelve hundred year old vampire resting somewhere down there.

I'd done a lot of thinking since chatting with Charlie the last time he visited. He'd been right that Variola needed to be brought down. She couldn't be allowed to stay in power, but I couldn't take her out on my own—someone much stronger had to help. If the shaman believed the older vampire could handle the job, and be a better leader, I had to hope he was right.

It couldn't be all about me and my concerns anymore. I needed to consider the innocent human lives in this region. The bodies Derrick and I had found showed far too many deaths had already occurred. We needed to put a stop to it. Charlie acted confident we could save Aniya. I had to believe he understood the dangers, or else my friend's life would be over.

Now to make it all work while being in front of Derrick's too perceptive eyes. My plan depended on him not alerting his superior to the importance of this place. I tapped him on the shoulder and gave him the turnaround hand signal since we'd gone past the vampire's location. Derrick indicated we should take our headsets off before leaning closer to me. Right—so the pilot wouldn't hear us. Of course, mine caught in my hair before I could get it free.

"Are you pickin' something up?" He barely spoke loud enough for me to hear him.

"Maybe," I said. "It's hard to tell, but something is underneath the ground back at the mine we passed a minute ago."

"You're not sure?"

I shook my head. "With all the earth in the way I can't say what it might be. It feels like a vampire, though. We need to at least check it out."

He raked a hand over his own tousled hair, giving a nice show of his large bicep, before turning back in his seat. I breathed an inward sigh of relief that he didn't question me further. With a word to the pilot, we flew back around.

Once we reached the site, I told Derrick to have the pilot circle around to help give us a better view. We would have to go down into the shaft and, based on the setup, it would take some special equipment to lower ourselves in. Plus it might have been blocked off, but I couldn't tell for sure from my angle in the air. I took a mental picture for later reference.

Derrick raised his brows after my gaze moved

from the site to him. A glimmer of hope reflected in his chocolate brown eyes. It almost made me feel guilty, but not quite. In the short time we'd known each other a sort of solid friendship had been built. We hadn't made any real effort toward it, but it came nonetheless. I hated having to deceive him. The man didn't deserve it, but his loyalty to Variola made avoiding the truth necessary.

"This could be the one, but I'm not getting a good sense of who it is," I lied. "I'm thinking it's better if we come back tomorrow with the right equipment and go down there where I can get in closer and confirm it."

My military days had taught me how to keep my expression clear so my thoughts couldn't be seen. You become skilled at tricks like that when you're forced to do absurd things like spray-paint storage sheds in the pouring rain. Commanders don't like it if you look at them like they're crackpots, or so I discovered before mastering the art of non-expression. I'd done many push-ups before learning to cover up my emotions. The skill came in handy now.

Derrick's shoulders sagged at my less than positive report, but he agreed with my recommendation and let the pilot know he could take us back. We had gotten a late start today and would need time to make preparations. You didn't go into a mine shaft without all the right gear or else you were asking for trouble. It didn't take prior experience to figure out it was dangerous. The occasional news reports on collapsed mines and men killed in them were warning enough.

***

I peered at the notebook paper before me, considering if the details appeared right. There had been a limited amount of time to study the mine shaft while flying in the Cessna. My drawing wouldn't be a perfect representation. I had to consider the sketch gave a view from above as opposed to ground level, which would be the way we entered tomorrow.

The shaft must have had a lowering device of some sort to take miners down, but I doubted it remained since the place closed. Some kind of rigging was still up top from what I'd seen, but the exact details were difficult to discern from so far above. They may have set up something to keep people out as well, but Derrick promised he would take care of it. He had a werewolf buddy who worked in mines as a day job and could help us out.

The planning side of me needed to draw things out when the details might be important. I also enjoyed the way sketching could help clear my head and allow me to lose myself for awhile. With everything that had happened in the last few weeks, that was more important than ever.

My pencil flew across the paper as nearby vegetation came to life on the page, making for a more complete scene. Sometimes adding those details helped give perspective. I wished I could have viewed the inside of the mine for a better idea of what we might be dealing with the next day. Somewhere below the place my drawing represented, an ancient vampire slept. Derrick didn't know it yet, but I would be waking Nikolas up and there would be no telling how that would go. I could only hope we survived.

"You have talent there."

I jumped when Derrick spoke over my shoulder. I had gotten so used to him being around that my senses were now dulled to his presence. He stood behind me where I sat at the kitchen table. Friends had complimented my drawings in the past, but something made me appreciate it more coming from him. When had his opinion begun to matter so much?

"Thanks, it's a hobby of mine." I didn't lift my head up as I spoke and let my hair keep my face curtained. He rubbed my shoulders and I tried not to melt into the soothing sensations. Derrick was a sup on a path for vengeance. There could never be anything more than friendship between us.

"That's the shaft we're going to visit tomorrow. You did a good job of drawing it from memory."

"It's not perfect, but close enough."

"Yes, it is. Would you mind if I took a look at that when you're done? Could help me on my end, seein' as how I got that friend I'll be meetin' up with for supplies in the morning."

"Sure, almost done with it now."

He watched me put the last details in, observing how it all developed. Having already studied the scene by drawing it, I didn't need the sketch so much after finishing and figured he might as well have it. When I handed it to him, something outside pinged my senses. It startled me so bad I shot out of my seat, knocking my chair back onto the floor. Derrick picked it up and frowned at me. This was something I did not need to deal with right now.

"Mel..." Emily called from the bedroom.

"Not now, Em."

Lisette headed directly our way. Her supernatural signature was one I would recognize anywhere. Why had she come here? It couldn't have been at a worse time. What if Variola found out? My panicked eyes settled on Derrick. I had no time to sugarcoat things. She was almost here. I grabbed the werewolf by both shoulders and gave him a pleading look.

"Derrick, a friend of mine from California is here. I don't want Variola using her against me like she is with Aniya. If you'll go along with what I say, we should be able to get rid of her. You won't have to worry about her being a problem. I promise. Would you please do this for me?"

I rushed out my request in a low tone, not wanting Emily to overhear. Lisette was pulling into the drive. He had to go along with this or there would be no getting rid of her. She had to believe everything we told her.

Derrick's eyes bored into mine. "Melena, you know I have to report everything to Variola."

My fingers dug into his skin through his black t-shirt. "And you know she is already using one of my friends against me. If we can make this one go away, at least she'll be safe. Please, I know you have a heart in there somewhere. I'm begging you to go along with this."

Whatever thoughts were going on behind his eyes, not even my senses wanted to figure them out. It seemed an eternity passed before he nodded his head. "I'll do it, but she better not stay after this or it's out of my hands."

"Thank you." I said, pulling him into a quick hug. It didn't even bother me to get close to him like it should have. He gave me a small pat in return, but didn't relax.

Emily popped out of the bedroom as we broke apart and moved straight for the window. New glass had been put in the day before while we were out shopping. She drew the curtains aside before I could stop her and peeked out. I grabbed her and pulled her away.

"Who is that chick, Mel? She has blue hair." She scrunched her nose.

"A pixie friend of mine from California. There aren't any of her kind around here." Better to clarify before she asked the wrong kinds of questions around Derrick. At least he hadn't noticed she'd picked up on Lisette's arrival at the same time I had.

Emily lifted her brows. "Is she going to be staying here with us?"

"Um, no," I said while ushering the teenager back to the bedroom. "She's going to be leaving. You stay back here until I get rid of her."

"But, Mel..." She whined as I shut the door. There might have been a loud sigh of exasperation coming from her direction, along with some grumbling, but at least there was no more arguing.

I grabbed Derrick's hand and dragged him with me, yelling at Emily to stay put and not come out for any reason. She had my laptop in there so at least it would keep her entertained for the moment.

"Just play along, okay?" I begged the werewolf.

Derrick inclined his head, reluctance written all over his face as we stepped outside. I pulled him along and kept his hand in mine, knowing this had to be believable. He'd played up our relationship in front of Matt and could do it again for someone else.

"Lisette!" I called out as she walked toward us.

Sure enough, blue hair framed her face. It would have surprised me more if she hadn't changed it since the last time I'd seen her. True to form, she'd chosen a small, flashy car instead of something more practical. The rental companies must see a lot of customers like her up here to bother having those types of vehicles in their stock.

"Melena?" Surprise showed on her face as she glanced from me to Derrick. I had leaned in close to him as we walked up in an attempt to imply something more between us.

"Hey girl," I said, letting go of him to give her a hug. She appeared too shocked to do much more than squeeze me back before we broke apart.

I smiled at my friend as if life couldn't be any better and returned to Derrick's side. He must have caught on to my plan because he put his arm around my waist and composed his face in an endearing enough manner that even I almost believed it.

Lisette's mouth opened and closed, but no words came out.

To be fair, Lucas might not have been that far off on my dating record. I'd never bothered to see a guy more than a few times and had never allowed one to get close. Seeing me hanging onto a man and appearing happy about it would send her into a state of major confusion, which was what I wanted—something to shake her up enough that she wouldn't question my actions too much.

"Derrick," I gave him my most adoring smile, "this is Lisette. The friend from back in California I told you about."

Following my lead, he held out a hand to shake hers.

"Nice to meet you. I've heard a lot about you," he greeted her in a pleasant tone. It was strange seeing him this way, like another man had taken over his body.

She hesitated, eyeing him up and down. I had to assume she'd detected what he was because her little pixie nose flared. Her kind didn't have a sense of smell like werewolves, but they could scent things out better than humans. She didn't appear all that pleased by my choice in men, but my prompting look forced her to shake his hand in return.

"And I've heard nothing about you," she turned her eyes on me. "Mel, want to explain this?"

I ducked my head and peeked at her through my eyelashes.

"Well, you know, it just sort of happened," I said with a timorous smile. "Things moved fast and I know you expected me to call, but it never occurred to me you would come up here. Especially with the shop and everything…"

"Email," she interrupted, putting her hands on her hips. "You could have emailed me. At least that much should have occurred to you after all this time. I got worried and so did Mrs. Singh. First her daughter, and then you, except now I see you're fine. So wanna tell me where Aniya is because she has some explaining to do."

Crap, should have known she would ask about that.

"Oh yeah, Aniya," I waved my hand in a dismissive gesture. "That's how I met Derrick. He knows her boyfriend, Phillip. She's fine, so you can go back and let Mrs. Singh know she'll be in touch soon, I promise."

Well, I hoped it would be soon anyway.

Lisette brushed her flat-ironed hair from her eyes and shifted her stance. "Mel, if she is fine then there should be no problem with me seeing her for myself. Where is she?"

Time to take a page from the deputy's playbook.

"Well, that is kind of difficult to explain at the moment, you see. Niya and Philip went on a trip up north to some cabin a friend of his let him use. You can only get there by plane and there is no cell phone reception or internet. They should return in a week or two. I'll have her call you when she gets back."

She twirled her hair around her finger. "A remote cabin, up north? Does it have electricity? Because we both know Niya is not an outdoor kind of girl."

"Uh, well..."

"It has solar power and a back-up generator. She'll be fine up there," Derrick interjected.

Lisette sighed and narrowed her eyes at me.

"Are you sure you're fine? This isn't like you, Mel. Relationships have never been your thing and now I find you with..." She waved her hand around.

"Derrick." She could never remember names.

"Right, so I find you with Mr. Macho here and I'm not getting it," she put a hand up when Derrick tried to cut in, but her eyes stayed on me. "Maybe Niya might have fallen for a man up here, since we know she has a romantic heart, but not you. Is this for real?"

I swallowed, not liking having to lie to her. Her voice had a note of hopefulness in it, as if she wanted it to be true. The one thing that kept me playing this game was if she didn't believe me, it could be dangerous for her. I had to convince Lisette of the story I'd concocted.

"It's true, Liz," I told her, using a high school nickname of hers she no longer used. "I'm happy with Derrick and there is really nothing to worry about. Please, go back and let Niya's mom know she is fine. You have too much going on in your life back in Monterey to be hanging around up here."

Lisette studied Derrick and me, as if trying to gauge the truth. Mixed emotions crossed her face. I held my breath while waiting for her reply. When she relaxed her shoulders, I almost let out a sigh of relief.

"Fine, I'll get a hotel room for the night and head back tomorrow. Looks like it would be too crowded to stay here anyway." An impish smile crossed her face. If her dirty mind had turned in that direction, she must be convinced.

"I promise, everything's okay," I hugged her once more. "Sorry you had to come all the way up here. I really should have called or emailed, like you said."

When we pulled apart, her eyes looked misty.

"It's good to see you happy, Mel. I began to think you would never find a man who could hold you."

She narrowed her eyes at Derrick. "Take care of her for me, okay?"

He gave her a solemn nod. "Will do."

"All right, well, guess I'll hit up a bar or something tonight. I imagine this town could use someone like me to liven things up." She giggled to herself and backed away toward her car.

I shook my head, imagining the trouble she could cause. "Lisette, don't go too wild, they might not be able to handle your kind of fun."

She grinned. "We'll see."

Derrick pulled me close when she gave one last look back at us. She seemed pleased by the gesture...and that I didn't fight it. Public displays of affection had never been my thing and she knew it. Despite the oddness of the situation, keeping up the act didn't feel as awkward as it should have. Derrick's musky scent surrounded me and I had to admit there were worse fake boyfriends to have. It was only once she was gone we each relaxed and separated. The alpha turned to me with a mystified expression.

"Blue hair?"

I shrugged. "She's a pixie."

He grumbled about the oddness of fae as we went inside.

Chapter Seventeen

The mine appeared dark and gloomy. None of the sun's rays reached beyond the entrance. One touch of the walls let me know they were frozen solid, despite it not being winter yet. I pulled on some leather gloves to protect my skin. No need to get cold weather injuries this early in September.

The narrow tunnel gave me a sense of impending doom and I wasn't the claustrophobic type. Derrick appeared calm on the outside from what I could see of him when my head lamp flashed in his direction. His emotions revealed something altogether different. He was nervous.

It had taken some convincing for him to limit his report to Variola so she wouldn't come down here with us. She'd been informed of what we were up to, but believed we'd pull back if the vampire was down in the mine. At least she couldn't come with us during the day.

My senses told me Nikolas was somewhere ahead in the dark caverns. Too bad they couldn't give me a handy map. I indicated to Derrick we should move forward. He led the way without needing his own headlamp. After a few minutes, he paused and turned back to me.

"Can you tell if it's him yet?" His voice came out

gruff. The longer we walked through the tunnels, the tenser he got. Werewolves were resilient, but not immortal. If the place caved in, we could both die.

"No, he's farther inside. A lot of dirt and rock are in the way."

Derrick let out a heavy sigh and moved on.

We had to take care with our steps. Some old supplies had been left lying around. I tripped over a pickaxe at one point and fell, making a bunch of noise as I slammed into the ground. The werewolf gave me a disgruntled look when a few choice words left my lips. I wondered if it was my cursing that offended him. He hadn't used profanity once since I'd met him.

Soon, a side shaft with a "keep away" spell on it opened up to our left. My senses revealed the vampire was in that direction. I turned to enter the tunnel. Derrick called out my name, trying to stop me. He hadn't done so well the last time we ran into magic like this, but at least he could recognize the feeling for what it was now.

I had to spend several minutes coaxing him through it. His steps were slow and reluctant as I pulled on his arm to keep him moving. He didn't growl at me this time, but as he passed through the spell's perimeter he muttered something about the dangers of old mines. At least it only stretched for about ten feet so he didn't have to panic long.

A short distance later a new shaft opened up to our right. It had been covered up with a glamour spell to appear like a smooth wall. I tapped on Derrick's shoulder to stop him. We both paused to stand before it. He gave me a dubious look when my headlamp's light bounced off the false barrier. The beam didn't shine through for him.

"There's nothing here," he said in a disgruntled tone.

"It's a glamour spell. Remember the last time we ran into something like this?"

He stared at the wall for a minute, studying it, before putting his hand up toward it. I grabbed his arm and jerked it back.

"No," I warned. "Don't touch it. The glamour is only part of the magic they used. There is also an alert spell that will let whoever designed this know if you cross it. We can't risk them coming with only the two of us here." *At least not yet.*

He dropped his hand to his side. "We must go back and bring the others."

Of course he would say that, but I'd committed myself to seeing this through. "Let me go in and check things out to see if there are any traps in there. It's better to be prepared."

Derrick shook his head. "No, it's too dangerous."

I heaved a mental sigh of frustration. "It won't be dangerous. Spells can't affect me and I doubt they would bother with physical ones since they could injure themselves down here just as easily. Don't worry, I'll be fine."

He glanced between the wall and me, doubt in his eyes. I didn't blink when he tried to stare me down. Our eyes battled it out for long moments before he averted his gaze.

"Go, if you're so determined, but don't be gone long or I'll come after you." That's what I was counting on.

"I'll be fine," I reassured him, taking the first step forward.

"Melena." He grabbed my arm. I turned back and saw the concern in his eyes. "Be careful. I don't want to see you get hurt."

I nodded, unable to speak through the lump rising in my throat. This would have been a lot easier if he'd been an asshole.

He let me go and I slipped away. Tingles raced over my skin as my body passed through the barrier, but my presence didn't affect the spell. Looking back at Derrick, I saw his brows were furrowed. The same worry still reflected in his eyes. He must have hated being left behind.

In front of me, the tunnel appeared like the others we'd passed through—narrow and dark. It veered to the left after I entered and went about fifty feet farther before opening up into a cavern. Not a large one, but bigger than the shaft I'd been traveling in. There were no other safeguards that I could find.

A shriveled vampire lay on the floor in the center of the open space. I'd never seen one like this. If not for my senses, I might have thought him dead—well, more so than he already was. His sallow skin had turned dried and wrinkled. An unpleasant odor permeated the air that was reminiscent of mothballs. Only his clothes and dark hair had stayed in semi-decent condition, if a bit dusty.

Putting my backpack on the ground, I dug out

two extra flashlights from inside. I pointed one up at the ceiling to let the light bounce off the frozen walls and aimed the other at the vampire. They lit up the chamber in an eerie glow.

I took a deep breath and knelt down next to the still body. Even at rest, he didn't look harmless. His grotesque features made me want to back out and run for Derrick. Waking him would be one of the most dangerous things I'd ever done, and I'd done a lot of dangerous things during my military career.

He could kill me. I wasn't stupid enough to believe otherwise, but too much depended on me doing this. It would take someone extremely powerful to take down Variola and her crew. The vampire lying before me had the potential to do it. Too bad no one else could break the spell—someone more resilient. I wished there'd been a way to bring Charlie, but that hadn't been possible either.

Time was of the essence. With Derrick pacing nearby, I couldn't wait any longer. I had to believe this would work. The vampire would be weak when he woke. My werewolf partner could handle him if it came down to it…probably.

My pocket knife cut through my hand in a smooth slice. I winced at the stinging pain. The blood rose up to coat my skin with a steady flow. I pried the vampire's mouth open to about half an inch and dripped it between his lips. How much he needed to break the spell I didn't know, but a full minute went by before a charge of awareness lit the air. I leaned back and pressed a cloth to my palm. Maybe a slow awakening? That would be easier to deal with.

One of his hands twitched. Okay, progress.

I thought I heard the beat of a heart, but it could have been mine. How long would this take? When his red-rimmed eyes flashed open, I scrambled for the wall. Shit, not long. The twin orbs were full of hunger as they followed my movements with frightening awareness. A predator sizing up his prey. I reached for the knife still laying on the ground a couple of feet from me. He leaped across the space between us. I didn't get to it in time.

He encircled my waist and flattened me to the floor. His creepy eyes met mine as he pulled himself up to be level with me. I pushed at his chest and felt my hands dip into his pliable skin before meeting solid ribs. Eww.

Bony hands gripped my shoulders and yanked me close. His fangs pierced deep into my neck. Sharp glass at my throat couldn't have been more painful. Most of his body might have wasted away, but his teeth sure as hell hadn't. I screamed for Derrick and struggled to get free.

He sucked in mouthfuls of blood, getting stronger with every pull. My blood could nourish him the same way as any other human's, but it would also weaken his supernatural powers. Some part of him had to recognize what I was—a factor I'd been counting on—but he didn't seem to care.

I thought of the knives under my sleeves, but couldn't get to them with one of my arms trapped between our bodies. Why hadn't I reached for one of those instead? My gun lay squished between my back and the mine floor, rendering it useless as well. None of my weapons were accessible. I had nothing.

My heart pumped harder as it struggled with the rapid blood loss. My ears were nearly deafened by the rising beats. I tried squirming away only to be pulled tighter in the vampire's embrace. With only one hand free, I couldn't get enough leverage. My throat burned where he tore through it. My life began to flash before my eyes. I couldn't die on a cold floor with a half-shriveled vampire pinning me down. My last moments weren't supposed to be like this.

I let out one last strangled scream, hoping for salvation.

My prayers were answered when the weight came off by an unseen force. Pure agony shot through me as the sharp fangs were torn from my already ravaged neck. I could hardly breathe from my throat being on fire. My vision faded, but I thought I caught a glimpse of Derrick's enraged face across the cavern before my mind drifted into a sea of indifference.

When the blackness engulfed me, it was a welcome relief from the pain. There may have been some shouting and scuffling after that, but it all seemed so vague as to be inconsequential. My body was floating to another place—a pain-free place. It was full of light and color.

I couldn't say how much time passed, but when I eventually came to, Nikolas sat with glazed eyes by my side. Lucas hovered over me. I knitted my brows in confusion. When did he get here? The nephilim seemed to always be popping up at the oddest times. Was I dead?

Was hell a place where I had to spend an eternity with him? No, I did *not* deserve that much punishment.

I blinked my eyes. The vampire's skin didn't look as sallow as it had before, though he still wasn't close to full health yet. Blood oozed from his wrist. That wasn't going to make things any better for him. A spicy taste lingered in my mouth. I ran my fingertips across my lips to find them wet. They came away covered in red. Ugh, nasty vampire blood. I rubbed my mouth with my sleeve to get it all off. Why would he have fed me? His lifeless eyes made me think he hadn't been all that aware of what he'd done. Someone else had made him do it.

Lucas sat on the other side of me wearing nothing but black. He looked like a specter of death. No wonder I'd thought I was in hell when I first woke up. A glimmer of relief reflected in his eyes as he rocked back on his heels. Emotion from him? Nah, it couldn't have been real. The blood loss was making me see things.

"We really have to stop meeting like this," I said in a scratchy voice.

A tinge of a smile might have ghosted his lips for a second, but I couldn't be sure.

"My reputation will surely be in shreds if you don't learn how to keep yourself alive without my help, little sensor."

His response was reassuring in an odd way. He hadn't mentioned killing me this time. Maybe there was hope yet.

"How did you get him calmed down?" I asked, turning my head as much as I could toward the frozen vampire.

"I compelled him and had him feed you his blood. I believe all your injuries are healed now."

"My injuries?" I couldn't think straight. It took a moment to catch his meaning.

My hand moved to my neck to find it smooth and whole. I lifted my shirt to find the claw marks from the bear attack closed up with only faint traces of them remaining. The healing process had begun over the last few days allowing a small amount of scar tissue to develop. At least it wasn't as bad as it could have been. The stitches had fallen out and lay against my skin. A swipe of my fingers brushed them off. I attempted to sit up, but my vision began to spin. I closed my eyes, half sitting up, and waited for it to pass.

Lucas put a hand against my back when the ground started to rise up toward me. He kept me from crashing into it. The warmth of his fingers reached through my jacket. The same tingles his touch always brought moved across my skin. I held back a shiver and tried not to wonder for the hundredth time why we had this odd connection whenever we were close together. As soon as I opened my eyes, he dropped his arm and moved away. He left a cold emptiness behind.

I shook my head, realizing my thoughts had turned to dangerous territory. Under no circumstances could anything other than cautious regard ever be directed toward this man. He only received that much because of his random acts of heroism.

I scanned the area around me and drew in my breath at the site of Derrick's lifeless form. He lay on the floor in a dark corner across the cavern. His throat had been ripped through much the same way as mine had. Except his hadn't healed. What had happened to him? I hardly remembered a thing after Nikolas bit me.

"What happened to Derrick?"

Lucas glanced over at the werewolf with a hint of disdain. "Nikolas needed to feed and couldn't continue to do so on you. This wolf came running in as if he planned to save the day. I thought I'd let him by being food for a hungry vampire."

"Oh, God, no."

I crawled over to him with a sick feeling in my gut. It occurred to me that my senses could still pick his essence up, but not by much. He would die soon if we didn't help him.

My hands shook as they grasped Derrick's pale fingers. They were cold. Werewolves should always feel hot...not cold. I looked at Lucas in desperation. He had to have some kind of powers that could help.

"You have to fix this," I demanded.

He scoffed. "You can't be serious."

"I am serious, Lucas. You have to make him better. He's as much of a pawn in all this as I am."

My voice came out pleading, something I'd never considered doing before when it came to him, but it was my fault Derrick had been hurt. The werewolf had come in here to save me. I couldn't let him die if I could help it. Even now, my senses told me his life was fading fast. He didn't have more than a few minutes left.

"Lucas..." I began again.

He heaved a martyred sigh and came over to crouch by the body. I suffered through annoyed looks while he put one hand on Derrick's chest and the other on his neck. The wound had stopped bleeding but remained open. A glow emanated from Lucas' hands and an incredible surge of power rose up. After a short time, the werewolf's life signs returned close to normal. A sigh of relief escaped my lips.

The nephilim had used up almost all of his reserves. He'd needed more power than I'd expected to bring Derrick back from the verge of death. I supposed healing must not be his forte, but he'd done it anyway for me. Without thinking, I hugged him. He sat stiff as a board in my arms.

"Sorry," I said, scooting away from him.

What was wrong with me? Why had I started acting this way around him? Saving me a few times did not erase what he'd done to Wanda. I needed to remember that and stop making up romantic notions in my head. If a knight in shining armor existed, this man would never be it.

"Don't ask that of me again," he said.

"I won't."

Avoiding his gaze, I turned my attention back to Derrick. Though his breathing and heart rate had returned to normal, he remained unconscious.

"When will he wake up?"

"Perhaps in a few hours. He's lost a lot of blood. I could only encourage the reproduction of it enough to stabilize him. His werewolf side will have to take care of the rest."

"What about him?" I nodded at Nikolas. The vampire still didn't look all that good with his ashen skin clinging to his bones.

"He is under my compulsion for now."

"How did you use it on him? Isn't he too old for that?"

"Under normal circumstances he would be too strong, but your blood weakened him. It made him susceptible to my power."

"Oh."

I had forgotten about that little detail with everything else that had happened. The vampire would suffer from taking my blood for a few days before returning to normal. Variola really couldn't find out what I'd done until he got his strength back.

"What are you going to do with him?"

"Bring him out of it, I suppose. He'll need to feed again first."

And who was supposed to do that? We'd run out of non-volunteers.

Lucas stood up and moved over to the vampire. With a fingernail he cut his own wrist and lifted it to Nikolas' mouth.

"Drink," he ordered.

My jaw dropped in surprise. I didn't think nephilim gave up their blood for anyone.

Twin fangs sank into his flesh and began sucking right away. The nephilim's blood did what Derrick's and mine couldn't have hoped to accomplish. It restored the vampire's body back to a much healthier state than before. It might have taken three or more humans to do the same job.

"How is that possible?" My voice came out in a

wave of awe.

Lucas shrugged. "The first vampire was born of a nephilim couple. As a child, it was their blood that nourished it, so therefore, that is the most potent blood for their race."

"But nephilim can't have children."

"No, not under normal circumstances," he agreed, "but this couple engaged the services of a black witch. It was through her meddling that the vampire race was born and because of her they must drink blood and avoid sunlight. There is always a price when you go against nature."

"So the first one turned more of them?" I asked.

"Yes, after he matured."

His answer brought a ton of questions to mind. I opened my mouth to ask them, but he held his free hand up.

"No. I have already told you more than most know."

Well, it had been worth a try. He usually wasn't even this forthcoming.

Lucas stopped feeding the vampire and moved to face him. Nikolas' skin didn't look pasty anymore and his muscles had filled out. With his gnawing hunger taken care of, I hoped he could keep himself together. I held my breath as Lucas said the words that would release him.

"Wake up, my friend. It's time we met again."

My jaw dropped. They knew each other?

Chapter Eighteen

Nikolas leapt up and attacked Lucas the moment the compulsion lifted. The nephilim blocked the assault, but didn't strike back. The vampire, on the other hand, attempted a round of vicious kicks and hits that would have pulverized a human...and most sups. My blood might have weakened him, but he remained a force to be reckoned with. He moved in a flurry of motions I had a difficult time following. I couldn't figure out why Lucas didn't stop him. He could have done it easily enough.

"You utter bastard," Nikolas yelled. "How dare you show your face here!"

The nephilim said nothing, letting Nikolas continue to strike blow after blow on him. It had to hurt but he didn't do more than flinch. The vampire might have been a couple inches shorter, with a slightly leaner build, but that just made him appear lighter on his feet. There was a slight British accent that came from him as he continued to let out his rage.

"Not even an apology? You got my sister get killed."

Lucas reacted. One moment he had his back to the wall and in the next he had Nikolas against another one. Dust scattered all around. That couldn't be good for the stability of the mine. The two sups were strong enough to bring it down on our heads if they weren't careful. I really had no desire to be buried in here.

"Hey, guys..." Neither looked at me.

"I'll tell you one last time," the nephilim growled out. "Gytha got herself killed. She was willful and disobedient. If she had listened to me and stayed home, she would be alive today. I regret that she died, more than you know, but I'm not going to apologize. She made her own choices. Do not hang her death on me."

Nikolas sneered. "That's contemptible rubbish. What was she doing that day, Lucas? Oh, wait, she was following you! If you hadn't gone after Henrik Nielson, Gytha wouldn't have been out there. You couldn't bear to let anyone else take him down, could you?"

They went back to fighting again and I put some of the pieces together. Over three hundred years ago my kind, sensors, had begun a supernatural war. Henrik Neilson had led it and many sensors followed him—all in the name of the church. It had been during the inquisition when religious fervor had been spreading across the world.

To my kind, it was an opportunity to get rid of all the non-human races they believed shouldn't exist. Thousands of witches, vampires, werewolves, and nephilim died—the highest concentrations were in Europe, but it spread everywhere. The fae were one of the few to be left alone but that was mostly because they had retreated to remote cities hidden by magic.

Sensors didn't fight the powerful races on their own—that never would have worked with their vulnerabilities. Instead they formed an alliance with angels who carried out most of the executions. Somehow, they could call on them when needed. Wherever a sup could be found, the sensors pointed their fingers and it died by angelic hands. The instigators of the widespread deaths were eventually discovered and the supernatural races struck back at my kind in revenge.

Within a few years, most of the races had been decimated. My own was reduced to no more than a few hundred, where before we had been in the thousands. The nephilim were almost wiped out since they were the biggest target. They dropped from somewhere around five hundred to less than fifty. Around two thousand vampires died as well, though a larger portion of their race survived. I didn't know all the other numbers, Wanda could only tell me what she had learned, but the fatalities were supposed to be staggering.

Some races made a comeback easier than others, though not mine. Sensors continued to be hunted down and killed. The fact I still lived, despite being discovered, amazed me. Most of my kind avoided revealing themselves—even if it meant turning a blind eye to the horrible things sup did to humans.

I'd been safer when I'd pretended not to see them either.

My attention turned to a new sup entering the area—her fairy aura filled my mind with sunshine and vitality. It took some of the chill from the mine away. Felisha headed in this direction at a speed no car could have managed. My shoulders sagged in relief. The mine couldn't take much more damage. Already too much loose dirt and rock had fallen from the men crashing into the walls.

I'd counted on her showing up at some point to check on things now that the hideout she'd created for Nikolas had been discovered. She and Yvonne, the woman from the tarot card reading place, had worked the spells that protected the place. That much had been clear when I'd read their magical signatures at the entrance. I wasn't surprised the mystic didn't come. If I was her age, I wouldn't have been rushing to the mine either.

Felisha moved in fairy form. It would reduce her size to a few inches and bring out her wings. It must have made maneuvering through the tunnels easier. I tried to get the two men's attention but had to jump out of the way when Nikolas went flying in my direction. He landed on his back at my feet. Lucas leaped on top of him and started slamming his head into the ground. I took a couple more steps away.

Felisha raced into the small chamber, transforming back to her full mass as she entered. Even her jeans and blouse made the change.

"Stop!" she yelled at the two men, sparing a brief glance at me. Her brilliant red hair swung with her movement.

They froze and turned their heads in her direction.

"Have you two no sense? Does this look like a place to let your tempers get out of hand?"

Lucas backed off Nikolas and stood, giving the vampire a hand to help him up. They dusted themselves off while Felisha glared at them. She moved forward and started running her hands over Nikolas' arms and chest. The man who almost killed me just a short while ago stood there and took it with a pleased smile.

Did she expect the vampire to have wounds? Her concern went above and beyond what I would have thought necessary, but maybe I was grouchy from blood loss.

After her examination was over, she stepped away.

"You're awake." A subtle awe came with her words.

Nikolas grinned. "It took long enough by the feel of it."

Felisha's beautiful face fell. "It would have been much longer if not for Melena." She turned to me. "We'd hoped you could do it. Thank you."

I settled on giving her a nod. It remained to be seen if the decision to wake a twelve hundred year old vampire was a wise decision on my part. Having one's throat ripped out tended to cast a shadow of doubt.

She turned back to Nikolas. "I worried you might be held under the spell forever."

He pulled her close and she fell into his arms. It was like watching one of those sappy romances. I couldn't decide what they were to each other, but their relationship couldn't be entirely platonic.

Lucas watched the exchange in amusement while leaning against the wall with his arms crossed. Our gazes met in a moment of understanding before we both realized what we were doing and turned away.

"Nik, I'm impressed," he said. "You managed to

lure a beautiful fairy to your bed, not an easy task."

I sucked in my breath. Nikolas set Felisha aside to get in Lucas' face. Angry black eyes clashed with flashing gold.

"Lucas," Nikolas growled out. "Felisha is a friend. You know she must mate with one of her own, or face the wrath of her elders. To imply otherwise would be dangerous for her."

The vampire took a threatening step toward the nephilim with his fists clenched. They were separated by no more than a few inches.

"And what about you? Would you care to explain why you went to such trouble to save this woman? You've always hated humans. Even if she does look like she'd be worth a toss," he stopped to waggle his brows at me, "she isn't the kind you would have considered before."

Okay, this conversation had gone way off topic.

I managed to stand up and not appear too weak while doing it. "Does men's maturity regress with age? Can we at least pretend you two are older than twelve? I think Felisha and I would both like to be left out of this pissing contest."

Nik turned his full attention on me. "Hasn't he claimed you?" He looked me up and down with small smile. "How very remiss of him."

I rolled my eyes and crossed my arms. "Not in this life."

Lucas frowned. "Nik, leave her alone. She has no interest in you."

"Oh, and why is that? Is she yours?"

The nephilim's shoulders rolled. "No, she is not. As you said, I have no interest in humans."

"Then what is she to you?" Nikolas asked. "She has to be something for you to bother saving her."

I would have liked an answer to that question myself. Lucas' eyes glowed as he pushed his power out so that everyone in the room must have felt it. I winced at the pressure on my head.

"That is no concern of yours."

No real answers forthcoming—big surprise there.

The vampire shook his head. "Keeping secrets now? I should have expected as much."

"Stop it, both of you," Felisha pushed them apart, putting her hands on each of their chests. "I don't know what is going on here, but this isn't the time or the place for an argument. Have a look around. You'll see we're in a mine shaft. The two of you fighting could bring the whole place down on us."

Nikolas had the good sense to look sheepish at her words, but Lucas didn't appear fazed at all. He did turn my way for a brief moment, but his gaze was unreadable. The way it seemed to me, if anyone would be dying from a mine collapse, it would be me. The others had immortality and accelerated healing on their side. Nikolas and Felisha might be able to survive and dig themselves out. Lucas could flash himself elsewhere, but I would end up going down with the first debris. A glance at Derrick made me think he wouldn't do well either. His body was having enough trouble recovering as it was.

The nephilim dipped his head in assent to

Felisha. "You're right. This isn't the time, but he's not going to be able to leave until sunset. I could move him to a safe location, if you have one in mind, but otherwise he'll have to stay here for the next few hours."

"I'm not interested in his help," Nikolas spat out.

Felisha rubbed his arm. "Nik, it might be for the best. Do you want to stay down here for three more hours until sunset? You've been in this place for five years."

He stiffened. "Five years?"

She nodded. "Yes."

His fist flew out at a nearby wall, but he managed to stop himself an inch before hitting it. He turned back to Felisha.

"It doesn't matter how long I've been down here. I will not be asking him for any more favors." He nodded toward Lucas.

Felisha sighed and exchanged a commiserating look with me. We needed all the advantages we could get right now if we were going to deal with Variola. Leaving out a potential ally who had lethal powers like Lucas would be stupid. Even I wanted the nephilim's help if it would mean getting Aniya back.

Lucas moved toward the vampire. "I'm willing to help if we could put the past behind us. Don't be a fool, Nik."

Another round of arguing began that escalated to a fist fight. Felisha had to leap out of the way to keep from getting hit as they zipped back and forth across the small space. I hid in the corner. Their anger was flooding my mind too fast. I was too weak to deal with the constant influx of powerful emotions the men put out. I collapsed to my knees on the ground, putting my hands over my ears in a vain effort to protect myself.

"Enough already," I screamed.

My eyes were squeezed shut, but I could feel everyone's attention turn to me. Felisha came first, putting a comforting arm around my shoulders. She attempted a spell to reduce my pain, but of course it didn't work. After a minute of intense effort, she stopped trying. The other two men moved close.

"She's weak. Her body has been through a lot," Lucas said.

"What happened?" Felisha asked.

Lucas gave her a brief overview of recent events. He included colorful descriptions of me such as foolish, bull-headed, and overly idealistic. Somehow, I didn't think he was saying them for Felisha's benefit.

I opened my eyes and focused on the wall beyond Lucas' shoulder, taking deep, controlled breaths to will away the pain. My voice came out weak when I spoke, "Can you guys...work this out later? Maybe we should worry about getting out of here first."

Nikolas shot Lucas a look before answering my question. "Of course."

"Thanks." I pulled my hands from my ears and rested them on my thighs, continuing to take deep breaths.

The vampire leaned forward and pressed his hands to my temples. I flinched. He ignored it and began rubbing both sides in slow circles. With the wall behind me, there was nowhere to go.

"Stop," I said, trying to force his hands away. He wouldn't budge.

"Relax," he told me in a soothing voice.

"Let her be, Nik." Lucas put a hand on the vampire's shoulder.

The gentle massaging didn't stop. "She needs this, Luc. Do you wish to do it?"

Lucas cursed and took a few steps back. "If she doesn't want it, don't force her."

Nikolas ignored him and kept his attention on me. "Tell me honestly, is this helping your pain or not?"

I opened my mouth to tell him it didn't, but that would be a lie.

"You did just try to kill me," I pointed out instead.

He dipped his head. "Yes...I was out of my mind—not that it excuses my behavior—but I can say it is something that will not happen again. Trust me, I'll not hurt you. Use your senses to judge my sincerity."

He meant what he said. I could even sense a thread of embarrassment on his part. Against my better judgment, I let myself relax.

"Keep your fangs to yourself."

He smiled in triumph. I pretended not to notice.

No one else spoke, leaving a peaceful calm for me to recover. Relief came in subtle increments. As the minutes dragged by, the pain eased. I put a hand on his wrist.

"I'm fine now. How'd you know to do that?"

He settled back to sit on the floor. "My family line carried sensor blood long ago. Though I did not inherit the ability myself, others did. It gave me some experience with the difficulties you face."

That hadn't been the response I'd expected. Maybe that was why Charlie trusted him.

"Well, thanks," I told him, not knowing what else to say.

Everyone managed to remain calm after that. If I'd known they would respond this well to my suffering, I might have manufactured an episode instead of waiting for a real one. Who knew they'd be so accommodating?

We worked out a plan for when the sun set. Felisha would drive Nikolas back to my cabin where he would set up his temporary headquarters. She lived in Fairbanks and didn't think it would be safe for him at her place, especially with all her human neighbors. Lucas offered to take Derrick and me back in my SUV since neither of us could handle the trip on our own at the moment.

"You can drive?" I asked him. With his ability to move around it seemed like a wasted skill.

Golden eyes bored into mine. "I can do many things."

Chapter Nineteen

Charlie and Emily were sitting together on the cabin steps when we arrived. She was giggling at something he must have said, but they both looked up as the vehicle drew close. I'd let the others know about her while we were still in the cave. Nik, as he insisted on me calling him, had promised he would be on his best behavior. I had my doubts, but Felisha assured me he would never harm a child. Her word meant more to me than his did.

Nik stepped up to the shaman with a smile on his face. They clasped hands.

"Glad to have you back," Charlie said.

"Damn good to be back," Nik answered as they let each other go.

The shaman and Lucas stared each other down. Charlie broke the visual struggle and lifted a brow at me. I shrugged and his mouth spread into a knowing smile. I pretended a sudden fascination with the ground.

Derrick brushed past me without a word and went in the house. Swirling emotions of anger and betrayal surrounded him. He'd regained consciousness thirty minutes before we left and had leapt up to attack Nik right away. Lucas was forced to put him under compulsion, though I didn't think it bothered him all that much to do it. I felt guilty for my part, but he didn't want to hear my apologies.

I moved over to Emily, at least she was happy to see me.

"How'd school go?" I asked her.

"Fine, but I was worried about you." She wrapped her arms around me in a tight hug.

"I'm okay, I promise."

She shook her head. "You look like a mess, Mel."

"It's nothing," I said, smoothing back her loose brown hair.

She raised a brow after studying my neck where some dried blood still clung to my skin.

"Uh huh, I can see that," a huff escaped her lips, "and adults say teenagers are difficult."

"That's because you are. Little miss run off in the woods by yourself and get attacked by a bear."

I was still worried about the responsibility of caring for a girl her age. It wasn't going to be easy under the circumstances. The idea had been to get her away from an abusive mother, but now the long term ramifications were setting in.

Nikolas cleared his throat. "I don't suppose you have a shower in your cabin do you?"

Only in Alaska would that question not be rhetorical.

Of course, he hadn't bathed in five years so it would be on his mind. That would be my priority too. I hadn't been able to determine much of his appearance, other than he was tall with a medium build. He was still rather filthy with all the dirt and blood covering his skin, clothing, and hair. He'd made quite a mess of himself while gorging on his unwilling donors. I pushed back that image; there were some things not worth remembering.

"Um, yeah." My voice came out in a croak. "Just go inside and turn left past the living room. There's a bathroom on the right off the short hallway before the bedroom."

He continued to stare at me and I wondered why he didn't just go in. Oh, right, vampires needed something more formal.

"Nikolas," I hesitated. "You are welcome in my home."

A small shudder went through me. I supposed there was a first time for everything, but it didn't make it any easier to let a vamp in after working so hard to keep them out. Of course, a werewolf had been living with me for over a week now and I'd gotten used to that. Nik nodded at me and disappeared inside.

Felisha's gaze followed him before turning back. "There are some clothes in my car I have for Nik. After Charlie told me you might be waking him, I went out and gathered some things he might need."

"Bring them in." The last thing we needed was a vampire strutting around in nothing more than a towel. "It's a good thing you thought of it, because I didn't."

She gave me a brief smile before heading off to her car. Emily followed her, asking questions about fairies. That worried me since no one had mentioned what Felisha was. The others didn't seem to notice her slip-up so I made a mental note to speak with Emily later about revealing things like that. It was a quick way to get discovered.

I searched for Lucas next, but didn't find him. He must have flashed away because his presence no longer came up on my radar. Charlie caught me looking around.

"Your nephilim protector has left for now." He grinned. "I believe he will return later."

"He isn't my protector."

The shaman shook his head. "He is something to you."

"Yeah, a pain in the ass," I grumbled. "What do you know about him anyway?"

"I know enough," he said. "The nephilim is not all that he appears to be, which you should keep in mind. A protector he may be, but a savior he is not."

I narrowed my eyes at him. "You know more than you're telling me."

"Perhaps, but it isn't my place to reveal such things."

"That's convenient," I said. "Kind of like how you failed to mention Nikolas would almost kill me by waking him up."

He cocked his head to the side. "You lived, did you not?"

"That's not the point."

Charlie took my arm. "Come, young sensor, let's get you inside."

I wanted to resist his efforts. All the comments about my youth were beginning to get to me. The temptation to shoot something back at him about being an "old man" rose up, but I refrained. My parents had taught me to respect my elders. Sups didn't normally count in my book, but Charlie looked older, which made his age feel more real compared to Nikolas and Lucas. They couldn't have passed for more than mid-thirties.

I let him lead me to the couch in the living room, lacking the energy to argue anymore. It might not have been the most comfortable place, but I didn't want to go to bed yet with so many people around. Not to mention I was filthy from the mine. Better to keep a close watch on everyone.

Despite my best efforts, I didn't last long before nodding off. About an hour later my senses forced me awake—a new presence had entered the area. Lisette was trying to sneak up on the cabin. She must not have taken mine and Derrick's word on our "relationship".

My eyes opened to find Nikolas sitting at the kitchen table, typing on my laptop. Guess he didn't need an invitation for that. I hated to think what his email inbox looked like. He turned his head when I failed to suppress a groan while getting up.

His thick brows knit together. "Did you need something, Melena?"

The shower had removed all the dirt and grime. His black hair must have been trimmed as well since the lengthy strands didn't stand out like they had before. They remained several inches long on top, and came down around his dark eyes. Vampires didn't have color around their pupils, as a rule, but this factor tended to work in their favor since it gave them a sexier appearance—assuming they had good looks to begin with, which this one did in spades. He almost gave Lucas a run for his money.

"We have a visitor outside," I informed him.

He stood up so fast it almost made me jump.

"What kind of visitor?" he asked.

"A friend who shouldn't be here. Follow me and don't do anything unless I tell you to."

He frowned, but didn't argue. I wanted to take Derrick as well, but he slept in the chair and needed rest even more than I did. Nikolas would have to take care of things this time. He remained weak, but he could still handle a young pixie.

If I hadn't been so tired, I might have questioned my sanity in using a vampire to deal with my latest problem. But right now it seemed wise to get this over with. I needed a shower and that gave me enough motivation to use him.

We moved past the lawn and into the trees, staying close together. Nikolas couldn't know the way to go and our quarry had used a camouflage spell native to her kind that would make it difficult to detect her by anyone aside from a sensor. I could feel her attention on us as we headed in her direction. The two of us stopped about ten feet away. She didn't budge from the tree she'd hidden behind.

"Lisette, come out. I know you're there."

A hiss of indrawn breath came from her direction. She stepped away from the tree and let down the camouflage spell.

"Want to explain how you found me, Mel? That shouldn't have been possible."

She had her hands on her hips and an annoyed expression on her face.

"Want to tell me why you haven't left yet?" I fired

back.

A flash of hurt flitted across her eyes. I almost missed it due to the low level of moonlight filtering through the trees. Her emotions confirmed my suspicion, though; she hadn't trusted anything I'd said before. There was pain and betrayal flowing from her in thick waves. It made my head ache again and I put a hand up to rub my temples. Nikolas saw me wince and made a move toward Lisette.

I grabbed his arm. "Wait. She's my friend and I want to hear what she has to say."

Lisette's head swiveled between the two of us.

"Mel, I'm not stupid. First you're with a werewolf, and now a vampire. I'm not dumb enough to think you don't know what they are with this many around. What is going on?" She tapped her foot in impatience.

Nik lifted an inquiring brow. I ignored him. Part of me wanted to explain things to Lisette, but her safety depended on her not knowing the truth. Pixies fought en masse together for their strength, but by themselves, they were vulnerable and could be killed without much difficulty. Even her camouflage trick had limits in the duration it could be used. Risking her would not be worth the potential loss in a fight.

I turned to the vampire next to me. "Nik, I need you to compel her to go back to her hotel and leave first thing in the morning. Tell her to forget she saw anything unusual."

A flash of surprise came over his face, but before he could say or do anything, Lisette took off running.

"Dammit," I said.

Nikolas raced after her, picking her up in no time, and bringing her back. She struggled in his arms, kicking him wherever she could, but he held her easily enough. He didn't bother to compel her until she began screaming at him. His command forced her to be still, but she still managed to give me an accusatory look. I diverted my attention from her and to the vampire.

He didn't appear happy. "I'm strong enough to make her leave, but it's impossible to alter the memories of anyone except humans. You'll have to live with this decision and she will resent you for it."

My shoulders sagged. In order to save her, I'd have to give up her trust. It seemed like an unfair trade—especially when my other best friend was being held as blackmail for my compliance. Why were so many of the difficult decisions hitting me now? I rubbed my forehead, hoping for the right answer to come.

"She'll be more of a liability than a help in getting your other friend back," he pointed out.

He had me there. We'd discussed a lot of things while sitting in the mine today with nothing but time to kill. Nik had been informed of all the stakes involved and had agreed we needed to cooperate together. I would help him get his position back as leader of the area and he would help me save Aniya. It came out as a fair trade. We couldn't afford complications like this.

I shoved all my personal feelings aside and met his eyes. "Do it. Make her go back home."

He nodded and forced Lisette's head to turn toward him. His gaze bored into hers. Unable to watch, I turned around and began walking away, but every word he said reached my ears.

Chapter Twenty

Derrick shook me awake the next day. I squinted at my watch and determined I'd slept about ten hours—twice as long might have been better. The room was dim. I realized someone had pulled the black-out curtains closed so light couldn't get through. Of course, there was a vampire in the house. Not the thing I wanted to consider upon awakening.

I'd fallen asleep on a make-shift cot we'd put together in the bedroom after I'd taken a shower the night before. Emily had gotten up from the bigger bed hours ago and left for school. Derrick and I were the only ones in the room.

His grim expression told me he must have regained his faculties since waking. Lucas had given him a few commands so the werewolf couldn't report our activities back to Variola, but it wouldn't change Derrick's opinions on matters. I was learning the limits of compulsion quickly.

"What's going on?" I asked him.

"Variola called," he said in a gruff voice. "She wants to see us at her house in two hours. You should eat something and get ready."

My stomach rumbled at the suggestion. I needed to get my strength up after all the blood loss from the day before. It had been awhile since I last ate. We'd brought some snacks with us yesterday when we went down into the mine, but those were long since digested. Of course, with Derrick angry at me now there would be no nice, cooked breakfast to enjoy. I missed the smell of it already.

He stepped out of the room after I got up. His rigid shoulders and lack of visible emotion told me he was holding his anger in check. To him, waking Nikolas and freeing him from the sleeping spell was a kind of betrayal. I'd known doing it would upset him, but hadn't seen a way around it.

If all went well, this whole thing would be over soon and there would be no more second guessing every decision I made and having to worry about which people and relationships I had to sacrifice in the process. The heaviness of my choices was weighing on me too much already.

Going into the closet to get my clothes gave me a start. I'd forgotten Nikolas had been relegated to sleeping in the small, windowless space. His body lay across the floor with one arm tossed over his head. It forced me to tip toe around him to find something to wear.

I supposed he'd wake up soon since older vamps didn't need to sleep much during the day, but he didn't stir while I moved around him. Of course, the guy had to recover from five years of malnourishment on top of the temporary damage drinking my blood did to him. He still felt weak to my senses and would probably remain that way for another day or two.

An hour later I was ready to go. I'd managed to

eat two bowls of cereal and a banana after getting dressed. Derrick sat on the chair by the window alone, staring out of it. Felisha and Charlie had left early that morning—they'd been the ones to take Emily to school.

He barely glanced at me when I walked up to him. I hated seeing him that way and wished it didn't have to be like that.

"What did you tell Variola when she called?" I asked. Lucas should have worked that out with him last night, but I'd missed hearing the details.

"She thinks we found a different vamp. A newbie I had to kill when he attacked us down there. I told her he was a squatter with no place to go. Don't know if she bought the story."

It wasn't like she could verify it since he'd be nothing but scattered dust now. I shrugged. "We'll have to hope she did because Nikolas isn't getting handed over to her."

He gave me a hard look. "Hope you know what you're doing, little girl. The stakes are high when you play games at this level and losers don't walk away."

"You think I don't know that?" I snapped.

He stood up. "You better."

***

We were greeted in front of Variola's home by three male werewolves who stood outside the main entrance. They stopped talking as soon as we walked up. I tried moving past them, but a guy with oily, blond hair grabbed my arm.

"Weapons."

Damn, I had hoped they wouldn't ask. My right hand reached back for the Sig and returned to set it in his hand. He tucked it in his pants and put his hand out again.

"All of them," he demanded.

I swallowed back a few choice expletives and jerked my jacket off to unstrap the wrist sheaths on my arms. The two pocket knives, along with another blade hidden inside the waistband of my jeans, came next. He kept putting his hand out. It reminded me that they had disarmed me after my capture and had discovered all my secret hiding spots. Better not to think about how they'd taken my clothes as well.

I knelt down and pulled the knives from under my pant legs, handing them over with reluctance. There was nothing left to give him.

"Spread your arms," he ordered.

I sighed and lifted them up.

His eager hands ran over my breasts, giving them a hard squeeze before moving downward. A shudder of revulsion went through me as he ran his hands along the waistband of the pants I wore, dipping deeper than necessary. My ass received the same treatment as he reached around for it while pressing up close to my front. His heavy breathing on my neck was hot and putrid. I turned my face away and gritted my jaw, wishing for it to be over as quickly as possible. The search came to a head when his intrusive fingers ran between my legs. Jeans did not provide near enough protection for what he was doing.

I let out a curse and shoved him away with all my strength. Even with wearing my pride like a shield, there was only so much I could take. Derrick growled when he heard my protests and leapt forward to take the man by his throat.

"I'd suggest you don't try anything that stupid again if you want to keep your head attached."

The weaker were dropped his eyes in submission. Derrick let him go with a grunt. The threat was enough for the guy to finish things up with a swift pat down of my legs and boots. One of the other werewolves waved us inside with averted eyes. I kept my chin up as I walked through the door and tried to ignore their following behind us.

The sight before me in the living room froze me in my steps. With so many sups in the house, I hadn't bothered to check who all was inside. It appeared the past had come back to haunt me.

"Noreen." My voice came out low.

The last time I'd seen her, she'd been lying on the floor of her club office in Monterey, unconscious from the wounds I'd inflicted on her. She looked fine now, in all her manicured glory, wearing a cream pantsuit.

I resisted the urge to run as I stared at her standing next to Variola, who wore her standard black leather get-up. The two women couldn't have been more different had they tried, but their stances were almost identical. They both stood with their feet spread apart and hands on their hips. It was a poor imitation of yin and yang.

Variola spoke first, "Melena, I do believe you've

met Noreen before. She was most anxious to see you again."

Pearly white teeth reflected from Variola's smile. No fangs yet, but the coldness in her dark eyes shone through enough to make me worried. Did they know I'd released Nikolas? I glanced over at Derrick, who had moved off to the side. He stood there with a blank expression that didn't give away whether he was paying attention to the exchange or not.

I turned back to them. "Yes, I remember her."

"Good," Variola said while moving forward to come closer. She stood several inches shorter than me, but the waves of power rolling off of her made up for the lack of height. Fighting her weaponless would be impossible and I hoped it wouldn't come down to that. Especially since another headache seemed to be coming on. I resisted the urge to rub my temples.

"What's this about?" I asked. "We're still looking for the vampire you want." Better to brazen this one out with the hope she didn't know the truth.

The witch-vamp's eyes hardened. "Derrick told me you were still searching. It seems to me you're taking far too long to find one vampire who shouldn't be that difficult to locate. Lucky for us, the perfect incentive arrived yesterday to help give you a little motivation."

I stiffened. *Incentive*?

"Robert," she called out to a vampire standing near the entryway. "Why don't you bring our guest?"

The man who'd brought Emily and her mother up to Fairbanks nodded and marched off. I recognized his name from her mentioning it several times. Robert wasn't much to look at—a small guy with history professor looks who was about ninety in vampire years, though he could pass for mid-forties in human. Before stepping out, his eyes had reflected a hint of cruelty. Variola only surrounded herself with the best.

For the next few minutes we stood waiting while the tension in my muscles continued to build. About a half dozen sups were in the room. Most were staring at me with expressionless faces. I tried to ignore them in favor of sending my senses out to find Aniya, but nothing came back to me. I had to hope they hadn't hurt her.

My head swiveled to the entryway as footsteps approached, signaling Robert's return with the "guest". I gaped at seeing Matt. He'd been worked over hard with a black eye, assorted facial bruises, and fang marks in his neck. He had to be in pain, but his eyes were filled with fury.

How could he put up such a brave front? Most humans would have been in a state of shock at this point.

"What does he have to do with this?" I asked, wishing I could pulverize the witch-vamp's triumphant face.

Variola laughed and Noreen stepped forward, running her gaze up and down my body. "You, little human, need a lesson in manners and obedience. This boy here will be the perfect training tool so there will be no more problems with you in the future."

Noreen walked over and kicked Matt between the legs with her high heeled shoes. He doubled over and cursed her. I leapt forward to try and stop the witch from doing anything more, but two vamps grabbed my arms and pulled me back. They avoided my flying feet and one of them punched me hard in the stomach. The air rushed out of my lungs and ribbons of pain sliced through my ribs. I had to wheeze through the pain.

"Leave her alone," Matt yelled out.

My head lifted to stare at him. How could he have any bravery left after what he'd been through?

Variola smacked him on the side of the head. "Young man, you've gotten yourself into enough trouble. If it weren't for your father, I'd kill you now, but don't push your luck."

His father?

Matt spit on the fancy Oriental rug laying across the wood floor before replying, "Not just my father, Theirn will be pissed at you too."

"Do not bring up Theirn with me! I'm free of him and his precious New Orleans. Your threats do no good here."

My head swung back and forth between them, trying to make sense of the conversation.

"What is going on, Matt?" I asked him.

Regret filled his eyes.

"I knew about them being here," he indicated the sups in the room, "but didn't know where to find them. When you showed your friend's photo, I didn't think about the guy with her being a vamp until later. Since you look human, I couldn't talk about it anyway. But then you started hanging around with that werewolf and I realized you had to know about them."

Derrick stood stoic during the whole conversation and wouldn't meet my eyes. Damn him.

Why wouldn't he say anything?

I returned my attention to Matt. "Okay, but how do you know about these people?"

He gave me a rueful smile. "My father is a werewolf and second to the head vampire in New Orleans. Last night, I saw the vamp who'd been with your friend and followed him here hoping to negotiate her release for you, but it didn't work out like I planned. These assholes have no honor." His angry eyes roamed around the room.

The werewolf next to him elbowed his gut. Matt didn't cry out in pain this time, but he did double over again. I hated to see him hurt over this. He'd been trying to help, though I wished he'd stayed out of it.

Even though he had a werewolf father, which I hadn't expected, he was human and vulnerable. For whatever reason, he hadn't been turned. Many were-parents bit their children once they reached adulthood, others refused to change their offspring, and some gave them a choice. His father must have chosen to leave him as a human.

"Wait, didn't you say you were from Texas?" My senses would have told me if he lied.

He nodded, having recovered from the latest hit. "I am. That's where my mother raised me. It was during the summer my Dad brought me to New Orleans where he lived. I met a lot of these guys from my visits there." He indicated Variola and a few others. At least that explained where they came from before arriving here.

"How did you find out about all this?" he asked.

"Oh, I've known about the supernatural

community for a while," I answered, looking away.

Variola laughed. "Still trying to hide what you are, sensor? I believe it's a little too late for that."

Matt's face reflected surprise. "Theirn has been looking for one of your kind for years. He said there aren't many of you left and the few who are still around get snatched up the minute they're discovered."

"More like killed," I muttered.

He shook his head. "No, they all think you're too valuable to be killed. You should have stayed hidden, Melena. These people will never let you go."

I swung my gaze over to Variola.

"Oh, poor dear, no one ever told you. There is always work your kind can be doing for the rest of us. What? You thought that war three centuries ago would keep us from using you? No, little sensor, the angels are long gone and they aren't coming back to protect you again."

I tried to jerk free, but the vampires held me in place. All this time I'd been running, thinking they would kill me if caught. Instead, they wanted me for some kind of slave labor. That didn't make it much better, but my perception of the world no longer looked the same. Wanda must not have known this or she would have told me. What more did they want? Would I ever be free again?

One look at Matt gave me the answer to my second question.

His eyes held sympathy in them. "I'm sorry, Melena. If I'd known what you were, I would have at least warned you."

His words rang as truth and it made me think he would have tried to keep my secret if I'd told him. Not that I would have. The instinct to protect my identity had long been ingrained into my psyche.

Noreen's insipid voice caught my attention. "Of course, we do have a problem now. If Matt knows about her, he'll tell his father. Then we'll have Theirn to deal with when he hears of this and we can't afford that."

Variola nodded her head and gave Matt a critical look. "We can't compel him not to talk either. Since his werewolf daddy makes him immune to any of our compulsions."

I guessed that to mean only a very old sup like Nik or Lucas could do it then. Another piece of information I hadn't known. It must be the older they got, the more effective and wide-ranged their compulsion.

Noreen smiled. "There are two choices—lock him up or kill him."

"No," I protested. Neither witch looked at me.

"You'll have to make sure it isn't traced back to us," Variola warned.

"Oh, I know what I'm doing," the younger witch replied with an anticipatory grin before sashaying out of the room.

Chapter Twenty-one

"Time for a little payback, sensor. We might need you alive, but the same can't be said about your friend," Noreen announced. She came in clutching a large, curved knife in her hand and eyed her prey with anticipation. Matt's eyes flashed with a fear he couldn't hide.

"Stop, don't do this." He didn't deserve this for trying to help me.

I tried to pull away from the vampires holding my arms. They kept me in place while everyone else ignored me. Derrick twitched, but otherwise didn't move. Only a trace of agitation came from him.

"You'll regret this," Matt growled out.

I gave him a desperate look, but he had focused his full concentration on his captors, struggling against them with everything he had. They were forced to hold his legs in place after he kicked out at Noreen, missing her by a bare inch. The witch stepped before him only after he'd spent some time wearing himself out. She traced his heaving chest with the knife, causing small rivulets of blood to seep out and stain his shirt.

I jerked forward with renewed strength when Noreen pressed the blade into Matt's abdomen, cutting him deep. Fingers dug hard into my arms to keep me from getting to him. I kicked the vamp on my right in the kneecap, distracting him long enough to get one of my arms free. The other vampire jerked my body close and locked me in a tight embrace.

"Stop," I gasped out. "Punish me if you have to, but leave him alone."

The knife moved clockwise as it went in, opening the wound further. Crimson flowed out to create a growing puddle on the floor. Every vamp in the room eyed it, and the victim, with undisguised hunger. Matt's face contorted until he let out a ragged scream. The men holding him kept their grips tight when his knees collapsed. Noreen pulled the blade toward his ribs in a final upward thrust.

"No," I screamed. Not one of the sups in the room acted like they heard me.

Blood seeped out of the corner of Matt's mouth and his face had turned a pale hue. Gurgling sounds reached my ears as his body moved in small jerks. I wanted to look away, but his gaze rested on me. Even now, there was an apology in his expression.

Within moments he exhaled his last breath. The life went out of his eyes as the men holding his body lowered him to the floor. Tears escaped me as I struggled to draw air through the tightness in my chest. He was gone and I hadn't been able to save him. Much of it was my fault for getting him involved, but the blame rested on others as well.

"You bitch. I'll kill you for this."

Noreen turned. Her hands were bloody but she didn't bother to wipe them off. Instead she walked up and slapped me hard enough to make my head cant to the side. I felt the wet splotches on my cheek where her hand had touched.

"Perhaps now you've learned your lesson. I suggest you do as we ask and locate that vampire as soon as possible."

Variola strode forward and took Noreen's hand, licking the blood off one finger at a time. The two women smiled at each other before returning their attention to me.

"If you don't want something similar to happen to your female friend, I suggest you get moving. She has no value to us outside of ensuring your cooperation. You have three days to find him and give us his location. Do you understand?" Variola's eyes promised further retribution if I didn't do what she wanted.

My body shook with anger. I wanted to say a lot of things, but knew arguing with them would do no good. In fact, it could make things worse.

"Yes," I said through clenched teeth.

"Wonderful."

She turned away and moved to a nearby divan to sit down. Her leather clad legs spread out into a blatant sexual pose. She appeared comfortable sitting there, despite the masculine tones of the brown leather furniture. Noreen eased herself into the seat next to Variola and managed to look as relaxed as her friend. Queens of the little world they'd made for themselves, but I'd make sure to change that soon.

"You may go," she announced with a dismissive wave.

The vampires didn't release my arms, but instead

pulled me along to the front door. We passed by Matt's bloody remains on the way out. No one had even bothered to close his eyes. A lump rose in my throat as I remembered the way he'd looked at me. I dug my feet in the floor, and turned back.

"What will you do with the body?"

Noreen rolled her eyes. "Make it look like a human killing, of course. Don't you worry your pretty little head about that. Just find the vampire."

"But..."

"Go," she interrupted.

Before I could get a chance to argue the matter further, the vamps pulled me out of the room. They threw me into the SUV and slammed the door shut moments later. Derrick climbed in on the other side, taking the wheel. I crossed my arms and sat rigid in the seat. Neither of us looked at each other.

About half-way to the cabin, he reached between our seats and pulled a cloth bag out. He handed it to me.

"Your weapons are inside," he said in a gruff voice.

I checked them over before shoving it all to the floor—too late to use any of it now.

"Did you know what they planned?"

Derrick's hands tightened on the wheel. "No, they gave no indication to me they would kill him."

"But you knew he would be there when we arrived?"

"Yes."

A blur of trees went by outside the window. "Why didn't you tell me beforehand?"

"Better you didn't know. You might have done something stupid and made matters worse."

My fist slammed into the dashboard. "Worse than dead? How is that possible?"

"In the supernatural world, a quick death is a blessing. It's the slow deaths that are the ones to be feared. I've known men who were tortured for years before being allowed to die. They thanked their executioner at the end."

I grunted. "Matt was human. They couldn't drag it out that long."

Derrick let out a pitying laugh. "Keep thinking that if it helps you sleep at night."

The cabin came into view and I hopped out of the SUV as soon as it came to a stop, grabbing my bag of weapons as I went. Sunset wouldn't be for a couple more hours and I wanted to be alone. That wouldn't happen in the cabin.

"Melena," Derrick called out as I began to stomp off.

I considered ignoring him, but an indefinable note in his voice made me turn back.

"What?"

"It's a full moon tonight. Try to return before dark."

I gave him a long look. Despite my knowing he was a werewolf all this time, I'd forgotten what that really meant. His warning reminded me. They all had a dark side and today I'd seen more than enough to prove it. Derrick didn't even try to stop them from killing Matt. The thought of it hurt me more than I'd expected.

During our short time together, we'd developed a connection—an understanding, which made it possible for me to live with him being so close all the time. Now the connection had been broken on both sides. I acknowledged my part in it, but at least the consequences of my actions hadn't been so high for him.

Maybe it was odd that I could care about him so much after such a short period of time, but he'd become a friend. A person who mattered. It seemed stupid now, considering who he worked for, but I'd felt comfortable with him from the start.

While out searching for Nikolas, we'd fallen into a natural camaraderie together. Back at the cabin, we worked out a system where he cooked and I cleaned. That was a big step for me in so many ways. Not to mention he could make me laugh, and Emily enjoyed being around him too.

Now Derrick stood looking at me with the same kind of regret in his eyes that had to be in mine. So many unsaid words lay between us. Both sides knowing we'd broken each other's trust, and feeling hurt by where that left us. Unable to bear it any longer, I gave him a brief nod and turned on my heels, heading into the woods.

As soon as I found a place far enough to be alone, I dropped to my knees and cried. Not the wracking kind of tears that could shake the body and let out loud sobs—that would have been allowing too much weakness. More like the kind that came slow and steady, coursing down the face, without a single sound to accompany them. Only the trees witnessed my meltdown, but their solid presence gave me some comfort. They didn't judge or ask for anything I didn't want to give.

***

Darkness washed over the land by the time Nikolas crept up. I sat on a log and stared at nothing in particular. My hand dug into the earth, crumbling whatever it could grasp. He took a seat beside me.

"Derrick told me about your friend. I'm sorry you had to go through that. You're right to be upset about it, but it won't bring him back."

I sighed and peered at him sideways. "There's always revenge."

His lips curved up on one side. "If all goes well, you'll have it. I wish I could say the same for all of my own grievances."

"Your sister?" I asked. Any topic that distracted me right now would be good.

"We never found out who killed Gytha. Because I sired her, the connection between us alerted me when she died. I felt it," he paused to press his hand against his chest, "right here."

I shuddered. Wasn't that kind of incestuous? I didn't know the full details of how a turning went, but now wasn't the time to ask. Better to stay on topic.

"Is that why you're so angry with Lucas?"

Nikolas grabbed a twig and began peeling back the bark. I waited through several minutes of silence before he answered, still not looking at me.

"Lucas and Gytha were seeing each other secretly

during the early 1500s when we lived in Italy. That's actually where I changed my name to Nikolas, though I've modified the spelling to suit my needs."

"What was it before?"

He wagged a finger at me. "That's one secret I won't tell. No matter how nice you ask."

"You know it's just going to make me want to find out more."

"The only one still alive who knows is Lucas. If you can get him to tell you, you deserve to know."

I sighed. "Fine, go on with what happened with your sister."

He cleared his throat. "I took her far from him after finding out, but she begged me for years to allow her to see him again. For vampires, we live so long that it's easy to forget the length of time that passes. I continued to treat my sister the same as the day she turned—no matter how many centuries went by. When we ran into Lucas some time later in what is now Germany, I realized the error of my ways and allowed them to be together."

At least he'd learned to let go of his cave man tactics. It still would have pissed me off if I'd been his sister. That's a long time to work on getting someone to change their mind. "So they were in love?"

He looked up to give me a rueful smile.

"Not in the way you think. At first they must have enjoyed the idea of a forbidden relationship, since they went behind my back to do it. Maybe they even fancied themselves in love, but it wasn't real. After I allowed them to be together, they fell apart. Gytha had always been too capricious for something permanent. Their break-up didn't hurt our friendship. The three of us stayed together and traveled around after that. They would have their occasional tryst, but nothing so serious you could call it love."

It was hard to imagine relationships spanning centuries for me, but I guessed immortals must form some close bonds with others in order to keep sane.

"You blame him for Gytha's death?"

The twig snapped in his hand.

"I trusted him to protect her while I went out to check on a woman, Josslyn, who I was intimate with at the time. So many of us were dying, and she hadn't contacted me for too long." A note of sadness came over his voice. "I never did find her."

He tossed the pieces of the twig away.

"Eventually, I had to return for my sister. I'd heard the latest deaths were close to our home, but discovered she wasn't there when I arrived. I searched the city only to find Lucas, bloody sword in hand, hovering over Henrik Nielson's headless body. The leader's guards lay dead around him with their hearts torn out."

Nik turned to look me in the eye. "There is only one way Lucas could have found him and that was by having a sensor lead him to the man. He'd planned it out and left my sister unprotected while he went after our greatest foe. The leader needed to die, but not at my sister's expense."

"You can't exactly kill Lucas as revenge, you know."

I'd fantasized the nephilim's death a number of times in my head, but I no longer felt the same need for revenge against him that I once did. My feelings about him had become a conflicting mess after recent events, but there'd been no time to sort them and figure out how much hate was left.

Nik laughed. "I tried killing him, believe me, but you must be aware of how difficult that is."

"Uh, yeah." I brushed my hair back out of my eyes. "Think you'll stay mad at him forever?"

The vampire's eyes bored into mine. "Mel...May I call you that?"

I shrugged. What could it hurt at this point? "Sure."

"Mel, when you're immortal, holding onto anger is easy. There is plenty of time compared to what humans have. But in this case I find myself in a quandary. It will be impossible for us to have our revenge on Variola and her supporters if we don't use Lucas."

"If it makes you feel better, I'm not any happier with the idea than you are."

Nik arched a brow. I told him my own history of dealing with the nephilim. At the end, he gave me an inscrutable look before taking my hand and brushing it with his lips. His touch felt warm, not cold like before in the mine. "I'd protect you from him, you know."

Okay, that was going too far. Sure, I was starting to notice how attractive he was, especially with his dark eyes and hair. The complete opposite of Lucas, I noted, but he was still a vampire. Their race and mine didn't mix—even if my body thought it might be possible. I pulled away from him and folded my arms. "I'm fine. Eight years and he hasn't killed me yet."

Knowledge reflected in his gaze. Like he knew exactly what I was thinking. "Perhaps it is time we both set aside our differences with him for now for the greater good. We can always pick them back up later when this is all over."

"I'd already come to that conclusion," I said, glancing at him. "There's no way around it."

Nikolas nodded and pointed up at the sky.

"The moon is out," he noted.

I drew my gaze up to see part of it through an opening in the trees. "The wolves will be too."

"Not to worry," he squeezed my arm in reassurance, "I'll keep the monsters away from you."

For someone who'd almost killed me only a day before. He sure did have an obsession with keeping me safe now. My senses told me he meant what he said, too.

"Are you flirting with me, Nik?"

He gave me an unabashed look. "What do you expect? It has been five long years and I have a beautiful woman sitting right beside me. What man in my position wouldn't try?"

I rolled my eyes. "You were asleep that whole time. It wasn't that bad."

He stood and lifted me up, drawing me close. "You're going to be a challenge."

I turned out of his arms, meeting no resistance, and started to walk away. As a parting shot, I said over my shoulder, "It isn't a challenge if you don't have a chance."

It was after I reached the cabin that it occurred to me my sadness about Matt's death had gone away—at least temporarily. Nikolas had helped me forget for a little while.

Chapter Twenty-two

My sword rang out with a metallic clang as it struck against Nik's. He parried it without effort and nodded for me to continue. My shoulders ached from hours of practice over the last two days, but he insisted on training me in the basics, saying they were necessary to use the weapon. The vampire had shown a strong resolve in making sure I survived the coming confrontation with Variola. This time tomorrow night, we would be in the fight for our lives as we attempted to wrest control from her. She'd called each evening to remind me of my duty to her. I was really sick of her speeches.

"Keep your arms in, don't extend them so far." Nik corrected my form.

I scowled, but bent my elbows and drew them in closer.

"Feet shoulder width apart. One of the most important elements of sword fighting is to keep your balance. If you can't remain on your feet, you'll lose the fight for sure."

I sighed and let the sword fall to the ground. At this point, I trusted he had no intentions of killing me and didn't care about relaxing my guard in front of him.

"Explain to me again why we are doing this. I

have a gun—a nice one that makes big holes in people. My odds are greater of hurting someone with that than with a blade like this." I gave my sword a disgusted look. Yeah, Wanda had said the thing about guns and vampires, but I still didn't have to like it.

Fighting sups with old-fashioned weapons didn't make sense. I'd suggested rocket launchers and grenades only to be shot down because they would create too loud of a disturbance. Far too many humans to compel if they drew attention. Lazy bastards.

Nikolas was sticking by his plan to use the old methods. I wasn't so sure about taking the advice of someone who was born before William the Conqueror invaded England. Battle tactics had changed quite a lot in that time. I believed my experience and training were more modern and useful.

He shook his head. "Mel, guns are too unpredictable in a fight with supernaturals, especially a large group. For one, we all move too fast. You could end up shooting the wrong person. For two, there is a good chance the witches will have spells in place to block your bullets from hitting them or their cohorts. A blade will be far more effective."

I put my hands on my hips. "But I'm immune to their magic, so that shouldn't be a problem. Plus you'd be surprised how well I shoot."

Nik gave a rueful smile and shook his head. "How many fights have you been in that are similar to the one we will engage in tomorrow?"

"None...like this."

He gave me a pointed look. "Exactly. In

comparison, I have been in hundreds, perhaps thousands. So who do you think knows more about which type of weapon will be effective?"

A mournful sigh escaped me. "My gun would still be better. We aren't going to make an expert swordsman out of me by tomorrow."

He took a step forward and put a hand on my shoulder. "Have faith in us. Lucas and I, along with the others, will handle all the more powerful opponents. We just need you to take care of Variola's witches, who won't be any stronger than you. I doubt they will be any better with a sword either, but there's always a chance. You need to be prepared."

I nodded my head and took a step back, pulling my sword into a fighting stance. At least it only weighed a few pounds, so it didn't feel too unwieldy. Nik had told me heavy swords, at any point in history, were a myth and the best ones often weighed no more than my current one.

"Let's get on with this," I told him, locking my eyes with his.

He raised his own sword again and went on the attack. I parried each thrust, but knew if he moved at his full speed and strength it would be impossible. Even when I failed to block in time, his reflexes were fast enough that he could pull back at the last second to keep from hurting me. I felt like a bumbling fool compared to his grace and agility.

"Keep your body turned to the side so as to provide a smaller target," he corrected when my tired limbs lost interest in our training.

I forced them back to work and strengthened my resolve. For once it would be nice to put him on his guard. His eyebrows rose when I went on the attack. He matched me thrust for thrust as we moved around the darkened yard, side-stepping the occasional tree. Dirt kicked up under my feet as I did my best to keep him on his toes. The man wouldn't give me an opening, but I kept trying anyway.

"Hey Nik," Emily called out from the sidelines. "You dropped your pocket."

He searched the ground in confusion. "What?"

"You dropped your pocket." She giggled.

I took advantage of the distraction and laid my sword flat on his neck. "Gotcha."

He looked between Emily and me.

"She helped you," he accused.

I shrugged. "You're the fool who's looking for your pocket on the ground. One would think after almost twelve centuries you'd have heard them all."

Nik pointed at Emily. "You'll pay for that."

She flounced up to him and stuck a finger on his chest. "Shouldn't have let a girl like me distract you. Seems you needed the lesson."

He gently removed her hand. "Don't you have homework you should be doing?"

Emily scowled at him. "Nothing that can't wait until morning."

"That's a lie, young lady." I put a guiding hand on her shoulder. "Go to the bedroom to finish it."

"Fine," she groused.

We watched her shuffle a path to the door at an

impressively slow rate, muttering the whole way before disappearing inside. Mine and Nik's eyes met. We smiled.

"Back to practice," Nik announced.

My smile dropped.

We picked up the previous rhythm we'd had before Emily's interruption and circled the yard in a dance I was sure he'd performed many times. A few minutes later our swords struck together with neither of us willing to give ground. He allowed his to slide along mine until they met at the hilt, drawing us close. My breath came out in short pants from the exercise.

"You're wearing me out," I said. "Not all of us have limitless energy."

He stepped back and gave me a sexy grin. "That's what all the ladies tell me."

I tried for a thrust at his neck, but he moved out of the way before it made contact.

"They're probably referencing your constant bragging, rather than anything else."

"I think not. They usually say such terms when they are every bit as sweaty as you are right now." His heated eyes perused my body with slow intent. "Minus the clothes, of course."

I cocked my head to the side, exposing my neck to his view. It drew his eyes right away, seeing my strong pulse beating there.

"Oh yeah? Do they do this as well?" came my own whispered voice.

I gave him my sweetest smile, sidled up closer, and kneed him in the groin as hard as I could before dancing back a few steps. Yeah, I was resorting to my usual tactics when overpowered, but it worked so well. He fell to his knees and clutched himself in pain.

A deep, full throated laugh came from behind me. Lucas had been watching us for the last few minutes.

"Well done, sensor. The man needs a good blow to his ego every now and then or it will grow overly large."

My brows arched up at Lucas. "I think it's already there."

Nik pulled himself back to his feet.

"Overly large? Are you really just speaking of my ego?" His eyes shot down to the appendage in question before looking back up at me with a grin.

I rolled my eyes. "Why did the witches do a sleeping spell on you instead of a death spell? Seems to me if they had enough power to do one, they had enough to do the other. And at this point, I'm thinking you drove them to it."

The amusement fled from his face. Nikolas didn't look too happy at the reminder of not being infallible. I had sensed some of the mechanics of the spell on him before breaking it. The magical signatures revealed five witches were involved. In my mind, that would have been enough to take him out if they'd wanted to.

"They could have," he admitted, "but the price for a death spell is rather high and all of them would have had to pay."

I furrowed my brows. "What price?"

Wanda had taught me a lot, but my knowledge of witchcraft still had its limits. She was only able to teach me so much about the supernatural world in three years.

Nik motioned for us to sit on the porch. We moved over to it and I gladly set my sword aside.

"Most of the time, the price of spells can be transferred to something else. Animals, plants, precious stones, and metals are all favored types of sacrifices. In the case of death spells, though, the witch must pay the price herself."

"What is the price?"

He gave me an amused look. "Their beauty, however much they have of it anyway. It ages them at least ten years just to eliminate a human and it twists their features. The more powerful the target, the more of a toll it will take."

I rubbed my chin. "More for a vamp, I assume. Not many people would be willing to make that big of a sacrifice in order to kill someone."

Nik nodded. "Exactly."

"Well, that explains what happened to the witch I killed a couple weeks ago."

His right brow lifted. "You're sure it was death magic?"

I described what I'd seen that night and how she used glamour to cover it up.

Lucas, who had moved over to the porch with us, spoke up. "I believe the sensor is correct. The woman must have used death magic at some point before."

Nikolas shook his head. "I'm glad there aren't more witches like her."

"So they put the sleep spell on you in order to kill you the normal way?"

"That is my guess. Variola didn't bother to

explain, as you might imagine. One minute we were sitting around having a good time, partying the night away. In the next, bitch-vamp and her temptresses were working their spell. They distracted me so well I didn't even see it coming."

Why he was surprised at being tricked by a bunch of women seducing him was beyond me. I managed to refrain from voicing that thought out loud.

"Couldn't you have stopped them, rather than running?"

A hard look came over his eyes. "No, they were well prepared with protection spells I didn't have time to break past them. Unlike you, I can't sense them. The rest of us have to discover these things the hard way."

I studied my hands, which were growing rough and cracked from our sword practice.

"At least you have the strength and speed to fight. I have the luxury of knowing what I'm up against, but don't have your advantages to do anything about it."

Nik put an arm around my shoulder. I stiffened but didn't push him away. The weaker side of me wanted the comfort, even if it came from a vampire. All my life I'd avoided getting into this exact type of situation and now I was right in the middle of it. Going up against humans was one thing, facing powerful sups was quite another. I didn't even begin to know how to prepare for what we were about to do. The rules were all different.

"You'll be fine, Melena. We won't let anything happen to you," he reassured me.

I glanced at Lucas, who had his usual expressionless mask in place. My gaze fell back on the vampire still holding me close. "Why do you accept me without a problem? Lucas here has wanted to kill me since the day we met."

Nik chuckled. "If he wanted you dead, Mel, you'd be dead. Believe it or not, he tolerated your kind well enough before the war. More than likely, it's your humanity that bothers him so much. Lucas has never been a fan of the human race."

The man in question spoke up. "That's enough, Nikolas. The only thing she needs to know about me is that I'll make sure she lives through tomorrow. Nothing else is any concern of hers."

Nik shook his head at the nephilim. "You haven't changed at all, Luc. Always one to keep everything to himself. I'll keep your secrets, but only because I need you tomorrow."

Lucas dipped his chin in an almost imperceptible nod of acknowledgment.

"Fair enough," he answered before stepping away from us.

"Lucas, wait."

He turned back to me, his blond brow raised.

"Some of Nik's people are coming now for the meeting. They should be here in a minute." My senses had picked them up a moment before as they entered the area.

Nik and I stood, dusting ourselves off as the vehicles drew closer. With Felisha's help, many of Nik's previous followers had returned after they'd been told he'd come back. In the past couple of days, those who were able traveled here to offer their support. I discovered most of them had relocated to remote areas of the state in the hopes Nikolas would come back. They were all that was left after Variola's take-over five years before. Despite the short notice, almost thirty of them had answered the call.

I braced myself for the influx of vampires and werewolves. Up to this point, I hadn't had to deal with so many at once. Not even at Variola's house. Nik put a hand on my shoulder—sympathy reflected in his gaze.

"Go inside and take a shower," he suggested. "The meeting won't start right away and it will give you time to adjust."

I let out a short laugh. "Oh sure, that's a great idea. Getting totally naked and sluicing myself with water while dozens of men stand around outside my cabin. Sounds like the perfect plan to make me feel more relaxed."

Lucas shook his head. The light glinting in his eyes should have warned me.

Nik put a hand on my shoulder and said in a solemn tone. "If you need protection in there, I'll be happy to offer my services."

Should have known he would say something like that.

"Never mind," I waved him away. "I'll go get cleaned up and be back out soon. At least the vamps don't have an invitation to come in, but I swear if you disturb me in the shower I'll revoke yours."

Nik put his hands up. "Not to worry, I don't go where I'm not wanted."

The statement didn't ring as complete truth. I

gave him a warning look before marching inside.

Chapter Twenty-three

Thirty minutes later I returned outside, wearing jeans and a long sleeve shirt with a warm jacket over it. A crowd of sups stood milling around the yard, conversing amongst themselves. Their numerous vehicles lined either side of the gravel road leading up to the cabin. Good thing it was late at night or some of my neighbors might have questioned all the activity. The cabin was about two hundred yards from the highway.

The overall mood felt tense, causing my head to start throbbing. I'd gotten used to having a handful of sups around, but this gathering was much larger. Nik left a vampire he was speaking with at the edge of the porch and took my hand to pull me to his side. My attempts to get free failed, forcing me to give up after a few tugs. He ignored my perturbed look and cleared his throat to draw attention.

It didn't need to be loud. Several dozen pairs of eyes stared up at us where we stood. Charlie, Yvonne, and Felisha had come, though they stood away from the others toward the back. Yvonne wasn't wearing her fortune teller robe. Instead she wore a long orange skirt with a loose sweater. I supposed the robe was part of her act for her day job.

Lucas positioned himself on the porch, off to the

side of us, with Derrick next to him. While the nephilim reclined against the wall studying the crowd, the alpha stood with his arms crossed and head down. I knew he wanted no part of this. Everyone else looked expectant at what Nikolas would say. I even caught Emily poking her head through the curtains of the bedroom window.

"As all of you know," Nik began in a formal voice. "I've been gone these past five years. The vampire-witch, Variola, and her following used treacherous means to take over our territory and kill many of our friends. They put me under a spell which left me incapacitated until it was recently broken. I would like to thank Melena, who at considerable risk to herself woke me from the deep sleep so that we can take back what is ours."

He raised the hand he held in his and kissed my knuckles with moist lips, looking deep into my eyes. I blushed, feeling stupid with so many people watching. I couldn't toss out a sarcastic remark at Nik this time to alleviate my embarrassment. The amusement in his eyes told me he knew that. He lowered my hand, but kept it in his as he returned his attention to the crowd. I forced my features to appear calm and composed, relying on my well-honed military bearing to get me through this.

"You all must know there is only one race who could have broken a spell as strong as the one that held me. She is a sensor, and though some of you continue to hold a grudge against her kind for their actions in the past, I expect you to treat her with respect. Melena is under my protection and any who threaten her will answer to me."

Nik's announcement, claiming me under his

protection, almost made me choke. I hadn't expected anything this extreme and gazed up at him in question. He met my eyes and lifted his lips in a reassuring smile before nodding to someone behind me. I glanced over my shoulder to see Lucas stepping forward from the dark place on the porch where he'd been hovering.

"I will give the same warning to you," his voice rang out. "As a long-time friend to Nikolas, I will tolerate none who do not give him their full loyalty. If you threaten him in any way, including through the sensor, there will be severe consequences."

Without warning, he pushed his considerable power out over the crowd. In all my meetings with the nephilim, he had kept it on a tight leash, but he really let it loose this time. Many in the crowd gasped and I clenched my hands, the pressure already tight on my head from so many supernaturals present. Nikolas didn't flinch at the grip I put on his fingers, but he did give a gentle squeeze in return. I took deep breaths, trying to ease the knives digging at my skull.

After everyone appeared properly cowed, Lucas pulled it all back in. I almost collapsed with relief. Maybe it had been a good thing Nik kept holding my hand because it helped keep me steady enough so I didn't embarrass myself by falling over. The nephilim gave me an unreadable look before moving back into the shadows.

I didn't know what to think of his show of support. His pronouncement had been even more unexpected than Nik's, but there must have been some purpose behind it—whatever that might be. All I knew was that he spoke the truth.

Charlie appeared in front of the deck and moved to stand next to us. He had a calming presence that somehow gave me further relief from the pain in my head. The muscles in my body relaxed by several degrees. He had a type of power I couldn't begin to comprehend.

When all eyes focused on him, he spoke. "As many of you know, I am bound to this land and all the people who live in it. For these last few years there have been great troubles with Variola. I did not support her rise to power and went so far as to ban her vampires from living in the city of Fairbanks, but could not stop all the heinous acts they committed, to my regret. Nikolas is a good leader, and has my support. If those of you here obey him, you will be welcome to live as you did before."

One of the older vampires, who was about two hundred years old, spoke up.

"Will all the same rules be in place as before?"

Charlie nodded. "They will."

I didn't know what all that entailed, but figured it had to do with the vampire's need to feed. Contrary to popular belief, they couldn't drink bagged blood. It had to be fresh from the source. Because of this, there needed to be a large enough population to draw from, or else the humans would be at risk from over-feeding. It was no doubt one of the reasons Charlie had allowed Variola's vamps in the city during the hours of darkness. Otherwise, they would have bled the surrounding area dry trying to meet their needs.

"Any other questions?" he asked.

When no one else stepped forward, Charlie gave a respectful nod to me and Nik before heading back to his place by Yvonne and Felisha.

Nikolas let go of my hand to address the crowd again. I took a step back, wanting out of the limelight.

"I hope everyone here will show their support by aiding me in my pursuit to regain leadership. Those willing to fight tomorrow night will be rewarded for their loyalty. Certain individuals will be asked to remain this evening so that we may outline the battle strategy."

His eyes scanned the people before him, picking them out one by one. Four men and one woman got the nod.

"There is a lot to accomplish. I do not wish to waste any more of your time. Those who were not chosen are free to leave and make preparations for tomorrow. Leave your contact information with Felisha so we can provide you with the exact details once they are ready to be released. Thank you all for coming."

Nik put a hand on my upper arm when I made a move to escape. I had expected everyone to head off to their cars when Nikolas dismissed them, but it didn't turn out that way. Instead, they all lined up and welcomed him back, swore fresh oaths of fealty, and even thanked me for saving their leader.

I stood in stunned amazement. It was as if Nik was a king, instead of a vampire leader for a small group. Only after each person had a few words with him did they leave, with the exception of those asked to stay back. I was happy to see the numbers dwindle. The large crowd had been overwhelming. Whether my head would manage to hold up under the pressure of tomorrow night's activities would be anyone's guess.

Nik turned his attention to me after speaking with a vampire who had to be almost four centuries old. "Mel, I need you to invite these three in. They are all vampires I turned myself. I assure you they won't cause you any harm."

I shook my head. No, I couldn't do this. It had gone against the grain enough to let him in when he arrived, but allowing another three inside was more than I could handle.

Nik's back faced the five. They couldn't see the imploring look he gave me. Only I could invite them in, except Emily. They had to know better than to bring her into it. I opened my mouth to refuse, but Lucas came up from behind and put his hands on my shoulders. The usual tingles ran through me even as he whispered in my ear.

"Do as he asks. I said no harm would come to you and it won't. Don't humiliate him in front of his people."

He had done another one of his special spells that allowed no one to hear his words but me. One of these days I'd have to ask how he did that. I felt myself wanting to give in to his wishes, not because of magic, but because he spoke the truth. Not to mention the whole lot of them could kill me if they wanted to while standing on the porch. Inside or outside made no difference.

Forcing years of ingrained fear down, I gave them their invitations after Nik provided their names. Those three, plus two alpha werewolves, stepped into the cabin. It became instantly crowded. Emily sat in the kitchen eating donuts, looking far too curious at the newcomers. I gave her an apologetic smile and told her to go to the bedroom. She let out a loud huff and stomped off. Something told me she would listen at the door. That's what I would have done.

We were short a few chairs, once you counted Charlie, Felisha, Yvonne and Derrick in on the crowd. I opted to sit at the kitchen table and Lucas stayed by me while Nik gathered most everyone else in the living room. Nothing hindered my view thanks to the open layout. Charlie and Felisha sat with me as well.

Nikolas went over the basic plan of attack for the newcomers. The rest of us knew the details and had already surveyed the site where the battle would take place. We'd all go out again tonight to do one last walk through. The additional five seeing the plan ensured the others who didn't stay would know where they needed to be once the time came. They would not learn the exact details until sundown the next day so as to prevent any information leaks. After five years, we couldn't be positive where everyone's loyalties lay. That is, unless we wanted to spend days interrogating people while I used my abilities to verify the truth. We didn't have that kind of time.

"What about protection? Variola's side is heavy with witches and we have to assume they will be using magic to attack."

The female vampire who spoke looked like an Amazon warrior. She had a large frame and a square face bordered by thick blond hair cut to shoulder length. Not an ounce of fat showed on her that I could see. Every inch of her body appeared to be solid muscle. At six hundred years old, I had a feeling she would be one hell of a fighter. I didn't ever want to get on her bad side.

"I have prepared special protection amulets for everyone to wear around their necks, Kariann," Yvonne answered her.

We didn't have witches on our side, but at least we had a mystic who could serve the same purpose.

"Will you be there tomorrow night?" Kariann asked.

Yvonne nodded. "I will be."

One of the alpha werewolves spoke up next—a sixty year old who hadn't aged past thirty. His power didn't equal Derrick's, but if he grew as old as him, he would come close.

"What about our weapons? They could be turned against us and the amulets won't do them any good."

Nik and I exchanged looks. We had already discussed this while working out the battle plans last night and had figured out a solution.

"Melena is going to donate some of her blood. It will be applied to each of the weapons. That will prevent any magic from affecting them."

Derrick stepped forward. "Wait a damn minute. Mel almost died from blood loss a couple days ago when you sucked too much out of her. A few days aren't enough for her to recuperate from that."

I had to admit, seeing that Derrick still cared touched me. Under the circumstances I was surprised he considered my health at all and wasn't just focusing his anger on our plot to take out his beloved leader.

Nikolas gave him a patronizing look. "We have been giving Mel iron pills every day to help her regenerate her red blood cells. I'll be monitoring her blood pressure while we draw out what we need. We'll stop if there is any danger."

Derrick shook his head. "That doesn't cut it. You'll be weakenin' her right before a battle. If she gets hurt, she'll go down that much faster."

I put my hand on Derrick's arm. "It's okay. I agreed to this. There is a greater risk with me not giving blood. If it comes down to it, Lucas will pull me out of the battle."

He shook his head. "Not good enough."

Emily stepped out of the bedroom. "I can give blood so Mel doesn't have to."

I covered my face with my hands, knowing everyone in the room had heard her. "Emily, go back to the bedroom please. We don't need your blood."

"Yeah, you do."

Nikolas lifted his brow in question. "Why does she think her blood would be useful?"

I shot Emily a quelling look. "She wants to help, but doesn't understand what this is about."

The teenager sighed in exasperation and thrust her hands on her thin hips.

"Mel, stop protecting me. I can't lose you now." There was a catch in her voice. "You have to let me help you."

Dang teenagers could be so convincing. I wanted to run up and hug her. Tell her everything would be okay, but I had to stand firm. She was too young to get involved in this.

"No, I don't, Em." I pointed to the doorway she'd come through. "Now go back to the bedroom."

She ignored me, looking instead at all the people gathered around the room. The attention didn't seem to bother her at all. It hadn't taken her long to come out of her shell.

"Everyone here," she announced, raising her arms up in a dramatic fashion. "I'm just like Mel. She is trying to protect me, but I'm a sensor too. I can help."

All eyes moved back to me. Now everyone in the room knew about her. How was I supposed to keep her safe if she wouldn't listen? Years of Wanda lecturing me against interacting with the supernatural population weighed on my mind. I couldn't shake that in the short time I'd spent with them.

Derrick spoke up first. "Is it true, Melena?"

A thousand lies flew through my mind, each more creative than the next, but everyone here would see through them. Instinct told me that much. Plus Charlie was giving me another one of his knowing looks. That shaman and I were going to have a serious talk one of these days.

"Can you grab me a beer?" I asked one of the werewolves. He was already digging around in the fridge.

He took out a bottle and handed it to me. I tried to get the cap off, but it was a pop top and my calloused hands were too sore to remove it without an opener. Lucas grabbed it from me and pulled the cap off in one swift move, even managing to catch it before the thing went flying into someone's eye.

I thanked him and lifted the bottle to take a drink. Nikolas stole it from me before it even reached my mouth. My scrambling attempts to get it back failed. He held it too far out of reach. Damn him. I didn't even like beer, but I wanted that one.

"Answer the question, Mel."

I gazed up at the ceiling as if divine intervention would surely come. Not surprisingly, it didn't. I leveled my eyes at a blank spot on the wall.

"Yes, she is a sensor too."

Nik grabbed my chin and forced me to look at him. "Why didn't you tell any of us this? She needs to be protected as well."

I pushed his hand away. "What do you think I was trying to do? If she would listen and keep her mouth shut," I glared at her. "Then no one would know and she would be safe."

Emily clammed her lips.

"Not telling anyone is not protecting her," Nik said. "She is too young, surrounded by supernaturals, and would have slipped up sooner or later. Why didn't you say anything?"

I shot a glance at Lucas. "He knows why. He has spent the last eight years terrorizing me for what I am and killed the sensor who was taking care of me. Wouldn't that be reason enough?"

Nik glared at the nephilim. "Perhaps you'd care to explain your behavior? I know you can be an absolute ass, but this is extreme, even for you."

Lucas took the beer from him and gave it back to me. "I like her better when she drinks."

I took a swig. At least I had his support this time.

Nik rubbed his face. "Never mind. It's too late to change anything, but Mel, we will be discussing this further later."

I wanted to argue with him and say that knowing most of these people for a few days did not garner instant trust. Yet with so many sups staring at me and needing to believe they could rely on me for the upcoming battle, it seemed like a bad time to have it out with Nik. We had to present a united front or I would never get Aniya back. They all had their motivations to fight this battle, but my friend was mine. I'd work with these people, but only because of her.

"Fine," I said. "But no one else can know about Emily."

"Agreed, but if Emily does want to help, we'll split the amount drawn between the two of you. It won't be that much, but this way neither of you should feel any ill effects."

"Works for me." Emily's face lit up with a triumphant smile.

I frowned and took another drink of my beer. If we survived this, I was going to the bookstore to pick up one of those guides for idiots who need to learn about parenting. A few days into it and I was already screwing it up.

Chapter Twenty-four

"Derrick, whose side are you on?" I asked. We were driving to Variola's house.

He glanced over at me with a startled expression before returning his attention to the road. A heavy sigh escaped his lips. "You want the truth?"

"That would be nice."

His right hand beat a staccato against the steering wheel for a few minutes before he answered. "I can't answer that, Mel. Variola has given me more than anyone else ever would have. That's not something I can just ignore."

My hand played with one of the pocket knives that would soon be handed over. I hoped to see it again after this. A good friend from back in the army had given it to me.

"Just because she's helped you doesn't mean you owe her forever, Derrick. There is a point where you get to walk away. I have a hard time believing you want to be on the wrong side of this. Think of those bodies we found. How many other evil things do you think she's done behind your back?"

His hand stopped moving to grip the wheel. "I've followed her for a long time, Mel. A man can't switch his loyalties overnight. You can't expect that."

A disgruntled sigh escaped my lips. "What does she have on you, Derrick? What makes you stay with her?"

He gave me a sharp look.

"She gives me time each year to search for my family's killers and helps me search for them. She also gives her blood to me on a regular basis so I don't age, which is something I need until I get my revenge."

"So that's why you stay with her? All this time and you still haven't found them. Are you sure she's really even helping you?"

"Melena, you don't know what you're talkin' about."

"Dammit, Derrick. Why didn't you step in the other day when they killed Matt?"

I expected him to strike out in anger at the question, but his expression turned remorseful instead.

"To be honest, I wanted to. I'd seen that kid grow up from back when Variola and the rest of us lived in New Orleans. Your nephilim compelled me to not do anything that might arouse Variola's suspicion. Stepping in would have caused her to lose trust in me and she was already headed in that direction."

"He's not my nephilim," I muttered. "So you're saying the compulsion held you back?"

"I don't think anything I could've done would have saved that boy. They wanted to kill him to hurt you, and anything I tried probably would've made things worse."

"Doesn't it bother you, though?"

"Of course it bothers me," he snapped, "but

sometimes you have to accept the things you can't change."

"Wasn't Matt's death enough for you to see how evil she is? How could you not turn against her?"

"Let it be, Mel."

A lump formed in my throat. Despite our differences, I liked Derrick and didn't want us to be on opposing sides. Nik had only compelled him to ensure Variola came to the meeting point, but beyond that, he was a free man.

That part of the plan had upset me, but the vampire had pointed out that he would never know where Derrick's true loyalties were unless he allowed the man to act on his own. He said it wouldn't be right to force anyone to fight on a side they didn't believe in. The concept came off as hypocritical to me since Lucas and Nik had been compelling the werewolf the entire time to do things he didn't like, but to them that didn't count as much.

"Am I going to have to fight you tonight, Derrick?" My voice came out low.

He let out an exasperated breath and pulled the vehicle over, heedless of the guy driving behind us honking his horn. Once we came to a complete stop, he set the gear shift in place and turned toward me.

"Mel, you and I are not going to face off. Despite your little stunt with waking the vampire, I ain't really mad at you. Might've done the same thing in your shoes. So get those silly thoughts out of your head. No matter how this turns out, things between me and you," his eyes bored into mine, "they don't change."

He closed the distance and pulled my body into a tight hug. His unique scent engulfed me, one that was all man. I embraced him back, hoping he understood how important he'd become. It didn't seem fair that we had to be on opposing sides, but I'd lived long enough to know life didn't always go the way you wanted it to.

Derrick didn't let go for a few minutes. Neither of us said anything, as if this was some kind of final goodbye. When we pulled apart, he kissed my forehead and ran a thumb across my cheek.

"If I can help it, you'll come out of this alive, you got that?"

I smiled and fought back tears. It was insane to think that a few weeks ago I'd rather have killed this man than touched him. My perceptions had come to a complete turn-around and nothing made sense anymore. We didn't even know if we would make it through the night, despite Lucas and Nik's assurances. I hadn't learned to trust them any more than Derrick had.

"Thanks," I gave him a watery-eyed smile.

"Anytime, Sensor Girl."

I laughed. Ever since the first time he'd called me "Sensor Girl" during the search, he'd kept doing it. At least, until things became complicated with Nik. The name came out whenever he wanted to lighten the mood and he always said it in a mocking voice.

By the time we reached Variola's house, I had my game face on. It was a few minutes after ten o'clock, which worked out well since Nik wanted at least an hour after sunset to get ready before we brought the witch-vamp over. Several of the same werewolves I'd seen outside last time waited for us now. We had called ahead and they were expecting us.

With a sense of déjà vu, I handed my gun and knives over. Giving them up brought a scowl to my face. At least this time I wasn't molested in the process with Derrick hovering close. I hadn't wanted to bring them at all, but it would have been suspicious if I didn't bring them with me. There really hadn't been a choice. We couldn't risk anything tipping Variola off ahead of time.

The house had a creepy feeling as we walked through the entrance. I'd never been upstairs at night, but the mood of the place didn't feel the same. Heavy curtains covered the windows at all times, yet it felt darker than previous visits. As we were led to the living room, I noted the large gathering of sups standing around. Way too many. The stirrings of another headache crept up my neck. It wouldn't get too bad, though, since I loaded up on ibuprofen before leaving the cabin.

Variola's lips lifted in a triumphant smile as we walked in. She had to have known the moment we arrived, but pretending surprise was all part of the game to her. She wore her full, leather regalia along with her multitude of braids looking fresh and tight. Noreen sat beside her and shocked me with her own attire. The prissy little witch had changed and now dressed in clothing similar to Variola's, except she'd added a leather jacket. A couple of warlocks were in the room as well, wearing their own version of leather attire.

"Do I need to go home and change? I feel under-dressed." The words popped out without thinking.

Variola laughed, waving her hand with black painted fingernails in my direction.

"Don't be silly, dear. Dress the way you like. It makes no difference."

In fact, I figured my clothes were a lot more practical for the evening. Jeans, an under-shirt, a long sleeve shirt, a warm jacket chosen for flexibility, and my trusty hiking boots completed my attire. It was cold outside, and while the vampires and werewolves could handle the lower temps, the mortal witches and warlocks could not. They'd be regretting their skimpy leather outfits later.

Variola's mood turned serious. "You've located the vampire?"

"I have."

She turned to Derrick. "Is this true? Are you certain it is him?"

"Yes. We verified it." He answered without blinking.

"Good," she stood up. "Then it looks like we have a spell to perform."

"Spell?" I asked. "Weren't you going to kill him?"

Variola clasped her hands together. "Of course, but only after we drain him of his powers. The accursed man ran off before we could perform the next step last time."

So that had been her plan. She wanted all of his powers for herself, which would be considerable since Nik was no lightweight. Even for being twelve hundred years old, he shouldn't have been able to reach the level he had.

Three more witches walked in, one of them being my former torturer, but the others I didn't recognize. They all wore leather too. Maybe they had a few dozen Harley Davidson motorcycles hiding around here we could ride on to keep with the theme.

I shook off that image and started counting. Seven of them were here to work whatever spell she had planned, though it'd been five for the sleep spell. She must have upped her numbers to be safe. There were thirty-two vampires and werewolves in the house now as well, quite a lot more than there had been in my previous visits. Nik's side would be about even with this one in the coming battle. Variola continued to remain the oldest of her group at four hundred, though, so at least we had age and power going for us. They had witchcraft, though, and that would make things tricky.

We sat around with tension stifling the air while Variola and Noreen went off to ensure whatever preparations they deemed necessary were in order. I jumped in surprise when Aniya came in. She ran over and pressed a hug before checking me over.

Relief washed over me at seeing her in one piece, though her complexion appeared a little pale. It was possible someone fed off of her today, but I didn't want to think about that too much if I wanted to remain calm. A thousand questions ran through my mind, and the look in her eyes told me she had her own. Both of us glanced at Variola's minions surrounding us and chose to keep silent after our initial greetings. She did grip my arm when we sat down, as if to draw courage from it. Nervousness and worry saturated the air around her.

Derrick didn't even glance my way. Instead he broke out the dagger he always kept with him so he could clean his fingernails. I always thought it odd how people used knives for that purpose, but I supposed it would be a handy tool if you were carrying one anyway. The two warlocks conversed between themselves in low tones while the three remaining witches gave me venomous looks. I supposed they weren't happy with me for killing one of their friends. I shrugged my shoulders and smiled at them. They would be dead soon enough.

Almost thirty minutes passed before Variola came back with Noreen. They were smiling a little too much for my liking. Derrick had given them the location where we would be heading so maybe they had been mapping it out. I had no idea what else they would be doing for that long. Their red lipstick didn't look any fresher than before.

"Let's get going," Variola ordered. "Aniya, you will be riding with me."

That caught my attention. "Why is Aniya coming?"

Variola didn't bother to turn around as she spoke. "No sense in keeping her here. As soon as you meet your end of the bargain she can go free, as promised."

I wanted to argue that plan, but it would arouse suspicion to say anything more. Derrick walked beside me and gave my arm a squeeze. The promise in his eyes said he'd watch out for her. I gritted my jaw and kept walking.

We came outside to discover it had begun

snowing. The temperature had cooled in the last hour or so, though it remained above freezing. I doubted it would stick to the ground or affect movement as we traveled. An earlier check of the weather report warned me of the chance for snow, but Nik had promised me the real stuff didn't come until October, which was almost a month away. I still shivered in anticipation of the coming battle and prayed the white flakes wouldn't affect things too badly.

As we came around the side of the house, a half-dozen SUVs and vans came into view. They hadn't been visible from the angle where we pulled up earlier, but it appeared there were enough of them so that all of us could fit in if we squeezed. It beat riding motorcycles in the snow, even if I did feel a little disappointment at the more traditional means of transportation.

Variola ordered Derrick and I to get in the lead vehicle. It made me wonder if she worried about an ambush along the way. The first vehicle was the most vulnerable in combat zones. The site where we were heading would take about half an hour to reach, but I got another surprise when we stopped a few miles into our route. Jack, the deputy from the police department, stood by his patrol car on the side of the road. He didn't have his lights on, but I recognized him easy enough. What was he doing here?

My palms grew sweaty as we waited in the vehicles. Variola led Aniya out and walked her over to the police officer. Her voice carried well enough to hear her words.

"Jack, I want you to take control of this girl and

move her away from here. If I don't call you in two hours, you will shoot her with your gun. Do you understand?" She had placed compulsion on him.

"Yes, ma'am."

My hands started shaking. I wanted to leap out and save my friend. Derrick's sudden grip on my arm stopped me before I realized what I was doing. My fingers were already touching the door handle. If Variola died in the battle, we would have no way to find Aniya in time.

The witch-vamp grabbed Aniya next and used her compelling voice once again. "You will not run or try to hide from the nice deputy. Do you understand?"

Aniya nodded in numbed compliance. "Yes."

"Good."

To follow that up, Variola put a charm on Aniya's wrist. My senses told me it would prevent any location spells from working on her. The witch-vamp gave me a pointed look as she passed my vehicle on the way to her own.

Derrick shook his head when I started to say something. His eyes said we had to carry this through to the bitter end. The amount of time we had might not be enough to find her, but if I made one wrong move now, the whole plan would be ruined. People counted on me to do my part. Yet I had a tough time getting past the possibility my friend might get sacrificed in the process. She was the main reason I had agreed to participate in this to begin with.

I had to control myself as the vehicles drove away, picking up speed. Derrick rubbed my hand in a gentle pattern, attempting to calm me down. It must have shown on my face how upset I felt, and even more so after I glanced at my watch. It was eleven o'clock. Would we get to her in time?

When we reached the old mine site, my emotions were reigned in tight. There was one way to solve all this, and that would be to get this battle over with as fast as possible. Saving Aniya was the only thing that would keep me going. She couldn't die. She just couldn't.

Chapter Twenty-five

The presence of numerous sups around the perimeter lit up my senses like a Christmas tree. We parked in a large area cleared of vegetation with the mine at its edge. Tall trees from the nearby woods surrounded us. Nik and his people were here. They hid nearby. Out of sight where Variola and her minions couldn't see or smell them, but close enough to move in fast.

Until the last of her minions arrived—a few were delayed for some reason—Nik's side couldn't attack. We had to draw all her forces in and lull her into a false sense of complacency. I knew the part I had to play in all this.

We climbed out of the vehicles and into the cold and drifting snow. The mood was tense with expectation. Derrick and I made our way over to Variola, who stood directing her minions on what she wanted them to do. Despite wearing a low-cut leather top with no sleeves, she didn't shiver. I envied her that. The cool, wet weather was making me uncomfortable. I was huddling in my jacket when she motioned us over.

"Derrick, is this the place where the vampire rests?" She pointed in the direction of the mine entrance.

He nodded. "It is."

Variola called out to a mixed group of

werewolves and vampires, indicating they should come forward. As they got close, their harsh visages came into view. Each one illuminated by nearby headlights that hadn't been turned off yet. All were in regulation leather gear and carried a plethora of weapons, including knives and swords, on their belts. My fingers itched to be holding my own gun.

"Very well," she said. "The sensor and these five men here will go in and bring him out."

Derrick took a step forward. "I should go in with her. She isn't comfortable in the mine, and she can't see well in the dark."

This was one argument I wanted him to win. He might be on the wrong side, but at least he wouldn't hurt me. The same couldn't be said for the others.

Variola waved off his concerns. "These men will help her find her way and she can bring a flashlight if that makes her feel better."

As if on cue, someone brought one over. I took it from them, gripping the cold plastic in my hand. It would help light my way, but it wouldn't make much of a weapon. Being a weak human really sucked.

"Better?" Variola asked. I could tell by the look in her eyes she saw me as pathetic too.

I nodded. She'd have her turn at the feeling later.

"Very well, sensor. Make sure you don't mess this up or it will be your friend's life."

Though she stood several inches shorter than my height, the woman managed to look down her nose at me with a warning expression. I kept my face impassive, refusing to give away a single one of my vengeful thoughts.

"Don't worry. I won't mess up," I replied.

At least, not according to my plans, but hers might not go the way she wanted. The witch-vamp would be battling for her life soon enough. Visions of her dying danced through my head. They made me feel warmer until I remembered her death could mean I wouldn't reach Aniya in time. There had to be a way.

Variola nodded, appearing satisfied with my response and ordered us to go inside. Her minions followed me as I led them over to the mineshaft. It opened up on the side of a hill, unlike the previous one that had been a hole in the ground. My flashlight clicked on as we entered, but it didn't provide much illumination.

I took care making my way through, thinking of my previous visits here and the random objects that had snuck up to attack me when I wasn't paying attention. A pickaxe had almost taken my leg out the last time. The sups behind me moved with ease and grumbled at my slow pace. I ignored them, happy the movement and lack of wind made the cold more bearable, despite the ice on the walls. Sunny California would have been really nice right about now.

After a few minutes, no sounds from outside reached us. Some of the guys began to get edgy. One of them remarked about a possible cave-in and the tension rose. The darkness gave the impression that the walls were closing in, but I'd already walked through this part of the shaft and didn't think it would collapse anytime soon.

A turn-off appeared to the left. I almost missed it with my attention focused on the ground. My hand dropped the flashlight so it rolled a couple feet before stopping with its beam reflecting off the wall. In the space of a heartbeat, Lucas appeared with a golden ray of light and handed me my sword. I grabbed it and pivoted on my heels, sensing him flash away to come up behind the five sups. Nikolas appeared at my side and gave me a brief nod before maneuvering himself into position. Variola's minions let out a slew of curses as we came at them from three directions.

No hesitation, I reminded myself.

The werewolf in front of me reached back to draw out a knife. I took advantage of his exposed torso and thrust my blade into the soft tissue of his stomach. The sword had been sharpened to a fine point and slid in with little resistance. Blood already soaked his front when I twisted it and pulled the blade back out, readying myself for another strike.

The man stumbled, clutching his wound as he looked at me with rounded eyes. Adrenaline coursed through my veins as I kept the sword tight in my hand. I expected my opponent to return my attack, but to my surprise, he fell to the ground. I'd thought his kind would be able to take more damage than that. His overwhelming pain hit my senses, proving it wasn't an act.

A sickening thud came from my left, drawing my attention.

Nik had relieved one of the vampires of his head. Both parts turned to dust moments later. He took a swipe at another vampire who'd been trapped behind his cohort in the narrow tunnel. The man ducked the blade and rushed forward with blazing eyes. Nik kicked his foot out and slammed the smaller man's shoulder, knocking him back. The movement was precise and graceful, though it flashed by, almost too fast to see.

I forced myself to return my attention to the werewolf I'd impaled. He was curled on the ground, struggling for breath while clutching his bloody wound. The damage might have been enough to kill a human, but he was already starting to heal. According to Nik, it was always better to take the head off or else a sup could recover and come back to attack again. I had no choice but to finish the job.

As the werewolf began to get up, I lifted the sword in a high arc and aimed for his neck. He raised his arm at the last second to block the blow, not leaving me time to readjust. The blade cut through his wrist and only made it partway through his throat. Blood splattered all over us both.

I tried not to think of the pain I was causing him. Killing an enemy was one thing, making him suffer was another. Dragging in a lungful of air, I sliced at him again, making it half-way through his thick neck. It took a third attempt before I managed to finish him off.

By the end, I was panting and covered with even more blood—most of it on my clothes and hands. It took some effort to keep the bile from rising up in my throat. Some people think the best fighters are the ones who kill without remorse. The day you stop feeling compassion for your enemies is the day you lose your humanity and need to be removed from society. I'd do what needed to be done, but I'd be damned if I let it harden me to the point that I no longer cared.

I looked around to see the rest of the fight was over. Two bodies remained, one of them the man I killed. A few piles of clothes from the deceased vamps littered the ground around us. Lucas had killed two of the sups himself in a flurry of motions that would have been impossible to follow—if there'd been a chance for me to do so. We'd needed it to be done fast in order to avoid damage to the mine. We'd also had to keep sounds to a minimum so Variola wouldn't catch on to our plan too soon.

Nik grinned at me after surveying the damage and my less than pristine appearance. He didn't have a hair out of place and only a splash or two of blood on the rest of him. His eyes lit up with amusement as I tried to use part of my shirt, which had remained clean under the jacket, to wipe my face. A few strands of hair had come loose from my pony tail and stuck to my cheeks.

"You're a right bloody wench aren't you?" he asked.

I rolled my eyes. His sick sense of humor came at the oddest times, but he did have a way of taking my mind off of things. For a brief moment, the carnage at our feet didn't seem quite so bad. He put an arm around me and drew my chilled body close.

"You did well."

I gave him a wan smile. "Thanks."

Lucas had his usual mask in place. "We're done here, let's go."

He didn't wait for a reply before turning and heading toward the mine entrance. I broke off from Nik to follow the nephilim, grabbing my flashlight before leaving. It occurred to me the shaft had been much brighter than it should have been during the fight. I vaguely remembered Lucas pushing out his golden glow. He'd dimmed it back down now.

We were half-way through the mine when a new group of sups entered the area. There must have been at least thirty of them and they were about to reach Variola and her crew. I pushed my abilities hard to check the mood in her direction. It had an air of expectancy. She knew they were coming.

I came to a sudden halt. "Wait."

Both men turned to me. I filled them in on the latest development, hoping it wasn't as bad as it seemed. Our side wouldn't attack until Lucas flashed over to give the order, but these new guys could mean a change in plans.

Nik frowned and looked at the nephilim. "What do you think?"

Lucas shrugged. "For me, it makes no difference how many underlings there are."

The pressure on my head grew as I concentrated on further activities outside. Protection spells were being set up that would prevent anyone or anything from breaking through. We were close enough to the mine entrance for me to get a good feel for their parameters. There were two circles, each about ten to twelve feet across. Both would need to be disabled before we could get close enough to attack the individuals inside.

Considering their small size and the locations of all the sups out there, the circles were only meant to hold the witches and warlocks while all the others on Variola's side were left to their own defenses.

According to Nik's description of the sleep spell, it appeared to be standard procedure for them to make the circles to ensure no one interfered with the magic they worked. Were the extra sups who'd just arrived a precaution or had Variola suspected an attack all along? I told the two men with me what I was sensing.

Nikolas reached out and put a hand on my shoulder. His eyes penetrated mine as I stared up at him. "Mel, I need you to break the nearest circle first. You'll have to use your blood to do it, but there is no other way. I'll take Charlie and we'll keep Variola and her warlocks distracted until you are able to come to us. Can you do that?"

Changing plans at the last minute. I'd grown used to that in the military.

"No problem," I answered.

Lucas shifted with impatience. "If you two are ready, I'll alert the others."

He would be fighting with our main group since he could reduce Variola's supporters faster than anyone. Now that her side was double what ours was, we needed his strength more than ever. Not to mention until I broke the circles he couldn't help against the main and most dangerous players. That didn't add to the pressure on me or anything.

After we nodded our agreement, the nephilim flashed away. Nik and I raced for the entrance, which came up after about a hundred feet. The snow continued to fall in tiny flakes outside, but still hadn't stuck to the ground. I braced myself for the wind and cold. It didn't disappoint, striking me as soon as I stepped out.

Variola laughed and clapped her hands as soon as we came out. I froze in my steps. She stood in her circle across the field, but I had a clear view of her.

"I knew you woke him days ago, little sensor," she spoke loud enough so everyone could hear her. "A smarter one of your kind would have known we'd be alerted as soon as the spell had been broken. Just because we couldn't find him didn't mean we weren't aware he was near. You should have considered all this, but I'm glad you didn't. Now we can finish this once and for all."

I'd never considered breaking the sleep spell would alert the witches. I wanted to kick myself for it. My senses had picked up the intent of the magic, but I hadn't bothered to study all the parameters. Now Nik's side would pay for that mistake with double the enemies to fight. I had to hope Aniya wouldn't pay for it too. I lifted my middle finger at Variola before racing toward the second circle.

She sent soccer ball sized flames out as Nik's forces descended on the field. Instinct made me want to duck, but that was a waste of time. They were bouncing right off me. Poor Nik had to do some impressive acrobatics to avoid them, though.

As I came behind the circle holding Noreen and the other female witches, I sensed they were beginning a vicious spell. It would weaken most of the sups on our side if they were able to complete it.

With no time to waste, I dropped the flashlight and used the sharp edge of my sword to cut one of my fingers. The sting made me wince, but I ignored the pain. Blood bubbled up in a sufficient quantity so when it dripped onto the line of the circle, the spell broke right away. All the witches turned to me at once with wrath-filled gazes. I straightened up and backed away. I hadn't considered no one would be nearby to help me. The muscles in my legs braced to flee, but I stopped myself from moving further. This was no time to turn coward. I'd never been one before and wouldn't start now.

Noreen held a six-inch silver knife, rather than a sword, and stood closest. I concentrated my efforts on her but took cautious steps to keep all the witches in my line of sight. She attempted to strike out at me in a clumsy move. I stepped to the right and swung at her unprotected side. The blade sliced into her left arm like butter.

She cried out in pain and dropped her knife to the ground to clutch her wound. My sword had cut deep enough that blood poured between her fingers. Noreen gave me a pleading look.

"Melena, you don't want to do this."

A part of me wanted to feel sorry for her, but then Matt's face flashed in my mind. He'd begged in the end and she hadn't shown an ounce of mercy. She didn't deserve any either. I raised my weapon once more.

"Actually," I said. "I do want to do this."

Even as she tried to back away, my blade cut through the air and into her neck. As with the werewolf, it didn't make a clean cut, but a second swing finished the job. More blood splattered on me, but I didn't bother wiping it off. Even with her head removed, the look on her face remained. It was frozen into a grimace with her forehead wrinkled and her nose scrunched up. I couldn't help but stare at her expression.

The brief moment of inaction cost me. My focus had been to the front when it should have been all around. One of the other witches had snuck up from behind. A vicious slice cut into my lower back. I arched away from the sharp blade, but it still penetrated deep into my skin and burned like flames had scorched it.

Breathing through the pain, I turned to face her. It was the same witch who'd tortured me not long ago in Variola's basement. She'd pulled the upper half of her stringy hair back, but it flew in wild abandon with the increasing wind. The third and fourth witches stood off to the side ready to attack as well.

I took a few steps back, trying to decide how to keep them at bay. From the corner of my eye I saw movement. Derrick raced toward us in full wolf form and leapt up to sink his jaws into one of their necks, tearing the throat out with a shake of his head.

I had to admire the shiny, black fur covering his alternate form. It hid any blood that might have coated him. He made for a pretty, if rather scary, wolf. After extricating himself from the dead witch, he moved to the next. She raised a short sword and eyed him with disdain, but he didn't look concerned with her bravado. His arrival left me with only one to handle. I focused my attention on her.

She scrunched up her face in fear and clutched her knife in a tight grip. The blade had to be eight inches long, with ridges on one side. My three foot sword could keep it out of reach if I was careful. The weapon sat heavier in my hands than before as I raised it and went in for the attack.

The woman shuffled back, holding the knife in front of her like a shield. I sliced along her chest, knocking her arm to the side. It didn't do more than give her a thin cut, but she screamed as if it had been much worse. I remembered what she'd done to me in Variola's dungeon. Her crying wouldn't save her. My body remembered the pain, even if the physical wounds didn't exist anymore.

She recovered herself enough to attempt a jerky swipe with her blade, but my sword blocked it. I swung the weapon again for another strike. This time it struck her below the ribs and sunk in deep. Sickening sounds came from her throat as she collapsed to the ground.

It looked painful. I finished her by hacking her head off. It didn't go any easier than the last two kills, and in fact took longer. I felt tired. After her head finally parted her body, I did a search of the surrounding area. It was just me and Derrick in the immediate vicinity.

He had finished off the last witch and began transitioning to human form. His strength and age made it quick. I estimated two minutes. It took all my willpower to ignore his very nude body as he moved toward me. Holy hell, he had a lot of muscles.

Focus on his eyes, Melena!

"Are you alright?" he asked in a gruff voice.

"I've been better," I answered, swaying a bit. His presence and my blood loss were taking a toll. "Thanks for helping me."

"Anytime, Sensor Girl." He gripped my arm. I managed not to let my eyes drop when he stepped closer. There were more important things to worry about than protruding anatomy.

I nodded at the remaining circle. We could see it through the drifting snow. Nikolas and Charlie had found a way around the witch's protection with their swords. The weapons had my blood coating them and were able to pierce through. They couldn't actually break the spell, since only fresh blood could do that, but it did give the guys an advantage.

Nik was springing about in lightening fast movements designed to keep Variola and her warlocks on their toes. She and her minions repeatedly tried to cast their spells but were interrupted every time. They had to keep shifting positions to avoid the blades coming their way. Nik had managed to nick them in a few places by the looks of their torn leather. To further frustrate them, Charlie was using his own magic to block the many fireballs they kept shooting out in retaliation. He moved fast for a man of his aged appearance.

The warlocks' faces reflected fear and frustration as they stumbled about the circle. Variola did her best to stand apart from them. It amazed me that the three magic users didn't shove each other out of the way to save themselves. A few of their fireballs had stung Charlie and Nik when the shaman couldn't block them in time, but neither of the men looked badly hurt from them. The singe of their clothes was the only evidence they'd been touched at all.

"I've got to go break that," I told Derrick.

Regret reflected in his eyes. Protecting me was one thing, fighting against his leader was another. The werewolf nodded and let go of my arm.

"Be careful."

"I will," I answered him before stumbling away.

Variola's circle laid half-way across the open clearing. The wound on my back pulled with each step, sending shots of agony through me. I had to work my way around mutilated bodies and piles of dust from vanquished vamps. Their scattered clothes fluttered in the wind and snow. A few small fires had broken out, giving the scene an eerie illumination. The smell of smoke reached me, but it didn't cover the much stronger scent permeating the air. Blood and death left a distinct foul odor you could never forget.

The fight was coming to an end, but over a dozen of Variola's minions were still left standing. Those among Nik's supporters, who were still alive and uninjured, continued to battle it out. No one appeared more savage than Lucas.

His short blond hair was plastered with blood and his face and hands were coated in it. The dark clothing he wore hid the rest. He had a disturbing look of pleasure on his face as he fought the vamps. They were lucky if they got one good swing of their blade, which he easily blocked, before he thrust his hand into their chests and removed their still beating hearts.

Silent terror reflected from their faces as they

stood frozen before him. They couldn't even flinch as the force of his sword cut through their necks and sent their heads flying dozens of feet away. He moved with predatory grace onto the next adversary without a backward glance. Nik's words returned to haunt me "If he wanted you dead, Mel, you'd be dead." A shudder went through me. If I hadn't believed his words before, I did now.

I dragged my eyes from the enigma that was Lucas to focus on the circle I'd finally reached. Charlie kept Variola and her crew distracted while Nik directed me to a specific spot.

"Break it there."

I nodded and moved toward it, wanting to get this over with. The line was wide. It would require even more of my blood than the last one to sever it. Variola and her warlocks eyed me with malicious intent and shuffled closer to my position. They stopped less than three feet away with their blades poised to strike. Nothing like having powerful enemies staring you down to make your job more difficult.

Lucas appeared at my side. He took an aggressive stance that had the witches hesitating to come any closer. I had faith he could keep them back. He didn't look all that friendly with the blood covering him and the dangerous gleam shining from his eyes.

All my wounds had stopped bleeding except for the one on my back. I ran my hand across it to get the fresh blood I needed and came away with more than enough. My head grew light at the sight of it.

Falling to my knees, I pressed my wet fingers to

the circle, running them across the thick line. It broke with an electrically charged snap. Derrick ran up and pulled me out of the line of attack, thankfully having found a pair of pants from somewhere, while Nik and Lucas moved in to engage. They dispatched the two warlocks with a few speedy slices of their swords, but Variola took off running.

The fear leaking from her told me she had no desire to stick around now that she had nothing and no one to hide behind. The more evil and cruel a person is, the less likely they are to tolerate being on the receiving end of retribution.

Lucas called out to her with a heavy note of compulsion in his voice.

"Stop."

She ground to a halt, straining against the pull of his compulsion with her back arched in an awkward position. She was a strong sup, and might have been able to fight it off if not for having wasted so much of her power earlier on spells and fireballs.

"Come to me," he ordered with even more strength.

Almost a minute passed while she attempted to struggle against the command, her body jerking as she resisted. In the end she turned around and walked back with the short, stilted steps you might expect from a zombie. Nik and Luc waited with their arms folded, wearing almost identical bored expressions. They didn't look to be in a hurry now that the moment of truth had arrived. I didn't have that luxury.

Derrick supported me with his arms, but I hardly

noticed. My vision was blurring and nothing appeared clear to me. The werewolf tightened his hold when he took in my weakened state.

"Nik...Lucas," he called out, "she ain't holdin' up. You two need to fix her before it's too late."

My eyes were now closed but my hearing continued to work fine. I heard Lucas curse under his breath. In what seemed like a flash, Nik kneeled beside me. I managed to crack my eyes open to watch him as he cut his own wrist. He held it to my mouth. Everything in me wanted to reject the offer, but I took it. Aniya needed me. If it required me drinking vampire blood to save her, so be it.

I pressed my lips to his wrist and grimaced through the first swallow. My initial reaction was to gag, but I got it down. A little more and it was no longer so awful. Maybe vampire blood was an acquired taste that took a few tries before it became more palatable. The spicy flavor transformed into something similar to honeyed mead, which made no sense because I'd never had honeyed mead, but that was the beverage that came to mind. I wanted more. No wonder some humans became addicted to this stuff.

Nik had to pull me away after what must have been close to ten swallows. I licked my lips, missing the taste already.

"You've had enough." The corner of his lip turned up.

I shifted in Derrick's arms in embarrassment, which made him chuckle.

"Not to worry, Mel, you'll be fine. I've got other

parts of me you can suck on once you're in better shape if you like."

"Jerk," I muttered. I pushed my arms out in an attempt to drive him away. Nik pulled them down and moved closer. I shrunk back into Derrick's naked chest, feeling caged between the two men.

Nik grinned and grazed his fingers across my cheek. "You bring out the best in me."

Derrick growled. "Don't you have something else you should be doing right now?"

Nik turned to view the gathering of sups waiting for him.

"Yes, I do." Nik nodded at the werewolf. "Thank you for protecting her."

Derrick dropped his intense gaze to mine.

"It wasn't for you," he said. I had to look away—way too much testosterone in this crowd for my liking.

"I know," Nik replied before going back to face his reluctant foe.

Lucas had been managing Variola during the delay. It took me a moment to realize they had stopped everything to take care of me. Why had they done that? They didn't need me anymore. My wounds could have been put off until after everything was over. I may have been bleeding out, but not enough to die in the next few minutes. I didn't know what to think of their behavior. Sups were supposed to be my enemies, but the lines had begun to blur.

Everyone's attention was drawn to the scene of Nik stepping up to the witch-vamp. Variola stood proud, no longer fighting the compulsion. I supposed she must have dredged up some courage from somewhere.

Nikolas paced around her. "Variola, you surely know the time-honored ritual for taking control of a region. It has always been the same. Though you chose to forgo it with me, I'll still give you a chance to fight to keep it."

She didn't move. Her pride cloaked her like impenetrable armor.

Nikolas waved over one of his supporters, who stood about ten feet away. "Give her your sword. We'll let her battle for her dubious honor."

The younger vampire stepped forward and held out the blade, hilt first. Variola stared at it. A small tremor may have shaken her hand as she took the blade. I leaned forward in Derrick's arms. Nikolas had raised his own weapon. I could see the anticipation written all over his face. Variola adjusted her position into a fighting stance and stuck her chin out. Yeah, she wasn't cowed yet.

Not so much as a shuffling sound could be heard across the clearing. One moment the two vampires stood still and in the next they were on each other. I couldn't tell who attacked first. The fight began that fast. They moved in a blur, never staying in one place for long. Neither combatant needed to stop for breath, but I was probably breathing hard enough for both of them.

Minutes passed. The clang of swords striking in rapid staccatos rang out. They didn't limit themselves to the ground. Both were old and powerful enough to fly. They hovered at least ten feet in the air, dipping and curving as they tried for each other's weak spots. I began to think the fight might never end, but then they suddenly dropped to the ground. Variola stood clutching her arm. Nikolas had cut through to the bone. It bled for a few moments before healing.

"Is that the best you can do, vampire?" I'd hoped to see her cowed more.

"This is merely a warm up," Nik flicked his sword. "I wanted you to feel like you were given a chance."

Variola gave him a condescending look. "Think you have it all figured out, don't you?"

"All of what figured out?" he asked.

"Why I came here."

His brows rose. "To steal my territory. That much is rather evident."

She laughed. "You know nothing, vampire. I was sent here."

"Oh," he replied. His eyes glinted. "Who sent you?"

"The same one who killed your sister."

Shock and anger hit the air so strong anyone could have felt it. Nik glanced at Lucas.

"Tell me who," he said through gritted teeth. His fangs cut his lips, but he didn't draw them back.

Variola smiled, giving a glimpse of her own sharp incisors. "I think not."

Lucas stepped forward and pushed his compulsion. "Tell us who sent you."

She shook her head. "Don't bother. It won't work. The one who sent me is stronger than either of you and she made sure I could never reveal her name."

My mind spun. Only someone older and more

powerful than Lucas could have placed a compulsion he couldn't break. Nik and Lucas began a wordless conversation I couldn't read.

Variola took advantage of the distraction and moved forward with a thrust of her sword. I wanted to cry out a warning, but everything happened too fast. Her blade aimed straight for his neck in what could only be a fatal blow. Nik pivoted at the last moment. With a raised arm, he blocked it so that it did no more than graze his skin, but it had been close. In the next moment he swung at her. He didn't miss.

Her head flew off and landed twenty feet away next to a group of werewolves. The largest of the group stepped forward with a look of disgust and kicked it off to the side. A moment later it turned to dust, along with the body. Her torn leather garments were all that remained.

Nik gave his arm a brief glance, but it had already started healing. Not much of his blood even stained his shirt. Lucas came over and patted him on the back. They appeared to be whispering something to each other but I couldn't make out the words.

They broke apart and turned to me.

"Did she tell the truth?" Nik asked.

I swallowed, hating to answer. "She told you what she believed to be true."

He ran a hand through his hair and groaned in frustration.

"We'll have to look into this," he told Lucas.

The nephilim nodded.

I wanted to feel bad for Nik. It was his sister we

were talking about, but we had more pressing matters that had to be dealt with now. A glance at my watch told me it was almost one o'clock. We were almost out of time.

Chapter Twenty-six

"I'm sorry about your sister, Nik, but we have to save Aniya right now."

Everyone's eyes fell on me.

"What are you talking about?" he asked, frowning.

I outlined what had happened before we came to the mine as fast as I could, not wanting to waste a minute. Derrick, whose arms continued to hold me, tightened in comfort.

"Mel, I don't think we can get to her in time," he said close to my ear.

I pushed his arms away and stood. The cold wind struck hard without his warm body close, but I ignored the discomfort. I ignored all the aches and pains. None of them mattered in this moment.

"There has to be a way."

Yvonne tapped her chin. "Do you know if the deputy had a charm on him to prevent the location spell?"

I reflected back to the scene and clued in on that small detail. "No, he didn't."

"Then we need only obtain the materials to place the spell on him."

I groaned. How were we supposed to do that?

She smiled. "Don't worry, I know where he lives. If I can get there soon, it will simply be a matter of gathering what I need."

"That will still take time," I argued.

"Not if I take her there," Lucas said. I glanced at him in surprise. He still looked rather bloody and I had to hope Yvonne wouldn't mind.

"You would do that?"

"I would, but you'll owe me a debt for it."

Of course, he wouldn't do me any favors for free.

"Fine, whatever, but do it fast. Niya only has five minutes left," I said after glancing at my watch again.

He nodded and turned his attention to Yvonne. "Tell me where you need to go."

She explained the details and I could see him working them out in his head. Did he have some kind of mystical map in there or what?

After being satisfied he had a lock on the location, he grabbed Yvonne and flashed them away. I began to pace, hoping they didn't take long. Every minute I glanced at my watch and let out an audible groan. A couple of times someone tried walking up to me, but I put my hand out to stop them. No one could calm me down and it wasn't worth letting them try.

With thirty seconds left on my watch, Lucas and Yvonne appeared again. She had the supplies in her hands and set them down to get to work right away. I didn't pay a lot of attention to how she did it, but my eyes willed her to finish as soon as possible. By the time she found the location, it was five minutes past the deadline and I was shaking with impatience and fear.

This time Lucas offered to go alone and get Aniya, saying he couldn't take anyone with him since he would need to be able to move her back here. I hadn't even known he could move a single person with him before tonight. After giving him my assent, he flashed off once again.

When he returned two minutes later, he held my limp friend in his arms. I gasped. She had a gaping wound in her stomach. She still breathed, but who knew for how long. She'd already lost a lot of blood if the deep red coating her faded jeans and cream sweater were anything to go by. I moved closer. Dread was closing my throat at seeing her olive skin with an ashen hue to it. Nik came to stand beside me and examine her as well.

"She has a thready pulse, Mel. Her heart is working too hard. I'm not sure she can be saved," Nik told me with regret-filled eyes.

"What do you mean she can't be saved?" I touched her cheek to find it cold. "Your blood healed me. It could do the same for her."

He shook his head. "You weren't this close to dying. She is dangerously low on blood and already in shock. If I give her my blood now, it will upset the balance."

"The balance?" I asked in confusion.

He nodded. "I'm not sure how much you know, but to turn a human into a vampire they must be bled out to the brink of death, and then be fed our blood. She is at that point now and wounded to the degree I would have to feed her a great deal of my blood to heal the wound."

"Okay," I said, still not getting it.

"If she lives, Mel, she'll turn into a vampire."

I dropped my head, not liking the idea of having to make such a decision for my friend. What if she didn't want it? There had to be another way.

"Wait," I looked at Lucas. "Can't you heal her?"

His eyes roved over Aniya still cradled in his arms and he shook his head. "No, she is too far gone for my skills."

"But you were able to save Derrick," I argued.

"He's a werewolf. His body merely needed a nudge in the right direction to survive. Your friend requires far more than that."

I turned away, frustrated. Would Aniya hate me for whichever choice I made? Was it right to not even give her the chance? Death was permanent, but if she didn't want to be a vampire we could deal with that later.

I swung back around.

"Do it." Resolve strengthened my voice.

"Are you sure?"

I nodded.

"You are aware that this may not work and she could still die," he warned. "Not everyone makes the transition."

"They don't?" I'd known changing into a hybrid was risky, but not that it was for humans. Wanda's teachings really left something to be desired.

"No, they don't. The best estimate is about half survive."

"I don't understand. Why would that be?"

"No one is sure, but we believe some people are fated to die and their death can't be cheated. A higher power decides, not us."

"You mean God," I stated.

He inclined his head. "That is what some believe."

Lucas snorted, but said nothing. Nephilim weren't in the best graces with heaven and didn't appreciate mentions of "the Higher Power".

Whatever the odds, she was going to die for sure if we didn't do something. "I still want you to do it," I told him. "We have to at least try to save her."

Nik nodded and took Aniya's body from Lucas. Her breaths were coming in too light and I felt guilty for delaying with all my questions. After he took care to lay her on the ground, he sliced his wrist for the second time tonight and eased her mouth open. His blood began dripping down between her pale lips.

With his other hand, he massaged her throat, forcing her to swallow. Within a minute, the cut on his wrist closed and he sliced it open again. This occurred several times as he worked to save her. The wound on Aniya's stomach didn't change at first, but after agonizing minutes of waiting the skin finally started to knit back together. I let out a sigh of relief.

Nik had paled considerably by the time he thought she'd had enough. One of the werewolves stepped forward and offered him his arm. He bit right into it.

"Will she live?" I asked Lucas.

He shrugged. "There is no way to know at this point. She took his blood well enough and continues to breathe, but the turning process is not easy. Your friend could die at any time in the next three days before she becomes a full vampire. All you can do is wait and see what happens."

"Thanks for sugarcoating it," I grumbled.

He lifted his brows. "Would you rather I lie?"

He had a point, even if I didn't have to like it. Time to change the subject. "What did you do with the deputy?"

A smile twitched at his lips. "He had an unfortunate accident with his gun."

I gazed at him in suspicion. "What do you mean...*accident*?'

He gave a light shrug. "His gun went off after I arrived. It happened to be aimed directly at his head when it fired, which was unfortunate."

Trust Lucas to create an "accident". The deputy had been under compulsion, and might have been innocent, but that wouldn't have mattered to the nephilim. He didn't see things the way I did.

"So what do we do now?"

Nik walked up and answered before Lucas could. "We take back control of my house."

Sounded like a plan to me.

Chapter Twenty-seven

"Well, this looks interesting." The familiar voice pulled me out of a comfortable sleep. I cracked an eye open to see Lucas standing over me next to the bed. His arms were crossed, but his lips were quirked in amusement.

"What are you doing in my room, Lucas?" I glared at him.

"Perhaps you should be asking yourself what *he* is doing in your room, sensor." He nodded toward the left side of my bed.

I slowly turned my head, not wanting to know what he meant—even if my senses were already telling me. One glance had me leaping from the bed, shouting as I went.

"Nikolas!"

The naked vampire lay there, not far from where I'd been sleeping, with his arms folded behind his head. I could see his pale, muscular chest and a light trail of hair leading lower before the sheet covered him up. His abs were the kind you could bounce a quarter off of and the rest of him looked every bit as hard...and rigid. He grinned at me, not even trying to hide his extended fangs.

I shook my head, trying to rid myself of the visual image he produced. How could a twelve hundred year old vampire have crawled into my bed and I not notice?

It was clear I had fallen off my game if this could happen.

"Nik, get the hell out of my bed." I swept my hand out in a shooing manner. "Now!"

He yawned and gave me an amused smile. "We need to talk."

I glanced at my watch. It was four o'clock in the afternoon. Since the battle with Variola a few days ago, my sleep schedule had gotten off track. I crossed my arms to glare at him.

"You couldn't wait until I woke up?"

His eyes dropped to fixate on my chest. My hand shot up to cover the small bit of cleavage I possessed that wasn't hidden by my tank top, but it only made him grin more. A groan escaped me—it wasn't like my curves were that impressive. Working out regularly kept me on the smaller side.

I stomped across the room to my overnight bag, grabbed a t-shirt from the top, and yanked it over my head. My glare didn't faze him. He skimmed his gaze down to my legs, bared up to my thighs thanks to the skimpy length of my shorts. He wagged his brows.

I huffed in indignation. "Nikolas, eyes on mine. If you must ogle a woman, go do it in Fairbanks."

He shook his head. "It's still daylight. For now, you're the most appealing female around."

"Go find Kariann, or the other five women staying here right now. I'm not the only one."

He frowned. "They shooed me away. You're the last one left."

I wasn't sure whether to be offended by being the last one or not.

Lucas cleared his throat. "You want to get to the point of this conversation?"

The vampire and nephilim's friendship had resumed in the past few days. I hadn't seen them work things out, but their getting along so well now worried me.

"Oh, right," Nik jumped up to stand next to Lucas.

I averted my gaze from his naked form to find a pair of my black lacy underwear resting on the floor. I worked at trying to shove it under the bed with my foot. Then I saw the matching bra a few feet away and didn't think they'd miss me getting rid of that.

"Wait." I held my hand up. "Give me a chance to shower. Whatever this is about, it can wait until after I'm dressed and had some coffee."

The two men exchanged looks in another one of their wordless conversations they liked to have. Nik had a glint of amusement in his eyes when he drew his gaze back to me.

"By all means, get yourself fixed up," he eyed me up and down. "We'll be out in the living room when you're ready."

I nodded and made a shooing motion. "Good, then go. And please, Nik, get dressed."

Lucas left without a word, but the vampire gave me one more heated glance before strutting away. His back looked as good as his front, I noted with annoyance. He left the door open, forcing me to close it myself.

Since the night of the battle, Emily and I had been staying at Nik's house. It would have felt like a betrayal to leave my friend to a group of sups she didn't even know. They had to keep her in the basement where she could be contained until her bloodlust subsided, but I couldn't bring myself to go back to the cabin. Emily had insisted on staying at the house as well. She'd explained Nik's friends weren't anything like Variola's and that she liked it here. I was too tired to argue or find someplace else for her to go.

Over the last few days Aniya had awoken several times screaming. I'd had to resist the urge to run outside and escape the agony I could feel in her voice. As it was, there were a couple indents in the wall where I'd punched it in frustration.

Nik had "recruited" a group of humans to donate blood, as it was the only thing that could relieve the worst of the pain for her. She wouldn't complete the change until tonight, but her body had begun needing human blood within the first twenty-four hours. Somehow, as Aniya's sire, Nik could control her enough to keep from killing her donors, but it took a lot of them to get her through the transition. I hadn't liked using innocent people, but he promised they would be returned to their homes after their donation, none the wiser as to what happened.

It had been a touch and go process. I hadn't eaten or slept much with all the guilt tying me in knots. Nik had assured me she would survive now that she was past the worst of it. We were waiting for her body to rest on this final day before she woke up fully transitioned. He promised her personality wouldn't be any different. I hoped he was right.

After showering and changing into a pair of

jogging pants and a loose sweatshirt—for Nik's benefit—
I headed downstairs and grabbed a cup of coffee.
Someone, probably a werewolf, had made a pot already.
The kitchen was on the opposite end of the house from
the living room, forcing me to walk some distance before
reaching the "meeting".

My previous visits to what was Variola's home
had been so limited I hadn't seen how many rooms there
were until we re-took control of the place. I'd also
discovered a security room filled with monitors. As it
happened, several cameras were pointed in various
directions outside. It explained how they'd known I was
out there a couple weeks ago. A few vampires and
werewolves were still here when we arrived, younger
ones who wouldn't have been much good in the battle.
They must have been watching for us because they fled
as soon as we got close.

Nik had them all tracked down and "dealt" with,
except Emily's mother who I insisted be allowed to go.
He hadn't liked it, but for the girl's sake he didn't argue
the point. I didn't like Stephanie either, but I couldn't
have that death on my conscience. She didn't stick
around or even ask to take Emily with her—not that I
would have let her. She packed a bag and left in under
fifteen minutes.

Now many of Nik's followers were staying here,
though some had already relocated to nearby houses and
cabins. Others planned to find their own homes soon so
that only a small contingent would remain before long.
There had to be at least twenty bedrooms in the house, if
you counted the ones in the basement, making it ideal for

a vampire leader's needs. We'd had to do some clean-up
that first day, but it was comfortable to stay in now.

Emily slept in her own room next to mine, and
loved the attention everyone gave her. She hadn't
seemed upset about her mother running off, but she
refused to talk about it when I first tried prodding her.
Sometimes we needed space to work things out on our
own. I'd made sure she understood she could talk to me
anytime, but I chose not to push her too hard.

The living room turned out to be more crowded
than expected. Hanging around sups all the time had
numbed me to the point I didn't pay as much attention to
their movements as I used to. Nik sneaking into my room
this morning had made that clear.

Almost all the key players since arriving in
Fairbanks were waiting on me. Charlie sat across from
Nik, both seated in high back chairs near a window
draped with blood red curtains. They spoke in hushed
tones. Felisha giggled with Emily where they sat next to
the fireplace. Luc stood alone next to an empty
bookshelf, drumming his fingers on the dark wood. I
missed seeing Derrick, but he'd gone back to his own
home after the battle and hadn't been seen since. He had
promised to visit me sometime soon, but I guessed that
day wasn't going to be today.

Every head turned toward me as I made my way
in. Something was up. Everyone's eyes watched me a
little too closely. I leaned against the wall near the
room's wide entryway and sipped my coffee. At least I
could make a quick getaway if needed. Throw the coffee
and run. That was my plan.

"Want to tell me what this is all about?" I asked.

Nik stood and moved over to me. "Why don't you have a seat?"

He grabbed my elbow and tried to prod me over to a stuffed leather chair. I didn't budge. When he pulled harder I let my coffee slosh a little. He blanched. All it took was a glance at his new furniture and rugs, delivered just yesterday, to make him back off. Nik liked nice things, but he hadn't wanted any reminders of Variola and her gang. Everything in the room had only been there for a day or two. It must have cost him a fortune.

"I hope you aren't going to make this any more difficult than necessary," he said.

"Stop the delaying tactics and tell me."

"We want you to stay here in my home on a permanent basis."

I lifted my brows. "We?"

He swept an arm toward the others gathered around the room.

"Yes, everyone here."

Well, that explained Derrick's absence.

"No." The word popped out of my mouth without a thought. I wanted to go home as soon as Aniya was ready to make the trip. There was no need to consider it further.

Emily spoke up, imploring eyes bored into mine. "Please, Mel. You said I'd be staying with you, but I don't want to go anywhere else. I like it here."

I could understand she didn't want to be uprooted, but that didn't mean I wanted to stay in this place. Enough bad things had happened here to last me a lifetime, and there were way too many supernaturals. My senses had begun to get used to the constant deluge of their signatures and power, but it still gave me headaches if their moods ran too high. Plus I didn't think it was good for Emily.

"Doesn't it bother you?" I asked her.

She shrugged. "It did at first, but I've been around them long enough it doesn't anymore."

Maybe with her youth she could adapt faster, but that didn't make it any safer for her. I gave her my most stern face. "Emily, it's dangerous for you to be living in a place like this. I don't like exposing you to so much on a long-term basis. It's bad enough you've been here for as long as you have."

Nik stepped forward. "I would protect her. You've proven yourself resourceful, but neither of you would be safe on your own. You have to know that."

I set my coffee cup down and moved closer to him. "What guarantees do I have that you would protect her?"

A flash of hurt crossed his eyes. "That's not fair, Mel."

I turned my head away; not liking the idea a vampire could make me feel guilty. That had to be a first.

Charlie spoke next. "I'm in agreement with him, Melena. Both you and Emily will be far safer here. I would watch over both of you as well."

"Why?" I asked him.

He cleared his throat. "Sensors are rare, but important. There are things you can do that no other race can; things that can protect the world from great harm by forces even more powerful than those in this room now. Whether you like it or not, you are one of the ones in a position to help the weak and innocent and should be willing to do so. Sometime in the near future you will find this to be true, but you must be alive to discover it. Go back to California now and your chances of survival will be slim."

His words rang as true, the same as Nik's had. Felisha stood up and walked over to me next, putting a delicate hand on my arm. Their "intervention" was beginning to wear on me. I gazed into her beautiful green eyes and tried not to be affected by her pleading expression.

"Melena, we would all be here for you and Emily. No one could harm you without going through us first. I know you've had some bad experiences in the past, but at some point you have to learn to trust."

Unfortunately, Felisha was too nice to argue with so I nodded and said nothing. She gave an encouraging smile before stepping back to give me room. My eyes sought out Lucas. His emotionless mask revealed nothing.

"What about you?" I asked. "Why are you here? Somehow I doubt you care what happens to me."

His golden eyes flashed for a moment before he answered. "I've made your safety my concern. That is all you need to know."

"That's a half-truth and you know it."

He moved forward until he was almost standing on my toes. "Little sensor, I've told you before. Don't push me."

I clenched my fists.

"Or you'll do what?" Might as well try and get him to spell out the truth.

He put his hand on my chin and tilted my face up. A cold smile spread across his face.

"Wouldn't you like to know?"

I grabbed his hand and yanked it from my face. He let me. "Actually, I would like to know."

"Better you don't, sensor, better you don't."

The others stood in tense silence. If Lucas made a move against me, none of them were powerful enough to stop him, even with their combined efforts.

I put my hands on his chest, which might have been a mistake because the touch gave me a certain degree of pleasure it shouldn't have, but my goal was to get his attention. He jerked. I didn't know if that was a good or bad thing. His emotions only revealed annoyance.

"Lucas, for once, give me a straight answer. Why are you with the others in wanting me to stay here?"

He gazed down from his impressive height. "My reasons are my own. Don't bother to keep asking."

That pissed me off. I was sick of his evasive tactics.

"Coward," I spit out.

Anger broiled inside of him. He took a step forward, making me take a step back with my hands still stuck to his chest. My heartbeat picked up as he continued maneuvering me until my back hit the wall. Maybe calling him a coward hadn't been such a good idea.

Lucas grabbed my head and held it between his large hands. My gaze locked with his. I almost could have sworn sparks flew from him.

"Little sensor, you demand an answer, so I'll give you one."

I swallowed, unsure what he meant as he stared down at me. So many emotions crossed his face that it was impossible to make sense of them.

"The one thing you need to know, above all, is that I will protect you. I will always protect you until the day comes when your time on earth is meant to end. Do not try to leave this town or I'll make you regret it. Count on this, if you cannot count on anything else."

And with those words, full of cold hard truth, he left. The flash of his light almost blinded me. My hands gripped the wall for support. Everyone else in the room appeared to be as shocked as me.

Emily was the first to break the silence. "Mel, I think he likes you."

I almost choked on her words. "What would make you say that?"

She shrugged. "In school, when a boy really likes a girl, sometimes he can be really mean to her. But sometimes, he does stuff that gives him away. I think that's what Luc just did."

"Luc?"

She shrugged. "He doesn't like it when I call him that, so I keep doing it."

I walked over to where she sat near the curtained window and gave her a hug. She meant well in her own way and I had to admit her funny logic had lightened the mood.

"So, are we going to stay, Mel?"

I leaned back to seriously look at her. The hope in Emily's eyes was almost too much to bear, and maybe a part of me had grown weak by having her around, but her safety was even more important than mine.

Everyone was right. I'd have a hard time protecting the two of us on my own. It hurt my pride to admit it, but we needed help to stay safe. Noreen might be dead, but the minions she left back in California weren't. They would always be a threat—one I couldn't fight alone. Here, at least, I stood a chance of survival and so did Emily. There would be other challenges to face, but at least we wouldn't be alone.

I smiled at Emily. "Yeah, we can stay."

She jumped up and let out a whoop before running over to Felisha and exclaiming her excitement. The fairy glowed under the girl's attention and I had a feeling they were becoming good friends. I might have considered letting Emily stay with her, except she needed sensor training and no one else could do that but me. At least I wouldn't be alone in figuring out how to raise a fourteen year-old. It was a daunting prospect.

***

A few hours later I sat on one of the new sofas in the living room waiting for Aniya to come upstairs. Nik had insisted on letting her wake up and get oriented first before seeing anyone besides him. He'd amazed me over the last few days at how attentive he was with her. I'd always pictured a more brutal process, but some of the other vampires in the house confirmed Nikolas took his role as sire very seriously. They said it made the transition process much easier and allowed the newly turned to adjust faster.

More than thirty minutes had passed and I began to get worried. My hand played with a mermaid figurine I found sitting alone on the shelf in the living room. I didn't know how it got there, but was glad for something to keep my hand busy. Everyone else stayed away so I could reunite with Aniya in privacy. It made the room seem almost too quiet.

Footsteps echoed on the wooden floor in the hallway. I put the figurine down and stood up. My senses told me it was her, though she felt different now. During the transition process, her personal signature had been in a flux, but now it had steadied into a regular vampire rhythm. When she came into the room, with Nikolas behind her, I had to admit she looked good. She walked with the grace given to all undead. Despite that, her movements were hesitant and there was a nervousness coming from her.

I took slow steps to close the gap between us, unsure how to behave. I didn't want Aniya to think I didn't accept her new status, but the change would still take some getting used to. This was the woman I had always known, but my senses were giving me the warning sirens that came anytime a vampire was close.

It was her spreading smile that did it for me. My behavior seemed ridiculous in the face of all we'd been through together. I stopped acting stupid and gave my friend a hug. After a brief stiffening of her body, she relaxed and put her own arms around me. She squeezed too tight, but I managed to handle it.

We broke apart to look at each other.

She must have cleaned up before leaving the basement because her hair was wet and she had new clothes on—a pair of dark slacks and a red blouse that complimented her complexion. Her eyes had darkened from brown to almost pure black, but her skin remained its normal olive tone. I assumed it took time after turning and being away from the sun before a vampire began to pale.

"I'm so sorry for everything, Mel," she told me in a tearful voice.

My head shook in denial. "Not your fault. You couldn't have known all this would happen. I'm the one who is sorry for seeing you end up this way."

"You're not mad at me?" she asked, surprise in her voice.

It almost seemed funny, considering all the worrying I'd done about her possibly hating me. She should be angry for getting her killed, well, mostly killed.

"Of course not," I answered her, "but how do you feel about being changed?"

He face dropped and worry came across her eyes once more. "You want the truth?"

My lips twitched. "If you haven't learned this already, you should know you can't lie to me or I'll know."

She frowned. "Have you always been able to do

that?"

I nodded and her eyes grew round. She covered her mouth as her face began to flush.

"Oh, God. You knew every time Lisette and I..."

"Yep," I nodded.

"But you never said anything," she whined.

"I couldn't. Now you'll have to learn to keep a lot of secrets too."

She nodded. Resignation reflected in her eyes.

"So you're okay with being a vampire?" I repeated.

After a brief hesitation, she smiled.

"To be honest," she flashed her teeth, thankfully no fangs showed, "I'm glad you told Nik to turn me. Remember all those vampire shows I used to watch on TV?"

I groaned. I'd blocked the memories from my head in the hopes she never got any funny ideas.

"Yes, I remember."

"Well, now I got my wish, even if it didn't come out quite the way I hoped."

Her boyfriend, Philip, had been among those we killed the other night. Lucas had recognized the guy right before removing his heart. Nik had said he broke the news to her when she asked about him during her transition. In my mind, it was for the best, but she might not see it that way. Philip had had plenty of time to brainwash her. Time would tell on that one.

"There is one thing I'll regret," she admitted. A wave of sadness swept over her.

"What's that?" I asked.

"There will be no way for me to be a teacher anymore, and my dreams of having children of my own are over. That's going to take some getting used to."

I sighed. She might have gained immortality, which she seemed okay with, but losing one's dreams would be hard to take. Neither of her biggest wishes could come true in any way I could think of. It wasn't feasible for a vampire.

"I'll be there for you," I reassured her. "In any way I can."

She nodded. "Thanks."

"I'll leave you two to talk." Nik spoke from a few feet away. He didn't move far, though, continuing to act as the protector.

Aniya and I didn't waste any more time before moving to sit and catch up.

Epilogue

Five days later I found myself at the airport seeing Aniya off. She was returning to California to pack up our apartment and ship everything to Alaska. I'd had no choice but to stay. Nik and the others had reminded me that Noreen's supporters remained there and they would be looking for me. The risk would be too great, they'd insisted. That left Aniya, along with two vampire guards, to go back and take care of everything. They didn't have a reason to attack her.

Aniya's mother would be coming back with her after some delicate compulsion was placed to gain her compliance. The woman would never leave any other way and Aniya understood that. She would also handle Lisette, since our mutual friend would no longer answer my phone calls. Her reticence hurt. I kept hoping she'd understand the position I'd been put in, but some offenses were easier to forgive than others.

Aniya was using a private jet Nikolas managed to borrow. It came from one of his vampire friends and was sun-proofed in case there were any delays preventing the flight from reaching ground before dawn. I watched it take off into the night sky before moving through the dark parking lot to my waiting vehicle.

Due to a recent rain, everything had a hazy

quality to it now. The weather reflected my mood. Some pressure lurking deep inside hit me as I realized for the first time in a while, I was alone. No one could hear me or see me. The part of the terminal I was in didn't have much traffic at the moment.

For a few minutes, I let my head rest on the steering wheel while music played at a low volume from the stereo speakers. At the house, too many ears could hear the slightest sound, leaving no room for privacy. I'd been holding it all in, not wanting anyone to think me weak. Now that I was alone, every emotion I'd kept bottled inside came surging up.

A lot had happened in the month since my arrival to Alaska. Everything had made so much more sense before, but now it no longer did, and I had no idea what to do except go through the motions and hope it all turned out for the best.

Tears ran down my cheeks as recent memories flashed before me, Matt's death the most vivid. He'd died because of me and there was no way to go back and fix it. His family would never know and I couldn't tell them. A sob escaped me and I let myself cry for a few minutes in the quiet of the vehicle. My soul needed the release. It had been stained by the things I'd done. It would take some time to get over the guilt, assuming it passed at all.

About the time I began to get myself together, I felt him. He hadn't come back since the confrontation at Nik's house, but he chose this moment to show up. A time when I least wanted him around.

"What do you want, Lucas?" I mumbled through the steering wheel.

"Is that any way to greet the one who saved your friend's life?"

Of course he would bring that up now. My purse was under the driver's seat, so I reached down and grabbed a tissue to wipe my face before bothering with a reply.

"You know I owe you for that. It's not like you did it for altruistic reasons."

"Perhaps not, but that's not why I came here."

I risked a glance at him. Lucas was reclining in the passenger seat—one leg cocked up while the other stretched out in front of him. He leaned against the door so his body was angled toward mine. His usual mask wasn't in place, but I couldn't read the expression he wore. His black silk shirt brought out the sharp angles in his face, and it came to me for the hundredth time how incredibly good looking he was. No other man could come close to him.

"What did you come here for?"

He studied me for a moment. "I think you're ready to know the truth about your Wanda."

My brow furrowed. "Wanda?"

His expression softened a degree and he put a hand out to push the hair away from my face. "You should know she planned to trade you."

I pulled away from him. "What do you mean?"

He sighed and dropped his hand.

"She spent much of her life aiding a particular group of powerful supernaturals. If you'll recall, she was growing old. What you didn't know was that she needed a replacement and when she came across you, she found one. Your parents, the adopted ones, didn't die by accident but by her design. She tampered with their brakes at a time when she knew you wouldn't be traveling with them. Once she had you to herself, she put the fear of all things supernatural in your head so you wouldn't befriend any of us before she sold you off. If I had not killed her, she would have handed you over two days later."

My chest tightened and I looked away. Everything he'd said rang of truth. How could that have been? She'd often been distant toward me, but could she really have been that cold?

Lucas was playing with my iPod. Our gazes met and I could see a trace of sympathy glinting from his eyes. I didn't want his pity. "If what you say is true, why didn't these sups come after me once she died?"

"Wanda wasn't a complete dim-wit," Lucas replied. "She'd planned to give you over as part of a trade for her freedom and a large cash payment. As a result, she couldn't risk them knowing your whereabouts, or hers, until the exchange."

My hands gripped the steering wheel and I leaned back, watching a plane take off into the night. Its lights grew smaller as it flew away.

"Lucas, why are you telling me this now?"

He set the iPod down. *A Drop in the Ocean* by Ron Pope began to play.

"Because, until this time, you weren't ready to hear the truth."

Sensor Series Reading Order:

Darkness Haunts
Darkness Taunts
Chained by Darkness
Darkness Divides
Darkness Clashes (coming fall 2014)

About Susan Illene

Instead of making the traditional post high school move and attending college, Susan joined the U.S. Army. She spent her eighteenth birthday in the gas chamber — an experience she is sure is best left for criminals. For eleven years she served first as a human resources specialist and later as an Arabic linguist (mostly in Airborne units). Though all her duty assignments were stateside, she did make two deployments to Iraq where her language skills were put to regular use.

After leaving the service in 2009, Susan returned to school at the University of Oklahoma to study history with a focus on the Middle East. She no longer finds many opportunities to test her fighting abilities in real life, unless her husband is demanding she cook him a real meal, but she's found a new outlet in writing urban fantasy heroines who can.

For more information visit:

www.darknesshaunts.com

Made in the USA
Charleston, SC
24 April 2014